Suddenly their kiss became so much more.

It was as if they'd been standing in a calm, sunny field, and suddenly a tornado had swept in and blasted around them. The wind caught, the weather shifted, and he and his emotions were whipped into a furious storm. The pressure of their mouths mounted, their lips pressed firmer and deeper and their tongues brushed. He wanted her.

Their bodies pressed closer, his hand dropped from her rib cage to her waist and down lower as he gripped her buttock and imagined what it might be like to throw her onto the bed and truly do everything he fantasized.

Break it up.... He must break it....

With a shudder, he tore himself away.

Cool air rushed into the space between them. He gazed down at her shocked expression. Perhaps it had been too much for her, too, the unexpected jolt of passion and desire that seized them.

"Welcome to Wyoming," he whispered.

"What a welcoming," she said softly.

* * *

W...... to Wyoming
Harlequin 14

Kate Bridges invites you to her

MAIL-ORDER WEDDINGS

From blushing bride to Wild West Wife!

The Great Fire of Chicago
might have changed best friends
Cassandra Hamilton's and Natasha O'Sullivan's lives
forever, but they're determined to carve a new future
for themselves as mail-order brides in the West.

Then along come their gun-slinging,
horse-riding, breathtaking new husbands—
it seems Cassandra and Natasha have got
a whole lot more than they signed up for!

RANCHER WANTS A WIFE
Already available

WELCOME TO WYOMING
April 2014

WELCOME TO WYOMING

—

KATE BRIDGES

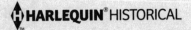 **HARLEQUIN**®HISTORICAL

Recycling programs
for this product may
not exist in your area.

ISBN-13: 978-0-373-29779-5

WELCOME TO WYOMING

Copyright © 2014 by Katherine Haupt

This edition published by arrangement with Harlequin Books S.A.

For questions and comments about the quality of this book, please contact us at CustomerService@Harlequin.com.

® and TM are trademarks of Harlequin Enterprises Limited or its corporate affiliates. Trademarks indicated with ® are registered in the United States Patent and Trademark Office, the Canadian Trade Marks Office and in other countries.

Printed in U.S.A.

www.Harlequin.com

Available from Harlequin® Historical and
KATE BRIDGES

**Did you know that these novels are also
available as ebooks? Visit www.Harlequin.com.**

For Greg, who loves a good adventure.

KATE BRIDGES

Award-winning and multipublished author Kate Bridges was raised in rural Canada, and her stories reflect her love for wide-open spaces, country sunshine and the Rocky Mountains. She loves writing adventurous tales of men and women who tamed the West.

Prior to becoming a full-time writer, Kate worked as a pediatric intensive care nurse. She often includes compelling medical situations in her novels. Later in her education, she studied architecture and worked as a researcher on a television design program. She has taken postgraduate studies in comedy screenwriting, and in her spare time writes screenplays.

Kate's novels have been translated into nine languages and studied in over a dozen colleges in their commercial fiction courses, and are sold worldwide. She lives in the beautiful cosmopolitan city of Toronto with her family. To find out more about Kate's books and to sign up for her free online newsletter, please visit www.katebridges.com.

Chapter One

Cheyenne, Wyoming Territory, August 1873

Simon Garr adjusted his hat, peered down the railroad tracks to the train chugging its way up the gulley and damn well hoped his bride-to-be wasn't on it.

They'd never be right for each other.

He was a liar and imposter.

She wasn't.

Other folks waiting on the platform jostled to look down the tracks. Simon bristled in his itchy wool suit. He'd feel more comfortable in denim jeans. He'd always worn charity-donated jeans while growing up barefoot on the plains, having to fend for himself since the age of eight.

No matter what he wore, it was hard to conceal his gritty determination, the need to be able to control everything around him, especially in dangerous situations like these. He enjoyed the weight and feel of his concealed weapons—the revolver in his shoulder holster, derringer pressed into his back, knife strapped to his ankle. He'd taught himself how to shoot when he was a kid. The first living thing he'd ever shot was a raging bear that'd mauled a friend. The second living thing, years later, was a man who'd murdered innocent villagers for three gold coins.

The checkered suit wasn't his usual style, but it *was* the attire that jewelers wore.

And that was what he was supposed to be. A jeweler. He was working undercover, impersonating a man named Jarrod Ledbetter, leader of the Ledbetter gang.

Ledbetter and his pack were not only jewelers, but clandestine train robbers. The real Ledbetter was dead. He and two other scum from their filthy group had been fatally shot last week in an undercover stakeout by Simon and other lawmen of the district. Word of their deaths was being closely guarded by authorities. The railroad bigwigs didn't want to release the information until they recovered the goods stolen days before the shoot-out, worth three hundred thousand dollars.

They'd hired Simon, a detective, to find it.

Simon cared less about the missing gold and jewels, and more about his two closest friends, also detectives, who were killed in the shoot-out. Simon winced at the awful memory of being unable to save his friends, of seeing the blood on their bodies. He looked at the faces of the people strolling by, sadly reminded that he'd never see Clay Holborne or Eli Remington again. He vowed to get even.

His mission now was to gain the confidence of the remaining two Ledbetter gang members, who hadn't been at the shoot-out, and uncover the stolen property.

Two days ago, Simon had made contact. The two remaining murderers had said they would be "honored" to finally meet Ledbetter in person to get their next assignment.

But the big surprise came when Simon had discovered that Ledbetter, before his death, had mailed away for a wife!

It was during a casual poker game last night that the two men had asked Simon if he was ready for her arrival this evening.

Hell no! But he'd bluffed his way through answering. He was deep undercover with no immediate means to inform his superiors. So, there was nothing he could do but stand here and wait. He'd brought a suitcase with him to add to the illusion that he did indeed expect her and wanted to whisk her away to the nearest hotel.

But who was to say *she* hadn't called off the wedding? Maybe Ledbetter was supposed to send a telegram this week to confirm and, due to his untimely death, hadn't.

What kind of woman traveled blindly to involve herself with an unknown man?

Maybe she was adventurous. Desperate. Or fleeing from something. Who the hell knew? All he knew was her name. Natasha O'Sullivan.

Women baffled him. Yet he had no problem lying to them. He'd done it countless times in the name of justice. He'd gone by more false names than truthful. The hardest thing about lying wasn't the actual deception—for it was always done in the name of good— but keeping the facts straight in his head about who he was this week.

Jarrod Ledbetter, he repeated in his mind.

He also couldn't control how some women would react to his lies. Men were more predictable. In his line of duty, being in command of everyone around him always had life-and-death consequences.

Hell. Just as they had for Clay and Eli.

Guilt consumed him again.

It overpowered his senses, made his throat constrict, his mouth run dry. He hadn't been able to save them. If he'd been faster, or stronger, or, damn, more aware of the hidden gang members on the cliffs...

The train, still half a mile off, blew its whistle. It caused a rush of excited voices on the platform. The early-evening breeze wafted through Simon's shoulder-length hair. It spun the leaves on the aspens and whispered through the tall pines and firs. Clay and Eli would never breathe air like this again. He tried to push the tragedy out of his mind. He needed his faculties clear and sharp.

The wheels of the locomotive screeched and the train roared past. It came to a rumbling halt and passengers disembarked. Simon peered up and down the platform, outwardly calm while trying to spot anyone who resembled a mail-order bride. He watched as folks were reunited, businessmen hired porters, cowboys slung their packs. No lone women so far.

Gratified that his bride wasn't here, Simon turned to go. But then he noticed the edge of a scuffed, brown leather trunk being pushed out of a rear car. The trunk's latch was busted. Clothing was visible through the cracked opening of the lid. A flurry of ropes held the thing together.

A female voice rang out from inside the car. "You ugly, uncooperative, good-for-nothing piece of trash..."

Then with a kick of her high-heeled black leather

boot, the trunk flew out the door and landed with a thump on the wooden platform.

He raised an eyebrow in amusement. He'd hate to be the leather beneath that boot.

But when she stepped out, his whole body tensed.

God, *no.* That wouldn't be her, would it?

The whistle blew again and the train rolled away.

He stood partially hidden by the posts around him and watched her.

She *was* the right age—twentysomething. And she was alone.

Dressed in a faded skirt and a formfitting bodice that was patched at her elbows, she brushed the shimmering brunette hair from her dark eyes and realigned her stuffy bonnet. It had fake fruit attached to the brim—cherries and grapes—and would appeal to a woman forty years her senior. *Donated clothing,* he thought. She glanced timidly down the tracks, head slightly bowed, and then adjusted her fussy white gloves in a prim fashion. Who was she kidding? She was no timid woman. She was a tiger in skirts.

The burly conductor in uniform called to her from the moving train. "Take care of yourself, Miss O'Sullivan!"

Simon cursed. So it was her.

"Bye, sir!"

He watched her wave. Her bright eyes flashed deep coffee-brown, and her expression rippled with warmth. Her skin was clear, her neckline plunged to a hint of cleavage and the cut to her suit bodice revealed tempting curves.

His jaw clenched.

She was innocent in all of this. That was what one of Ledbetter's men, the more brutal one, Kale McKern, had implied in the poker game last night—that Ledbetter had fooled her. As he'd fooled lawmen for years, men much more experienced with criminals than she was.

All Simon had to do was walk up to her, tell her he'd had a change of heart and put her on the next train home.

Simple.

But it looked to him as if all her dreams were packed up in that battered old trunk. And now he was about to tell her he didn't want her. He swore. He wasn't here to cause trouble to any woman. He was here to find justice for his friends. No doubt Simon would cause her heartache and embarrassment by turning her away, but he couldn't disclose he wasn't the real Ledbetter, for there was no telling who she might talk to on the return journey home. Then his life would be in danger. Maybe even hers.

This way, they'd both be spared. Only her feelings would be hurt. Feelings healed a lot faster and better than gun wounds.

But damn…he was about to give her one big invisible bruise.

On the bright side, in a few weeks when this was over, she'd likely read in the papers that the lying and murdering Jarrod Ledbetter had died in a shoot-out, and she'd be relieved she never got involved with him. She'd be free to marry in a more normal sense.

Mail-order brides were common in parts of the West where there was a high ratio of men to women, but why would any female feel the need to marry by mail? Especially one as good-looking as Natasha O'Sullivan.

She turned around to deal with her trunk. The glossy ring of curls she'd pinned up at the back of her head bobbed. Her bosom moved up and down, accentuating her slender waist. With a swallow, he glanced away and took a step closer to the ticket counter, annoyed that the train she'd pulled in on had just left. He glanced at the chalkboard and the schedule for the next one.

Today was Wednesday, almost seven in the evening. He scanned the departure times. The next one was Friday, then Sunday. There was no train leaving for two days?

He rubbed his bristly jaw. How was he supposed to get her out of here?

Stagecoach, he thought, or wagon train.

He turned around, steeled himself, adjusted his hat and strode toward her. There was no chance Ledbetter would've sent a photograph of himself—or even a description—for fear that his criminal face would be plastered across the country. So there was no way she'd know Simon was a liar.

A crazy thought hit him.

Nah. Couldn't be.

Or could it? Could she have been more involved with Ledbetter than even McKern had suspected? Could she have been in cahoots with Ledbetter? Did she know anything at all about the stolen gold and jewels? She *was* a tiger in skirts. She had a temper she was trying to conceal. What else was in her character?

His cowboy boots thudded on the platform. She looked up in his direction, seemed to sense who he was and smiled. Loose strands of brown hair twirled across her face and over her freckles. Lips the color of sweet raspberries parted.

Hell, he nearly melted.

She might be a criminal, he repeated in his mind. Before he could respond to her, other footsteps shuffled to his right and she turned to look that way.

Simon frowned and turned his head to see who it was.

His muscles tightened in warning as he spotted the two men from Ledbetter's gang—Kale McKern and Woody Fowler. Simon had told them to stay put, that he would pick up his bride alone and see to them in a couple of days. What were they doing here?

Then he recalled all the lewd remarks they'd made during the poker game—about what the mail-order bride might look like and how fast Simon could get her to bed.

They'd likely had a few drinks and came to see for themselves.

These weren't stupid men; Ledbetter himself had gone to Harvard. In a time when few people were educated, Ledbetter's wealthy grandparents had sent him to the best college in the country. He'd learned everything from books; Simon had learned everything he knew from the streets. Ledbetter had demanded that the men who worked for him be college educated, too, not only because he preferred the company of intelligent men, but as a cover. What sheriff would suspect a group of well-educated men to be cutthroats and train robbers? McKern and Fowler had gone to school in Upstate New York, violent thieves and scoundrels from an early age.

Simon kept walking toward the woman, firm and steady. He was reassured by the weight of his concealed guns and knife. But McKern and Fowler also carried hidden weapons. Simon tried to think fast. He couldn't turn Natasha O'Sullivan away in the presence of Ledbetter's men, for that would raise suspicion that Simon wasn't who he said he was. Then both he and she might get a bullet to the skull.

So now he had to pretend to be the ever-lovin' groom.

Damn. This mission just got a lot more complicated.

Three men were walking toward her, and suddenly Natasha O'Sullivan was no longer sure if one of them was her groom.

She had thought it was the tall, muscled one with shoulder-length dark blond hair, but it might be the thinner gentleman in the bowler hat or the heavyset one with the dark mustache. Her nerves took hold. It was one thing to write confidently to a complete stranger but quite another to be here in person. Surrounded by unfamiliar things and faces, she was scared and intimidated and lonely.

Evening light shimmered through the canopy of leaves above them and danced across the wooden platform. The breeze brought a heavenly relief to the back of her sticky neck and the perspiration that clung between her breasts. She'd worked up a sweat due to the blasted trunk that had nearly made her miss her stop.

The three men reached her at the same time.

The tall, handsome one in the checkered suit held out his hand and smiled. "You must be my lovely Natasha."

Goodness. Relief washed through her, loosening her rigid shoulders, unlocking her knees and lifting the corners of her mouth in a very grateful smile. He was here. He'd come for her just as he'd written he would.

She slipped her gloved hand into his large palm. *My, what a firm grip.* She turned her face to look into the warmth of his green eyes. Her stomach clenched with the intensity of his gaze, the strength of his profile and the thought that he was hers.

For one thousand miles, she had hoped and prayed that she would feel some connection to him when they met. She'd felt that connection seconds ago, when they'd first locked eyes across the platform. She was blessed. Not only was he an educated man from Harvard, but about as sturdy and healthy as she could imagine.

"I'm Jarrod Ledbetter," he said with a deep rumble. "I could hardly wait to meet you, darlin'."

Her heart skittered at the endearment. "My pleasure, Mr. Ledbetter."

"Jarrod, please."

She inhaled a breath of fresh Wyoming air, laden with the scent of fir trees and pines. "Jarrod."

The man was intimidating.

If she had to say, she'd say he was affected by her, too. She could see it in the heated manner of his gaze, the upturn of his silky lips, and how he slowly dropped his hand and rubbed the back of his neck. And yet he took a step away from her, his stance detached.

Jarrod cleared his throat and then introduced the other two men.

"These are my associates. Kale McKern and Woody Fowler."

They were all roughly thirty years of age, give or take a couple. Neatly shaven, well dressed, inquisitive.

The thin man in the bowler hat stepped forward to shake her hand.

"Mr. Fowler, how do you do?" she asked.

"Welcome to Wyoming Territory, ma'am."

Then to the other she added, "Mr. McKern."

"You arrived on a right beautiful day." His mustache

wiggled as he chewed on a piece of grass. She thought she detected the scent of alcohol. Maybe they'd had dinner while they were waiting for her.

"You all work together in the jewelry business?" she asked politely.

The two men shoved their hands into their pockets and deferred to Jarrod. He was obviously the leader of the group. He likely employed them, judging by the respectful way they looked at him.

"Yes, we do," Jarrod said boldly, half a head taller than his associates and much more muscled. Goodness, by his letters, she'd never realized he'd be so handsome. "Pay no attention to them," Jarrod continued. "They just came to say hello. Now they'll be on their way." He seemed to give them some sort of signal. "As soon as they pick up your trunk and deliver it to the hotel across the street. Right, fellas?"

"Yes, sir." Mr. Fowler heaved on one end of the trunk, and his friend the other.

Jarrod was trying to get rid of them, she thought, likely so that he and she could be alone. It made her flush to think she would be alone with her future husband soon. There was only so much they could get across in letters. His had been rather formal and very proper. She was not expecting this bigger-than-life red-blooded male with rather long hair standing in front of her. She wondered what he had in mind for this evening, and when they would be talking to the minister. She had been expecting one final letter from him this week before she left Chicago to clarify those details, but it hadn't come. He likely hadn't had the time to write it.

As the men hoisted the trunk, she gripped her satchel.

It contained her coin purse, travel documents and derringer.

Jarrod held out his elbow and she took it with an appreciative smile.

He was unexpectedly charming.

They strolled ahead of the other two, making their way down the platform toward the stone-built depot.

Jarrod patted her fingers that encircled his arm. Even though she was still wearing gloves, it was such a tender gesture and made her insides flutter.

Lord, she was going to be sharing her bed with this man. Sharing her body with his. Back home in Chicago at Mrs. Pepik's Boardinghouse for Desolate Women, she'd met a lot of women from ragged backgrounds, some worse off than her, hearing all sorts of tales about men from different segments of society, rich and poor. All sorts of talk about the pleasures and dangers of intimacy. She hoped that Jarrod was what he appeared to be in his letters: well educated, finely bred, a gentleman in every regard.

She did admit, he looked wilder and more untamed than she'd imagined. Much more physically in shape than someone who spent a lot of time reading books and studying jewelry. And what was it about him that made him seem so distant from her?

"How was your trip?" he asked. "Not too tiresome, I hope."

"It was a little rough, I'm afraid. We had problems with the locomotive."

He raised his eyebrows. "You don't say."

"Luckily, I took an earlier train from Chicago—one day earlier because train schedules can be so disruptive—so I had time to spare when we broke down yesterday morning outside Omaha. We had to wait an entire day for new parts. The railroad put us up for the night. I nearly didn't get here."

He raised an eyebrow. "How unfortunate."

"Yes, it could have been. My friends in Chicago sometimes tell me I get too worried over fine details, that I'm always expecting trouble, but thank goodness I had the foresight to leave earlier this time. Otherwise you'd still be standing here, thinking I stood you up!"

Jarrod nodded. "Good thing you're resourceful."

"I try to be," she said. "Thank you kindly for noticing." Her skirts picked up as her enthusiasm bounded.

"Always expecting trouble, you say?" He peered at her oddly.

"It's in my nature. I don't trust easily. My friends in Chicago say it's because I grew up with my grandfather, who was overprotective and worried about every little thing. You know how older folks are."

He blinked. "Right. And yet here you are."

"Oh, I know it must seem to you that it's a contradiction. That I don't trust easily and yet I traveled a thousand miles to marry a stranger. But as I said in our many letters, I had to get to know you first. That's why I needed to ask you all those questions."

"I guess I passed your test."

"You most certainly did." She rubbed away a fallen hair from her cheek. "And my friends, of course, helped me pick out the most eligible bachelor from all the responses I got from the ad."

"And you trust your friends."

She smiled. "Yes. We help each other. So far, six of us have placed ads as mail-order brides." It was their way of escaping the tragedy of the Great Chicago Fire two years ago that had charred the city, leaving behind death and destruction and forcing them to make new lives for themselves all across the country. In her heart, it was also to get away from the loss of her grandfather, and the burden of feeling like a wild bird in a cage. She'd always wanted to travel and feel the ripple of adventure in her pulse.

He pulled in a breath that made her wonder what he was thinking.

She added in a whisper, "This is the most daring, craziest thing I've ever done, though. Coming to meet you. My grandfather would roll over in his grave."

"Then I'll have to take good care of you for the sake of your granddad." He patted her hand again in a most detached, grandfatherly way, much to her puzzlement. "You likely missed dinner. Are you hungry, darlin'? I thought I might book you a room across the street. The Mountain Hotel has a beautiful view and a fine restaurant."

She thought she heard a snicker behind her. With a frown, she spun to look, but the men behind her were straight-faced, shuffling the heavy trunk between them.

She tensed over the fact that he wished to book a room. One for her and one for himself? Surely not one for them together, for there didn't appear to be enough time to wed first. As eager as she was to get to know him intimately, she wasn't the type of woman to do it before marriage. She'd met lots of women like that at the boardinghouse, though, many who became dear friends. Ladies of a "certain kind" who taught her things about what pleased men in the bedroom—tips she would surely try out on Jarrod. Perhaps he would stay at his home tonight, although she didn't know the particulars of where he stayed when he traveled. He'd written that he owned a few homes, modest homes little more than cabins that he wished to make bigger and brighter with her as his new bride.

"You didn't have dinner yet?" she asked him.

"I was waiting for you."

"How considerate."

They stopped by the outer stone wall of the depot as he picked up a fine suitcase befitting of a jeweler. She gathered his things were inside. Perhaps they would marry quickly and honeymoon somewhere?

They walked through the crowded station and came out on the other side at street level. The boardwalk was teeming with folks in all directions. Wagons loaded with ranching supplies rolled along the dirt street. Storefronts were strung with banners that read Shovels for Sale, Sandwiches Till Midnight, Gold Nuggets Weighed and Exchanged, Copper and Silver Bought and Sold.

Some of them had help-wanted signs tacked to their doors and windows. Natasha glanced across the street to the left, to the river valley lined with plush green trees. In the center of the greenery sat one outstanding hotel. It was built of stone and timber, and sprawled across an acreage. A wood-burnished sign hung over the entrance. The Mountain Hotel.

Gracious. It was massive and more luxurious than any building she'd ever spent time in.

The two men lugging the beat-up trunk weaved around two cowboys and planted the case behind her.

"Why don't you fellas go on ahead to the front desk?" The brim of Jarrod's black hat shielded the setting sun behind the mountains. "I'll be in touch in the next few days."

"Take your time getting back," Mr. Fowler said. The other man nodded and they soon disappeared through the horses and pedestrians, carrying her trunk to the hotel.

She brightened, pleased that he would be spending a few days with her. She clutched her satchel to her waist. "Jarrod, have you had an opportunity to think more about what we discussed in our letters?"

"How's that again?" He turned toward her with a twinge of concern. Did the question bother him?

"The letters," she repeated softly. "What I asked you in my last one?"

"I'm…I'm still giving it some thought."

"I see." She puckered her lips.

Had they hit a little snag in their communication? She wished to make it clear how involved she wished to be in this marriage. And now, upon meeting him, she wondered again why he had replied to her advertisement for a bride. He seemed so attractive and intelligent and successful, her doubts rose again. She had asked him precisely this in one of her letters, and he had responded that he'd been engaged once but it hadn't lasted due to her unfaithfulness, and that due to the nature of his business, he traveled so much that he didn't have the opportunity to meet many women. Combined with the fact that the ratio of women to men was somewhere in the neighborhood of one to twenty.

Jarrod seemed distracted. His gaze moved over her bonnet to the other side of the street. She turned to see what held his dire attention.

A team of horses were rearing up at a water trough. An elderly man was holding tight to their lines, but he turned pale as one horse neighed, fell down hard on his front hooves and bucked.

Her body stiffened in fear for the man.

Jarrod muttered, "Excuse me," and dashed to help.

Jarrod took control. He grasped the reins from the elderly man, calmly speaking to the horses as he pulled tight against the power of the beasts. He finally got close enough to pat the shoulder of one. The jittery white one settled first, then the chestnut mare. They were magnificent animals, muscles gleaming in the faded golden light, accentuating the muscled lines of Jarrod's legs, the strength of his shoulders and width of his chest.

His tanned hands were utterly commanding, yet soothing at the same time. She wondered where he'd mastered his skill with animals.

When it was apparent that the mares were settling, other folks rushed in to help. Jarrod never released his hold. He kept control of the situation, even turning to the frightened elderly man to calm him, too. They talked, laughed some and kept talking low and serenely.

The picture was comforting to her, that she had chosen to marry a man with integrity and capability.

Yet oddly, the scene also caused a rush of homesickness.

She would likely never again see the dozen women she'd made friends with in the past two years at Mrs. Pepik's Boardinghouse for Desolate Women.

They'd all suffered through the Great Fire. One-third of the city had lost their homes. One hundred thousand people homeless. Dozens had died. Natasha had been living with her grandfather at the time. They'd lost their house in the fire, and his jewelry shop with it. She had mistakenly assumed that because they weren't physically hurt by the flames, they'd be fine.

However, three days later, her grandfather had suffered an apoplexy from the stress—a sudden paralysis of half his body, as well as slurred speech. The next day, she lost him.

It still misted her eyes.

Women with no other means to support themselves had turned to Mrs. Pepik. The kind widow hadn't allowed anyone to feel sorry for herself. Her late husband, a policeman, had taught Mrs. Pepik how to shoot a gun, and she made sure every woman there knew how to handle one in self-defense. Then at the beginning of this year, the women had decided to place ads in the Western papers as mail-order brides. Suddenly their futures turned brighter, and no one could stop talking about where they wanted to live, which state, which man.

Natasha yearned for love, for intimacy, for family. She yearned to be free from what had always been expected of her in Chicago.

She'd had several men to choose from in the letters. In the end, she'd decided on Jarrod Ledbetter because he had replied to her ad that he was an educated man and a jeweler. She wished with all her heart to join her new husband in his ventures. Here in the West, she hoped to run her own jewelry shop—or a partnership with Jarrod—not only to prove herself, but in silent honor of Granddad. He had, after all, trained her in everything she knew, and she had become just as skilled in jewelry repair and knowledge as he had.

In the distance with the sun nearly set, Jarrod turned over the reins to the now-calm owner and made his way back to her.

"Where were we?" Jarrod asked when he reached her. Heavens, he was so rough and energized from his adventure with the horses. "Let's move on to that hotel. We'll enjoy a nice meal and get to know each other."

Her throat welled with a lump when she thought of the tender friends she was leaving behind in Chicago. She tried to overcome it by reminding herself that she would write letters home to them and that she was with a good man, in a good place.

She'd never been in love before. Could she drop the shield of protectiveness that her grandfather had instilled as second nature to her heart, and fall in love with Jarrod Ledbetter?

Chapter Two

Simon pleasured in the way the candlelight from the restaurant tabletop shifted across Natasha's face. The glow brought out her lively eyes, outlined the fine arch of her brown eyebrows and warmed the contour of her lips. It was late evening. Darkness engulfed the window next to them, dampening the view of the river below, but he was enjoying the view in front of him.

He'd hooked his hat on the wall behind him, but she was still wearing her bonnet with the fake grapes and cherries. They bobbed on her head as she ate her meal.

Remain in control, and never leave anything to chance. That was the simple rule he'd lived by ever since he'd turned eight. Those words had put food in his belly, kept him safe, protected his heart.

And it was why this situation made him bristle.

Don't hurt her, he thought. *If she's innocent and not a criminal, she doesn't deserve to be hurt.* In order to find out, he had to ask more questions.

He planted one large elbow on the white tabletop and leaned in toward her bosomed silhouette. What exactly could he say that hadn't been said by Ledbetter in his called letters? How could Simon now pretend to know what had been written between them, so that he wouldn't alert her that he was an imposter?

He'd start with something tame. "Where are you from originally?"

She inhaled, and when she did, her chest moved up and down, accentuating the slimness of her waist. He noted how nicely she moved and the sensitive sweep of her dark lashes over her face as she answered.

"Chicago. And you?"

She brought the glass of ice-chip water to her lips and sipped, making him wish she'd do all sorts of devilish things to him with those lips. He swallowed hard, cursed himself silently for noticing her womanly charms and glanced away to the other customers in the crowded room to distract himself.

Waiters in black suits hustled to deliver wine and liquor, soups and main courses of roast venison and wild duck.

"I'm from the Midwest. Raised on a farm. Before I moved to Boston, of course." He and Ledbetter had both been raised in the Midwest. Simon in southern Dakota Territory, Ledbetter in Nebraska very briefly till his parents had died and he was whisked away to Boston by his wealthy grandparents. The grandfather, apparently, had made his fortune from pirating ships in the Caribbean. The nasty streak was either in the bloodline or was taught to his grandson. Simon's parents weren't around long, either, but he'd had no one to whisk him away to safety.

"Natasha. That's an awfully pretty name. Where'd that come from?"

She flushed at his attentiveness. "My father was Irish, but my mother was Russian. She named me."

"Ah," he said with humor. "Irish and Russian. That makes you a person with quite a hot temper."

Her brown eyes lit with amusement.

"And," he continued, pleasuring in her reaction, "your Russian blood would explain the high cheekbones. Very lovely."

"How about you? What's your family heritage?"

"We can trace our lineage all the way back," he said, proudly speaking the truth, "to George Washington's house."

"Truly?" she said. "You're related to George Washington?"

"Well…one of his servants."

She smiled. "What made you want to go to Harvard?" She looked so nicely at him, he found it hard not to scoff at her curiosity. However, the question made him realize why he was here. Not to flirt with her, but to fool her. The closest he'd ever gotten to stepping foot inside any college was riding past one in a locomotive. He hoped his speech and mannerisms didn't give him away. He tended to cuss more than he should, and he could never sit calmly in a suit.

"I always had the urge to study," he lied smoothly. He shifted his too-wide-to-get-comfortable shoulders against his chair and tried to straighten his cramped leg under the table. There never seemed to be enough room for him in these fussy places.

She played with the stem of her water glass but gazed intently at him.

"Studying came naturally," he lied some more. Ha. He had counted down the days in school when he wouldn't have to pick up another pencil. Although he *was* excellent with numbers and calculations, and figuring out what sort of gun he'd need to shoot what distances, and how much gold bullion a two-foot-by-two-foot safe could hold.

She scooped the white napkin from her lap and dabbed her lips. "That's incredible. Your parents must've been so proud."

"I reckon." He realized she was referring to Ledbetter's departed parents, but Simon was thinking of his own. His mother would surely be proud, if it were true and if she were still alive. But his father—the no-good son of a bitch—wouldn't give a cow's scrapings. After all, the bastard had walked out on Simon and his mother when he was just a kid.

"And pray tell," she said, returning the napkin to her lovely thighs, "what subjects did you study?"

He blinked at her. How the hell should he know?

She must've taken his hesitation to mean that the question needed clarification. "I know you studied economics, but do tell what precisely you covered."

"Ah, I see." His hair brushed against his shoulders. "Economics of the United States. Of our natural supplies, and the upticks and downticks of the market, and our trade with the richer countries of the world. For example, England and France."

"France? Don't tell me you speak French?" Her lashes fluttered. How engrossed she was with her imaginary, dearly departed Ledbetter.

To be frank, Simon was a little put off at how much she seemed to worship him. Who the hell cared about someone who'd studied at Harvard? The man had fleeced old women of their wedding rings and slashed the throats of railroad passengers who wouldn't co-operate. Education was no substitute for character.

"Nah, no French." He shifted his long arms as the waiter brought glasses of red wine that Simon had requested. He'd selected French wine from the Burgundy region. She'd been impressed by that, too.

"Cheers," he toasted, "to us."

"Oh, Mr. Ledbetter, yes, to us."

"Please, it's Jarrod."

"Sorry, it slipped out. It's just so strange to be thinking we're to be married shortly when we've never met before. Jarrod," she corrected herself, clicking her glass against his. "May we always be this happy." She lifted the glass to her mouth.

"Hmm," he said softly, thinking of her comment, then took a swig. Not bad stuff. He preferred wine from the new vineyards of California, but he'd had a sense he needed to show off by asking for an imported bottle. It was what Ledbetter would have done.

He schemed as he twisted in his prickly wool suit and stared at the enticing person seated mere inches away. How exactly was he going to get through to this woman without arousing her suspicions to get what he wanted?

Something was off between them.

Natasha had felt it ever since his two friends had left them alone, and she and Jarrod had headed here to the hotel. She was trying awfully hard to be congenial and friendly, but something was holding her back.

What was it?

She lifted a piece of grilled fish to her mouth and tried to enjoy the meal, the restaurant, the company.

Perhaps it was a reaction to *his* behavior.

She had a sense that Jarrod was sizing her up rather harshly. That now that he'd met her face-to-face she wasn't perhaps what he'd been expecting?

She wasn't as formally educated as he was, granted, but she was well aware of the world, very well-read and inquisitive about business and jewelry. Her grandfather had taught her much about the business world, about delivering fine goods, about keeping his word on delivery times and being honest in a business deal. She hadn't gone to Harvard, but she would love to read some of his texts to learn the finer details of economics, to be privy to what men were educated on and perhaps the economic secrets of the world.

No…she didn't sense that he was lording over her that he had a college education and she didn't. It was something else.

In his letters, he'd been keen to list what he wanted from her, declaring his desire of starting a family together, of bonding as husband and wife, but now in person…she sensed none of that. Every time she caught his eye, he was the one who looked away first. He had seemed open and friendly at first glance, but only to a point, for any intimate talk she was hoping for—about weddings and ministers and how many children they'd like to have—was not materializing.

It chipped at her confidence.

Was she emitting involuntary signals that she herself was hesitant of this marriage? That now that she'd arrived and met him, perhaps they were doing this too quickly?

Nothing easy is ever worth having. That was what Granddad had always said.

Perhaps she should take in the evening more slowly,

not let her nerves run away with her senses. She would strive to be observant, to ensure that now that they'd met, she still did truly wish to marry him for him, and not because a stranger had simply responded to her letter.

What were her alternatives if she chose *not* to marry Jarrod Ledbetter?

She knew a trade. Jewelry repair. She'd read in the newspapers that many women here in the West ran their own businesses. That they even had the right to vote.

She had little money in her pocket, which was frightening on its own, but outside the train depot, she'd spotted two signs in storefront windows saying Help Wanted. She could apply for one of those positions to make sandwiches, or for a jeweler's shop assistant, or any number of small jobs until she decided how to open her own jewelry store.

But…she was being ridiculous. Things were going as planned. She was here and her fiancé across the table was prepared to marry her. How on earth had she allowed her mind to wander off in this manner?

Because she was seeing it through the eyes of her protective grandfather, who'd always warned her not to give her heart away too freely. Any man who came into the shop and gave her a second glance got a cold stare from him in return.

Not until you're sure of his intentions, Natasha, he'd say, *should you ever allow a man to court you.*

But Jarrod had given her no reason to doubt that he still intended to marry her.

"Tell me something more about yourself." He seemed to be enjoying his roast venison and took another bite.

"Such as?"

"Anything and everything. Start from the beginning."

"But you already know so much from my letters. I have to apologize how much I poured onto those pages."

"Nonsense. I liked that. And now that you're here in person, I want to hear about you all over again." His green eyes flashed with flecks of deeper colors. His gaze lowered to linger on her lips.

Her pulse rippled. "You sure I won't be boring you?"

He shook his head. His dark blond hair shifted about his broad shoulders, and she very much enjoyed the absurd length of it. All the cultured men in Chicago trimmed theirs short. But this was the Wild West.

"I'm mesmerized," he murmured.

She smiled. He was definitely more charming in person than he'd been in his letters. His letters had been intense and serious. She had detected no sense of humor in them, but then, what man showed his humorous side on a page? It wasn't as if she was marrying Mark Twain, for heaven's sake.

"Well, as I said, I was born in Chicago. My parents died early, sadly, both from tuberculosis." When she was fourteen and had never even heard the word before. She'd become their caregiver for a solid month, getting instructions from the doctor and learning how to make chicken soup on her own, change bedsheets with a person still in them, and sit in the darkness night after night listening to their rattling breathing and praying they'd make it. God had never answered her prayers, and it had taken her years to forgive him.

"I'm sorry to hear it."

She frowned gently. She'd already told him that in her letters. Didn't he remember?

He seemed to, for he corrected himself. "I mean to say—sorry to hear it in person." His mouth twitched in genuine sympathy.

"Thank you," she said sincerely. "But I had a lovely upbringing with my grandfather. We didn't have much, just each other. We lived above his jewelry shop."

"His jewelry shop. Tell me more about that."

"I thought you'd be interested in his business, seeing how much it is that you and I have in common."

A line in his cheek flickered. "My thoughts exactly."

"His shop wasn't big, but he had a lot of customers. At first, I'd help him by working the counter. You know, taking in the cash, putting it in the drawer, making change. A couple of years later, I helped him with the watches."

"The watches?"

"Pocket-watch repair. Cuckoo clocks. Grandfather clocks. He wouldn't let me do much but hold the pieces for him. But I studied what he did. Sometimes if we were behind, he'd let me do an order. Then we expanded to repair gold rings. To reset loose stones in other pieces of fine jewelry. The business got bigger and bigger."

He frowned. "And then you must've…you lost it in the Great Fire?"

She nodded.

"And your grandfather passed away…." He prodded for more.

She promised herself she wouldn't get weepy. His death was more painful to her than her parents'. "That he did, unfortunately. A few days after the fire, when things had cooled down and it was safe, we were sweeping the streets of charred debris. One minute he was teasing me that I looked like a chimney sweep, and the next he was clutching his heart and falling to the ground. Apoplexy. His speech was so slurred I couldn't understand him. We never got a chance for another conversation."

"That is a shame." He reached over the tablecloth and touched her hand. His large, warm fingers pressed against her slender ones. Such a difference in size. Such pleasure in his touch.

"Then I placed the ad," she said on a brighter note. "And here we are."

"Yes, indeed." He pulled his hand away. "Tell me again why you chose my letter," he said, "above everyone else's."

"But I've already told you."

"Tell me again. A man likes to hear in person what his bride thinks of him."

"There were dozens of respondents, as I mentioned, but yours stood out. It was so well worded. Your education truly does you justice with the written word. When I discovered you were putting your business education to good use in your jewelry enterprise, I thought I could be very supportive to you."

"Supportive. Hmm."

"And that's why I posed the question. The one you're still thinking on."

"Ask me again," he said softly. "Tell me more directly so I get a true sense of what's on your mind."

She inhaled. "Well, it's just that I believe that you and I could build quite a business establishment as a couple. We could do this together, Jarrod. We'd be twice as good, twice as big, twice as profitable. I *know* the jewelry business."

"And so…?"

"I'm asking you if you'd please consider letting me join you in your travels. You know, do whatever needs to be done?"

She sipped another smooth mouthful of red wine as he leaned back in his chair and stared at her so intensely that she thought he would shatter his wine goblet.

She was in on it, thought Simon with rising anger. Sure as thunder came before lightning, Natasha O'Sullivan was devoted to helping Ledbetter's criminal jewelry business. How much more obvious could she be?

He tried not to moan. He tried not to flinch as he sat watching her. He tried not to move a muscle in his face to indicate in any manner that he was affected by her request to join him. She knew about jewelry repair and was quite willing to indulge her would-be husband by jumping in with 100 percent enthusiasm.

How could a man from Harvard accomplish so much and yet now be so dead?

Why did Simon feel such disappointment in her?

She had many positive attributes. Why did she wish to become a criminal herself?

Greed?

All right, he'd play along. After all, she might know the whereabouts of the missing three hundred thousand dollars' worth of cash and jewels and lead him directly to it. In fact, if she was guilty, that would let him off the hook for how he should treat her. He'd met criminal women before, and they were just as vicious and deadly as men. Didn't he owe it to Eli and Clay to put her behind bars? Some of her cohorts had shot them in cold blood! They'd made Simon go mad at the scene, trying to stifle the flow of blood from Clay's neck where a gunshot had severed the artery. And poor Eli with a bullet straight through the heart.

If this woman was involved in any manner, she deserved what was coming.

Simon could only pray that she wasn't too bright and wouldn't pick up on the fact that he wasn't really her beloved partner in crime, Ledbetter.

But maybe he was jumping the gun. Maybe he was assuming too much, assuming that she knew what she was getting involved with, that it was a criminal enterprise with Ledbetter.

Slow down, he told himself. *Let's not pull the trigger yet. Give her the benefit of the doubt.*

How much, thought Simon as his pensive gaze swept over the caring eyes and the pursed feminine lips, did she know about Ledbetter's business? The lawmen were still looking, but as far as they could gather so far, they hadn't been able to uncover any stores that Ledbetter had actually opened in any town. Yet he'd claimed he had several. The man knew a lot about jewelry, but maybe only because he'd been a thief.

But surely the man hadn't written too much in his letters for fear of incriminating himself. Or maybe he had. Maybe the braggart couldn't help himself. All he had to do, once he'd trusted her and revealed his hand, was tell her to burn his letters.

"Well?" she prodded. "What do you say? Shall we run this business together, Jarrod?"

In all the years he'd been chasing criminals, he'd arrested only two women. He'd never injured one before,

for neither had resisted arrest. Laws were laws and whoever broke them would come to justice.

"Before I answer that," he said, bringing the French
Burgundy to his lips once more, "I need to ask if you've
kept any of our correspondence."

She frowned at the question and lowered her voice.
The grapes on her bonnet flashed in the candle's flicker
of light. "I did as you asked. However, I don't see why I
needed to burn them all," she whispered, "even though
I do understand your need for privacy and security, seeing how many jewelry shops you intend to open. And
how you've been robbed yourself just recently."

He quirked an eyebrow. So he'd been right. Ledbetter had asked her to get rid of all his letters. "Thank
you kindly for understanding."

"I admit, I thought it odd at first. But the more you
explained, the clearer it became."

Clearer? His side was getting murkier. They were
speaking in riddles. How much did she know? Was she
a criminal or simply in over her head?

Hellfire. He couldn't send her home on the next train
or stagecoach yet. He had to find out how much she
knew and whether she could lead him to the jackpot. It
was what his superiors at the detective agency would
expect him to do. To follow through on every lead,
and certainly not to feel sympathetic toward a possible
criminal only because she was a head-turning female.

He pushed away his plate and tried to act civil and
calm, as Ledbetter would do in this situation. All in a
day's work for that bastard. "Would you care for anything sweet? I saw raspberry pie on the menu."

She leaned her pretty frame back against the chair
rails, smiled down at her empty dinner plate and sighed

in contentment. "I don't think I can fit another morsel. Thank you for the wonderful meal and the wonderful company."

"Pleasure's all mine, Natasha."

She kept flushing at the mention of her name. It did feel rather intimate to him, too, sitting here across from a seemingly lovely lady who soon expected to be his bride.

If these were normal circumstances, if he was allowed to be himself as Simon Garr and she was his mail-order bride, he'd be as nervous as a trapped cougar. He'd seen what sort of marriage his parents had had: his father walking out, his mother drinking herself to death. No way on this earth he ever wanted that.

She lifted the white napkin from her lap and folded it across the table. She looked rather nervous, pursing her lips as though straining to find the right words. "What—what did you have in mind for the wedding ceremony? How soon would you like to do this?" The smooth muscles in her throat moved up and down with her delicate question.

Everything about her was a trap. Her smooth voice, the soulful brown eyes, the scattered freckles on her face that made her seem so innocent.

He silently cursed. There'd be no damn wedding.

He was saved from answering by their waiter.

"May I offer you some coffee?" the man asked as he gathered plates. "Perhaps some pastries, miss?"

She shook her head and nervously brushed her sleeves. Pastry was the last thing on her mind, he guessed, for she had a marriage to pursue.

"Please send the bill to the front desk," said Simon,

pushing his long legs back from the table. "I'll settle up when I pay for Miss O'Sullivan's room."

"My room?" Those cinnamon-and-brown-sugar eyes flashed at him again as if to add, *Not our room? We won't be married tonight?*

"I thought you might like to settle in. Find your way around town, rest up a few days before we plunge into this."

She might be beautiful and tempting, but he was not Jarrod Ledbetter. Fortunately, she was not his mail-order bride and it was not truly him who needed to make decisions about an upcoming wedding.

He wanted no part of wives and obligations and possible children who'd grow attached to him and…and detective agents who'd deliver the news, as they had to Clay's widow and Eli's mother, that their loved ones had been killed in gunfire in the line of duty. God almighty, Clay even had a young boy, Tucker, who'd been left behind. Simon knew all too well how it felt to be deserted by a father.

He reminded himself again.

Natasha O'Sullivan was poison.

Chapter Three

He wasn't that taken with her. The hurtful thought rippled through Natasha's mind at dinner and became even more apparent as Jarrod walked her to her room.

Her high-heeled boots padded along the carpet runner behind him as her disappointment grew.

At dinner, there had been moments when he'd looked across the table and she had sensed that he was drawn to her. He'd waited for her to answer some of his questions as though there was nothing more important to him in the world. But at the end of their meal, she had noticed a slight hesitation, an almost-imperceptible coolness that seemed to blanch his heart. It was almost as though he'd been testing her in some way, and she had failed his qualifications.

Why? What could it be about her that he disapproved of?

She couldn't help it, but she was also ruffled by the fact that he took charge without much discussion with her—he'd told the front-desk clerk that he'd like one room with a pretty view for an unspecified period. Why not discuss the waiting period with her? Why did he think she wished to rest up before "plunging" into this? The bellboy had left to deliver her trunk to the room, while she and Jarrod remained to fill out the guest register.

She stepped beside him and decided to voice her opinion. "Jarrod, it's not that I wish to rush into a wedding, but it's not precisely rushing into it when we've been thinking and anticipating it for three months, now is it?"

"Huh?" He rubbed his bristly neck. "It's just that I wish to give you time to settle in."

"Perhaps it's a silly notion, but I fantasized that upon meeting you, you might lift me in your arms and tell me how you couldn't wait to be with me. That you had a minister waiting this minute."

"Ah. I see." He gulped. Why was this conversation making him nervous? "This way," he said, motioning with his hand and making a sharp left.

She followed in the narrow corridor. Why was he so controlled with his feelings when all she wanted was to be encircled by his arms and held for a little while?

She hadn't been held for a very long time.

But perhaps she should be happy that he wasn't rushing her into marriage. That he wished them both to take their time. Perhaps she should learn to temper her loneliness and her desire to connect with another person. It would come in due course. Impatience on her part wouldn't help.

Her folks had never talked to her about boys. They'd had a loving relationship with each other, and with her, but the pain of losing them made her wary of getting close to a boy and possibly losing him, too. The last man who'd kissed her had been a young man who'd come from an upstanding family her grandfather had known. Granddad had rarely introduced her to potential suitors, had never rushed her nor tried to force her to marry young.

Wait for the right one, he'd often say. *Be guarded like your grandmother, dear Elizabeth, was until we knew each other well.*

Natasha had liked her last suitor well enough, but there'd been no mad rush to see him, no quivering in the pit of her stomach when they kissed. It had been more brotherly—playing checkers and strolling along the river together. Before him, she'd known several boys while growing up, but none she'd dreamed of with wild intensity. She had wondered if there'd ever come a time when she would meet a man who would turn her heart and soul upside down. She'd wondered it on the entire train journey here. She wondered it now as she watched Jarrod's thigh muscles flex beneath his wool trousers, as she watched his shoulder blades move beneath the shadows of his jacket.

"I think we're close," he said, turning his cheek slightly as he looked at the numbers on the hotel doors to match the one on the key.

They passed the bellboy. "Folks, it's straight ahead and to the right." He pointed that way.

Jarrod tipped him some coins, and they continued down the hall.

What had Jarrod thought when he'd first read her advertisement in the paper?

Looking for a man of solid worth. I am a hardworking young woman of good moral standing and excellent health. I adore children. I also have skills in jewelry repair, can handle a revolver and a horse, and would dearly love the adventure of living west of the Mississippi. Please write to Miss Natasha O'Sullivan…

Now that she'd left Chicago, however, she felt an ache in her heart she couldn't suppress. Her friends were left behind, and she hadn't realized how much she had relied on them. They were trusted souls who gave her straight answers.

She thought she would find all of that and more with Jarrod. His letters had been cordial and, although a bit detached, had filled her with an intense desire to join him in his travels on the railway, tending to his jewelry shops across the West and scattered over the Rockies, and creating an empire of prosperity.

Yet why was there such a chasm between them?

Granddad would never approve of her becoming a mail-order bride.

Perhaps that was why she'd done it. That thought burned inside her. But there were extenuating circumstances, she reasoned, trying to push away her shameful feelings that she wasn't quite good enough for her grandfather's standards.

She'd always tried to be such a good girl, abiding by his rules, listening to all of her elders with politeness, being ever so demure. It was her time now, wasn't it? Time to do as she pleased with whom she pleased. Time to follow her heart and any desire to fulfill her life with her *own* dreams, no matter how silly or outlandish they might appear to any onlooker.

She had that right.

"Ah, here we are. Room 208." Jarrod inserted the key into the door at the end of the corridor.

He turned the knob, swung the door open and stepped aside for her to enter.

"Is that it, then, Jarrod? No more talk of wedding plans?" Why was he elusive?

"Only until tomorrow. It's been a long day for both of us."

"Long day?" she snapped. "That's how you think of this? Of me?"

"Of course not, darlin'." He swooped in to brush his lips against her cheek.

The light kiss was unexpected. A sexual current rippled between them, hot and fierce, as she wavered past his looming body, inches close to his chest and his firm, square jaw.

His skin, bristling with unshaven shadows, held the scent of fresh outdoor air mingled with leather. She inhaled sharp and quick, and his gaze snapped down to hers. A moment of fire burned between them. Who were they to each other? Soon-to-be husband and wife?

The thought that they would soon share a bed made her tremulous. Heat shot through her chest, flushing her skin and heating her limbs.

She was so inexperienced yet so lonely that she couldn't wait to share her nights with Jarrod.

Her nostrils flared with the heady scent of his masculine presence, and she stepped past him, desperate to breathe neutral-scented air. It was almost as though she couldn't think straight when he came too close.

And she had to think straight to surmise her next step. What would be the proper requirements to set her mind at ease that he was indeed the man she should spend the rest of her days with?

"Jarrod, I don't wish to be one of those couples who pretend for appearances that we are happily wed, when beneath the surface we might live in separate homes in separate towns in separate beds."

"You have given this a lot of thought."

She frowned. "Haven't you?"

He seemed to be getting exasperated. He tugged at the collar of his shirt as if it were too tight. "Yes, it's all I've been thinking about. For *days*."

"Only days?"

"Weeks. Three months." He groaned. "What do you want me to say?"

She opened her mouth in disbelief. "How can you be so...so detached?"

Still looming at the doorway, he held up his palm in a sign of forgiveness. He seemed sincere as his voice softened. "I'm sorry. Let me rephrase this. Since the moment you stepped off that train, I haven't been able to take my eyes off your beauty. Since the moment you kicked that trunk halfway down the platform, I thought there's no other woman in the world for me."

"You truly mean that?"

"And every word I said in my letters."

At his bright expression, she felt buoyed. Then somewhat embarrassed. "You saw me kick the trunk?"

"Uh-huh."

"Oh." So much for appearing ladylike.

She stepped into the large room, her skirts and petticoats swirling about her ankles. It was a fine room. Large and airy, decorated in clean white linens with fresh-cut flowers on the nightstand and a lantern lit on the wall above the bed.

Her trunk had been placed at the foot by the closet door, and the bed had been turned down. The pillows had been fluffed and patted and looked inviting after her long, tiresome journey. Comfortable feathers awaited her.

She tossed her satchel onto the bed, lifted her arms to unfasten the pin holding down her bonnet, removed it from her head and turned to face Jarrod.

Staring at her from several paces away, he pressed a bulging shoulder against the door opening, one massive cowboy boot crossed over the other. He studied her as she patted down the unruly hairs that followed her bonnet, and mistakenly knocked out a pin from her hair.

One side of her curls fell to her shoulder, so she quickly unfastened the pin on the other side till it tumbled down, too. The weight of her hair fell onto her collar and spine.

He was watching it all, as if he'd never seen a woman fix her hair before.

The lapels of his suit jacket opened. She got a glimpse of the shoulder holster crossing his chest and swallowed hard at how intimidating he looked. The men in Chicago rarely displayed their weapons. She wasn't naive enough to think the men in the East didn't carry any, but this vision of Jarrod made her realize how rough and crude and lacking in the law the West was. She'd observed it on the train ride here. Every man had the right and duty to defend himself, and most carried guns.

She placed her bonnet and hairpins on a stand.

His posture stiffened, as if watching her made him uncomfortable in some way, as if being here in her room made him uncertain how to proceed. But, Lord, he hadn't even crossed the threshold of the door. How tense would it make him if he moved closer?

"I trust you'll be comfortable tonight, Natasha. I'll swing by in the early morning."

Startled that he was leaving, she asked, "Where will you be tonight?"

"Right next door."

Her eyes widened. "Next door? In this hotel?"

"I thought it would be more convenient if we could spend more time together. No sense going back to the cabins with McKern and Fowler. I'm here to spend time with you."

Her pulse hammered in her throat. So he did care.

Her lashes lifted as she walked closer, experimenting with this new relationship, this new man. What did he want to know about her?

And what did she wish to know about him?

The answer was quite simple, really.

She wanted to know what he truly thought of her as a potential bride, beyond their cordial first greeting and the predictable words of *How was your trip?* and *How do you do?* There was one quick way to find out, and he seemed to be too shy, or too much of a gentleman, to make the first move.

Her lady friends of a certain kind back at the boardinghouse had often told her that some men, especially upstanding gentlemen, often needed a nudge to know when a woman wanted to be touched. And where she wanted to be touched.

Natasha stepped close, craned her neck to stare up at him and tangled her slender fingers into his. An invisible current shot through her at the contact. She tugged in a breath of air. He froze.

Kiss me on the lips, she thought. *Show me what you truly feel and kiss me properly.*

Her touch was unexpected.

Simon's initial response was to pull back. He wasn't here for this; he was here to get into her mind and motivations, and not be affected by her damn presence.

She pressed her soft lips together as she stood assessing him, their fingers entwined. The warm light from the lantern danced across the bridge of her nose and lit the soft details of her cheek. Her dark chestnut hair, slightly ruffled from the hairpins she'd removed, swirled about her creamy throat.

Why did she have to be so luscious?

She slid her hand into the nook of his firm waist, her light touch caressing his skin, sending a jolt riveting through his gut. She stood so close he could breathe in the scent of her fresh skin and the lemony rinse she'd used on her hair. His pulse drummed hard beneath her touch, and when their eyes met, hers were clear and sharp and inquisitive. No woman, no innocent woman, had ever offered herself to him in such a tender manner.

She was poison, he reminded himself.

And yet he needed this, needed her. He needed tenderness and warmth and gentle understanding. Lord knew he'd had none of this on the road for the past ten years, only hard work, distance and no attachment to any upstanding woman he might have met in his line of duty. There had been saloon girls and hard-core drinkers who could guzzle a bottle of whiskey as fast as any man, but no one with any lick of sensitivity or class.

He swallowed hard at what he could not have.

A night with her would be filled with a hell of a lot more consequences than with a pretty barmaid. This woman would demand things from him he wasn't willing or capable of giving. Just as his father hadn't been able to give to the woman he'd married, and to the son they'd had.

Maybe that made Simon selfish. So what.

He was protecting her by not giving in, by not succumbing to her charms. He was also protecting the soreness in his heart that would surely rise if he ever became involved with a decent woman.

Huh, he thought, realizing for the first time in his life that he'd never been with a decent woman.

He'd slept with painted ladies, barmaids and drinkers. No one like Natasha O'Sullivan.

His jaw muscles tightened.

He should have broken free of her grasp then, for when she slid her other hand along the other side of his waist, his sexuality awakened, and the lonely boy who'd grown into a lonely man could not resist her.

With a firm grip, he anchored his hands at the sides of her face and lowered his lips to hers. It began as a graze, a soft, teasing pleasure, warm and delicious. His mouth slid across hers, tasting and pleasuring in the feel of her femininity, marveling at how lightly she could kiss, and yet how firmly his body responded. It was instant arousal. He had an immediate need to take it further.

Expertly, he moved her, stepping into the room just enough so that he could kick the door closed with his big cowboy boot and press her against the slab. Her hands slid up over his ribs, making him burn with a palpable need. He cupped the back of her neck, twirling the silky strands of her hair beneath his fingertips, gasping at the sound of her soft moan and then boldly shifting his palm to cup her breast.

He could feel the rib cage of her corset, the shallow waist, the whalebone strips that tilted her breasts upward. The cup of her breast was large and firm beneath his hand, a wondrous mound of beauty. The bud of her firm nipple arched beneath the fabric into his palm.

And suddenly their kiss became so much more. It was as if they'd been standing in a calm, sunny field, and suddenly a tornado had swept in and blasted around them. The wind caught, the weather shifted, and he and his emotions were whipped into a furious storm. The pressure of their mouths mounted, their lips pressed firmer and deeper and their tongues brushed. He wanted her.

Their bodies pressed closer, his hand dropped from her rib cage to her waist and down lower as he gripped her buttock and imagined what it might be like to throw her onto the bed and truly do everything he fantasized.

Break it up...I must break it...

With a shudder, he tore himself away.

Cool air rushed into the space between them. He gazed down at her shocked expression. Perhaps it had been too much for her, too, the unexpected jolt of passion and desire that seized them.

She slid the back of her palm against her red and swollen lips. She stared at him in amazement. Or was it shock?

He couldn't apologize! He was supposed to be her beloved groom, so how could he say he was sorry for his display of obvious desire?

"Are you all right?" he managed to gasp.

"Yes," she murmured, her brown eyes as round as chestnuts, her nostrils flaring as she caught her breath. Her fingers trembled as she lowered her hand to her waist.

"Welcome to Wyoming," he whispered.

"What a welcoming," she said softly.

"You've had a long journey. I'll leave you to rest. I'll be back in the morning and we can have breakfast."

She nodded, stepping out of the way to allow him to open the door. Her hair was totally disheveled, buckling in waves along her shoulders. Her skin was flushed and she herself was as breathless as though she'd been riding a galloping horse for hours and had been abruptly pulled off.

"Good night." He strode out of the room and wondered what on earth had just happened between them.

What the hell did he think he was doing?

Chapter Four

Jarrod was definitely attracted to her, thought Natasha with a combination of pleasure and confusion an hour later. Judging by the kiss that still had her stomach in knots every time she thought about his handsome face and his roaming hands, there was no doubt about his physical attraction to her. She pulled her thin robe tighter to her damp, bare skin. She'd just bathed in the hotel's Spring Room for Ladies and had returned to her room to unpack.

So the hesitation she'd felt from him at dinner was not a physical one. That left her to wonder what precisely it was.

Wasn't he pleased with their friendship and looking forward to a much deeper relationship? Falling in love? Having children?

Then what in blazes was wrong? One minute he was keeping her at arm's length as though he didn't know what to do with her, and the next, he was grabbing her by the behind and making it very obvious what he'd like to do with her.

"I don't understand," she grumbled, tossing aside the

ropes from her trunk and lifting the monstrous lid. She didn't know a lot about men from personal experience, but she was ready and willing to learn about Jarrod.

Rummaging through its contents, she tossed aside the worn blanket, then the patched dresses.

She reached for her jewelry box. She didn't have an overabundance of jewelry, but there were some fine pieces given to her by her grandfather, and others that she'd taken a shine to at his shop. She had saved for some of it herself, investing her hard-earned wages into precious metals, gemstones and pearls. Sadly, over half of her items had been destroyed in the Great Fire. And she'd had to sell most of the few remaining pieces from his shop over the past two years as she struggled to make ends meet.

She spotted the exquisite wedding gown she'd tucked in the middle of the trunk, between the other clothing for protection.

Gingerly, she slid it out and stood up to assess it.

The gown was more beautiful than anything she'd ever owned. It had been bought just for her and graciously sent by train to Chicago by her dear friend Cassandra Hamilton in California. Cassandra had also been a mail-order bride from Mrs. Pepik's Boardinghouse, the first one in fact, and was now happily living with her husband in the vineyards of Napa Valley. Cassandra and her husband were doing very well to be able to afford such an extravagant gown for Natasha.

"Oh, Cassandra, thank you."

The billowing white satin wasn't too wrinkled; nothing that hanging in the closet couldn't solve.

Natasha spread the gown onto her bed and smoothed the front. The bodice was tailored and beautifully fitted along her bosom and waistline. The square neckline swept low. Mounds of bustling white satin formed the lower half. And, Lord, the train! Who would've thought she'd be wearing a ten-foot train? It was embedded with lace and pearls and cut-glass crystals. There were jewels of red glass sewn into the hem and trim around her long sleeves.

She vowed she'd be a good wife. She'd be respectful of Jarrod's wishes and dreams, work hard to better both their lives, and the lives of their children when that time came. She'd fall into step beside him as his equal partner and lover.

Her pulse bounded again at the thought of that fabulous kiss. And the heart-pounding love affair they might start.

Could she allow herself the freedom of trusting Jarrod? If she couldn't trust her husband-to-be, then whom could she trust? She'd never relied on a man before, not a suitor. She supposed she did follow by her grandfather's example of never being able to fully trust someone who wasn't family. The older he'd gotten, the more protective he was. Near the end of his life, he'd turned everyone away. She tried not to be like him in that regard, but it was difficult to peel away that layer of self-protectiveness that had been ingrained in her since she'd been fourteen and faced with the loss of both parents.

What if Jarrod's indecision in setting a date was a hint of a deeper problem? Why didn't he wish to talk about any details of the wedding? Was she being stupid in ignoring the signals that he didn't want to marry her?

Don't be a fool, girl. If a man doesn't wish to marry, walk away quickly and find yourself another. That was what her friend Valentina Babbs, in her fifties and a

former lady of the night, used to tell her at the boardinghouse.

"But when do I walk away, Valentina?" Natasha
asked aloud. "How do I know if it's time?"

*You can tell how they really feel about you if you
ask them about their mother. If they open up, it means
they trust you more than they do her.* Valentina gave a
lot of odd advice.

Sighing, Natasha brushed at the creases of her lovely
gown and wondered when or if she'd get the opportunity
to wear it. She tried to ignore the feeling in the pit of
her stomach, that troublesome anxiety that was building every time she thought of Jarrod.

She reminded herself that she had options here. She
had to ask herself whether *he* would be a great choice
for *her*. She wanted an incredible partner, someone to
watch out for her as much as she would for him. If he
wasn't committed to that loyalty and to her in every
way, then perhaps she shouldn't select him.

It wasn't too late for her to back out. A feeling of remorse lodged in her throat. Surely it would not come
to that.

She was ashamed to think of what her grandfather
would say, to know she'd come all this way in a bid to
marry a stranger—only to be sorrowfully disillusioned.
Not to mention embarrassed, unprepared, broke and in-
describably hurt.

Simon hadn't slept well. After rolling for hours, he
was relieved when the sun finally came up and he could
rise out of the damn bed. He tried not to think about
her. She was the reason for his tossing and twisting
last night.

He thought about his jewelry assignment. For the past few years as a detective, jewelry missions had become his specialty. Some detectives knew all about livestock, others the construction and valuation of houses, and for him, it was gems and gold. He'd had an early interest in the field since he was kid, bartering and selling watches and gold chains in train stations with other runaways. Some became pickpockets. He'd picked a few fine pockets himself, but it had always left him with too much guilt, so he'd stuck to lawful trade.

He shoved aside the covers and planted one hard foot on the soft rug. Naked, he stood up, walked to the windows and peered through the sliver of curtains to the street below. The cool air in the room ruffled the hairs on his torso. He assessed the hustle of the street vendors and listened to the clomp of horses as strangers went about their business.

He felt nothing.

Just as every other morning when he rose and wondered what town he was in, there was no stirring in his heart that he might belong here, that there might be someone important waiting for him and binding him to this place.

No one was waiting for him. No friends, no work colleagues, no woman, no wife.

He wondered how it could be possible to meet as many people as he did in his line of work as a detective, traversing the country on covert missions, yet still be unconnected to everything and everyone.

Except there'd been Clay and Eli. They'd been his close friends. And look where that had gotten them. Knowing Simon meant death and destruction. *Don't*

*depend on Simon Garr as a friend. He'll watch you
get killed, then brush off his trousers and walk away.*

He sighed.

Lately, it was hard to know who he was anymore and
where he wanted to go from here.

"Oh, don't be stupid," he mumbled to himself. All this
soul-searching because he'd met Natasha O'Sullivan?
When it came to women, it had taken him years to get
his life to this point where he liked it. No attachments,
no responsibilities, no damn obligations, no one to live
up to or to possibly disappoint when they truly got to
know him.

He veered away from the window to dress.

The full-length mirror tacked to the armoire re-
flected his nakedness as he got into his trousers. He
buttoned them, the muscles of his torso flexing in the
coolness of the morning. He took out a neatly pressed
white shirt, shoved his arms into it and repositioned his
concealed weapons. Derringer behind his back, dagger
to his ankle, shoulder holster across his chest.

Even a sauna last night in the Gent's Spring Room
and Sauna hadn't been able to calm him. What the hell
had he been thinking, kissing her like that?

Blazes. He was an idiot.

Did he want to sabotage his own assignment?

Sure, no one had told him a mail-order wife was
on her way, but he'd dodged plenty of women before,
hadn't he?

She was no different from the dozens of others
he'd come across in his years of travel, he tried to
tell himself. Some women had thrown themselves at
him, depending on who he was supposed to be while
undercover. Posing as a rich and powerful man always

seemed to make him the biggest magnet. Other women preferred him when he was impersonating a drifter, whom they thought needed love and attention. Once he pretended to be a schoolteacher, and that had uncovered a woman twenty years his senior who kept surfacing every time he was alone, putting her hands all over him and trying to woo him to her place for dinner.

He'd never taken pleasure or spent the night with any of the women in his line of duty, only the tougher ones he met in saloons, the ones he knew could handle his leaving and didn't expect much in terms of settling down or his making false promises. There'd been some humor in the delicate situations he'd sometimes find himself in while undercover, but he'd never been truly distracted to the point of losing control.

He'd come awfully close with Natasha O'Sullivan last night.

Yes, she was different from all the rest, he admitted. What was it about her?

Something in her eyes. A glimmer of vulnerability.

He reached into his armoire and pulled out a black suede jacket that had fringes hanging from its sleeves. He tugged into it, donned his black hat and told himself that he knew exactly what he found attractive about her. Why he'd kissed the hell out of her last night.

Because he'd sensed the same thing in her that lately seemed to be engulfing him.

Loneliness.

That deep, throbbing ache in the pit of his soul that always came out late at night to whisper, *Hello, I'm here again to keep you company.*

He swore and pushed the ache from his heart. He'd been alone since he was eight years old. He was tough and impenetrable and didn't need anyone. To hell with everyone who might think differently.

He wouldn't get close enough to the O'Sullivan woman to kiss her again. In fact, he would try to physically avoid her so there was no opportunity for him to be drawn in. If he kept his cool and stayed his distance, he'd get the information he damn well needed to get from her—the location of the railroad's stolen property—and be on his way to the next assignment.

It was simple. And simple plans always worked the best.

At the sound of the firm knock on her hotel-room door, Natasha's pulse leaped. It rattled her composure. She reached to open the pine door and found Jarrod Ledbetter on the other side.

He was dressed more casually today, in a black suede coat and hat that might belong to a cowboy, but a crisp white shirt and tailored wool trousers that a businessman might wear. In the light of day, he seemed more alive and intimidating than ever. Good heavens, she thought, her mind racing with sensual thoughts of what it might be like to disrobe him of those fancy clothes.

"Good morning." He gave her a charming smile that in no way alluded to any uncomfortable regrets he might have about the intimate kiss they'd shared last night. Her face, however, flushed with heat at the searing memory.

"Morning, Jarrod."

His gaze sharpened over her plain calico dress. It had been a hand-me-down gift from one of her friends at the boardinghouse. It was a size smaller than she usually wore and therefore too snug in the bodice. However, she would take her shawl with her and drape it over her shoulders for modesty. She'd leave her hair loose, too, in the manner she'd noticed other younger women wearing last night at dinner.

"How did you sleep, Natasha?"

"As deep as an ogre. Utterly wiped-out. You?"

He shrugged. "I never seem to sleep well."

"That's a shame. Perhaps it's because of all the traveling that you do. Have you ever tried camomile tea or—"

"That's a lovely cameo," he said, glancing at her throat.

She wondered if he'd purposely changed the subject. "Thank you."

"Made of pink shell," he said, "mounted on a black velvet ribbon. The scene depicts 'Rebecca at the Well.'"

Her hand sprung to the nicely weighted oval above her cleavage. She was pleased he knew so much about jewelry and that she could share this love of the craft with him. "I thought the length of the ribbon nicely balanced the size of the cameo."

"Very becoming. And cameo earrings to match."

"Do you like them? They were originally mounted on posts. I converted them to fish hooks so they dangle, more in keeping with the length of the velvet ribbon."

His penetrating eyes flashed. "Very simple, yet very elegant."

The heated manner in which he said it made her feel as though he was appraising her, not her jewelry. Either way, she was flattered. His opinion meant a lot, since he was such a fine and experienced jeweler. He didn't wear much jewelry himself, besides the handsome silver buckle on his belt that was engraved with his initials, J. L., and encrusted with studs. Most men did not wear a lot of jewelry, but she truly enjoyed seeing the occasional lapel pin or watch fob on a well-suited man.

"Ready to go?" he asked. "I thought we might take a stroll and have breakfast outside in one of the cafés. The food's not fancy, but the sightseeing is grand."

She was relieved to take the focus from herself and happy to explore the town.

She took her white shawl and exited the room. He tugged the door closed for her, and she turned to lock it with her key. Their fingers brushed accidentally. Her belly rippled with sensations, but he removed his hand so quickly from hers that she felt the space between them rather cold. When she turned around and placed the key in her beaded handbag, he was already standing several feet away.

Oh.

Such an abrupt parting.

He seemed more relaxed when they got outdoors. He smiled at her and motioned her to pass first along the crowded boardwalk and shops, all with the good manners of a schoolboy.

This man was no schoolboy.

She swallowed hard at the glint of metal in his eyes. There was something hardened in him, something she feared might be impenetrable.

Valentina from the boardinghouse popped into Natasha's head, reminding her to ask about his mother.

"Jarrod, I—I was wondering if you might tell me more about your family. I realize your parents passed away when you were rather young. Six, right?"

He nodded, his expression remaining hard. "Barn fire."

"I'm awfully sorry. Do you recall anything about your mother?"

He shook his head.

Nothing? Six was old enough to have some memories, wasn't it? Valentina wouldn't want Natasha to give up on the line of questioning. "How about your grandmother? What was she like?"

"A nice lady." Jarrod ushered her through a crowd of people coming at them at the boardwalk, then changed the subject. "That's an unusual clasp in your hair."

The signs were not good. He wasn't letting her into his world.

"Something my grandfather gave me," Natasha answered sadly due to Jarrod's refusal to confide in her. "My most valuable piece, actually." The stones were modest in size, but beautifully set, and she recalled how delighted her granddad had been when he'd presented it to her. "It contains four precious stones, set in eighteen-karat gold from the new mines in California. The brooch means the world to me, not because of its monetary value but its meaning."

"Of course. The gems are arranged in a secret code to spell out a message from your granddad to you."

My, she thought as he continued to elaborate, Jarrod Ledbetter was very keen to notice details, wasn't he? She tried to understand that it might take some time for him to open up about his family. His mother's passing must've been tragic for him.

That's all it is, Valentina.

Jarrod elaborated on the one topic he seemed quite pleased to pursue. "The first letter of each gemstone spells out the word *DEAR*. There's a diamond, emerald, amethyst and ruby."

"He was sentimental," she explained. "An excellent goldsmith and gem setter. He made it himself."

Many people from many different countries used gemstones to spell out words in their jewelry. It was a common practice, and if the message was written in a different language, extremely difficult to decipher.

"I once repaired a ring that I secretly deciphered," she recalled. "It spelled out *FOREVER*. And a lapel pin that spelled *APOLOGY*."

He quirked an eyebrow. "Did you share the information with the owners?"

She shook her head. "That would have been indiscreet. They more than likely already knew the messages, and I was simply the hired help."

"Ah, the ethics of jewelry repair. You must keep your eyes and ears closed to the secrets of others."

He was teasing her. A rush of excitement coursed through her at the possibility of what the day might bring.

It was interesting to discuss jewelry with him. She had always been thrilled in learning and practicing what she'd learned with her grandfather. Intimate messages and meanings in jewelry were also represented with symbols, not only spelled out with words. Shamrocks were symbols of luck, for instance, and mistletoe represented a desire for a kiss.

Jarrod strode beside her. It seemed that he was being very careful to leave several inches between them as they walked. She could understand his desire to be a gentleman, but she wouldn't be put off if he were a bit bolder. She might not be very experienced about what exactly would happen on the wedding night, but she did yearn for a display of affection, to be romanced.

The August sky was clear and sunny. The day was already warming, and the bustle of cattlemen and miners and shoppers enthralled her. There were so many different types of people here. Most were men, but occasional women passed by, too, dressed in various tastes ranging from simple country fashions to elegant coiffures and wealthy dresses.

Soldiers from nearby Fort Russell strode by, dressed in uniform and headed toward the livery stable across the street. A church sat nestled next to it, and a gambling hall next to that. What a mix of affluence and attitude.

Two men in shiny jackets and cravats mused at a jewelry-store window. She glanced at the gold chains that draped across their ruffled shirts, the diamond lapel pins, the silver-tipped watch fobs, the ruby cuff links and golden rings. She'd never seen any men wear so much jewelry.

"Heavens," she whispered in surprise, trying to fathom who these flashy men were.

"Gamblers," Jarrod whispered back.

"Ah." She glanced at the jewelry-store window as they passed. George's Fine Gold, the swinging sign above them read. When she turned the corner, she realized there was an entire row of jewelry shops on this street.

"Oh, my." Such wealth.

Close by, near the Union Pacific Railroad Depot, where she'd arrived yesterday, tents were slapped up with makeshift bakeries, coffeehouses and cafés. There were market stalls of all sorts of merchandise being sold from coffeepots to snowshoes to hammers and mining equipment. One man specialized in ropes, and all sorts of these fibers, in various thicknesses and colors, dangled from the top of his awnings.

What interested her most were the jewelry stores ahead of her.

"How on earth do you compete, Jarrod, with all these shops?"

He had a ready answer. "My stores have been around longer than most and I've got established customers. I give them expertise in the field. Honesty and value in transactions. Half of these shops are nothing but fronts for dishonest thieves."

She frowned in surprise and scrutinized the customers going in and out. Many were what seemed like hard-working folks dressed in everyday work clothes, some were travelers with luggage, others were more wealthy folks dressed in finer clothes. It was disappointing to know that some of them were being hustled and cheated.

"There's a nice café around the corner, but if you're appetite's not burning yet, I thought we could investigate one of the larger shops."

"I'd like that." She was curious to see how the shops and the jewelry compared with Chicago's.

"After you," he said, flagging her into the wide storefront ahead. The sign read Wyoming Jewelry Exchange. "It's the busiest exchange in the territory."

Lanterns hung over glass cases, illuminating the sparkle beneath. The room was four times the size of any jewelry shop she'd seen in Chicago.

"Goodness, you could fit my grandfather's entire shop in one of these glass display cases."

"It is impressive. Is this what you had in mind, us working together?" he prodded. "In what role do you see yourself exactly?"

She was a bit flustered by his direct question. She'd been hoping he would embrace her in his business, but his scrutiny gave her the impression she had to prove herself. She tried not to be annoyed that he didn't trust her without question.

"Well, yes, I would love to work the counter at any of your stores. Direct customer interaction. I found that in Chicago, customers purchasing jewelry often open up to a woman more so than a gent."

"Good point. The more trust you can create in that sales transaction, the more they are likely to spend."

Spend? She wasn't precisely focused on moneymaking. "I'm more concerned with providing something of quality. Of building our reputation as fine jewelers."

"Building trust first. Income will follow after that."

"Precisely," she said, although he seemed to be much more practically minded, businesswise, on sales. She supposed that's what made him so financially successful. Granddad had never concerned himself with finances, and she supposed that's why his shop had never thrived. He never charged enough for his services. Jarrod had the opposite philosophy. She would have to learn to think more like a businessperson.

They walked between rows of gold and silver necklaces, copper jewelry, beaded bags and buttons, precious and semiprecious stones. Signs that proclaimed they could make handcrafted jewelry designed to customer specifications, and an area where gold and silver ore was weighed and bought.

Two armed guards stood at the entry and another at the back door—which seemed to lead to private rooms.

Natasha wiggled her way among browsing customers to the display of black jewelry. It was very fashionable to wear necklaces and earrings made of black jet or vulcanite. The style had come from England; Queen Victoria had been in mourning over the death of her beloved Prince Albert for more than ten years now. Her mourning jewelry—black in color—was now fashionable for all wearers and not only for sad occasions, but happy ones as well. Natasha had never seen such a magnificent display of black graduated beads, elaborate settings and decorated links.

A plump woman bumped into Natasha's elbow while speaking to her husband. "Beuford, won't you buy me this brooch? You know how smart black looks on me." She glanced up at Natasha. "Pardon me, miss. Terribly sorry to have bumped you."

Natasha smiled at the woman's enthusiasm and nodded to indicate no harm done. Natasha inched away to peer at a jet snake necklace with a heart dangle.

"That's pretty," said Jarrod, inching to her other side.

"Oh," said the woman, gazing to another display case. "Look at those rubies, Beuford." She pointed to a necklace as a thin salesman removed it from the glass display so she could try it on.

Natasha couldn't help but overhear.

"This is it, Beuford."

"You sure it's what you want?"

"Absolutely. I adore rubies."

When the price tag flipped over and Natasha could read it, she frowned at the low price. She discreetly caught the eye of the woman, and signaled to her that the price was too low.

The woman frowned back, as if trying to comprehend.

The salesman was momentarily called away and Natasha whispered to the couple, "Those can't be real rubies. Not at that price."

"What do you mean?" said her husband. "The sign in the window says they sell at wholesale prices. That's why the price is low."

Natasha stepped closer. "May I?" She indicated that she would like to lift the piece from the woman's hand.

The woman nodded and Natasha lifted it to her cheek. She pressed it there for a moment and quickly returned it to the woman's hands. "Not real," Natasha declared.

"But you didn't examine it," Beuford protested. "You didn't even look at it closely through one of those eyepieces."

"I don't need to," Natasha whispered. "Those rubies are paste. Made of colored glass."

"How can you be certain?" asked the woman.

"Glass stones like those heat up quickly against the skin. Real gemstones remain cool for quite a while longer. Different thermal properties."

"Well, I'll be danged," said the gent. "Hey, mister, what're you tryin' to sell us here?"

The salesman returned. "Sir, I assure you this is top-quality gold."

The couple turned to Natasha. She nodded to confirm it was real gold.

"But not real rubies," Beuford declared.

The salesman sputtered, "Well, nowhere does it say... I—I wasn't finished showing you the necklace, sir, and was quite meaning to tell you that these are exquisite replicas of Indian rubies."

The salesman tried to placate Beuford while Jarrod whispered in her ear, "I'm impressed with your knowledge."

Natasha flushed at his compliment. "A good quality in a partner?" she asked him.

He blinked. Something in his expression flicked with disappointment, but then it must've only been a figment of her imagination, for he smiled. "Absolutely."

She should be happy at his response, but instead she was confused. Why was she getting mixed messages from him? What did she have to do to prove she was valuable? Or was it her? Was she reading things into his words and expressions that weren't there?

She concentrated on the jewelry. Since the price tag did not state that they were rubies, there was no outright lie told. No crime committed. The salesman would simply go along with whatever the customer assumed—that they were real rubies—the customer none the wiser, but his wallet a whole lot lighter when he left the premises.

There were, of course, very expensive real pieces here, Natasha observed. There was just so much of it, one had to know what one was buying.

The salesman left with the "ruby" necklace and the middle-aged couple turned back to Natasha.

"Do you mind advising us while we shop, dear?" asked the woman. "We would, of course, pay you for your time. It wouldn't take you long."

"An hour at most," said her husband.

Jarrod interjected, "We were just leaving for breakfast."

The woman's face flattened in disappointment. "I see. Didn't mean to trouble you."

Natasha softened. The couple reminded her of many

folks she'd dealt with back East. "Where are you from?" she asked them.

"Boston," declared the woman.

Jarrod's city.

"I suspected you were from the East," said Natasha, having recognized their accent. "I'm newly arrived from Chicago. But my—my fiancé—" she stumbled over the new word, although was pleased at its sound "—is from Boston, too."

"And we really must be going," said Jarrod.

Why the rush?

"Where from in Boston?" Beuford asked eagerly. "Perhaps we know some of the same people."

Jarrod groaned. He seemed perturbed. Why was he so impatient to leave? Because he wanted to spend time with her alone? It was truly sweet of him, but she found it very interesting that this couple hailed from the same neck of the woods as Jarrod. The more she learned about her future husband, the better. She would love to hear more about their fine city, and would love to hear an exchange between them and Jarrod.

"I'll tell you what," said Natasha. "I'd be happy to advise you on your purchase, if you'd do us the honor of joining us for breakfast when we finish."

Chapter Five

"My apologies, Natasha," Simon interrupted, trying to think fast on his feet to extricate himself from this potentially damaging interchange with the middle-aged couple from Boston. "But we do have important plans to make, darlin', and we simply don't have the time to spare." He tipped his hat to Beuford and his wife. "Have yourselves a pleasant day."

"We do have the time," Natasha insisted as the older couple watched.

Simon tried to temper his reaction. Why did she have to be stubborn? He was supposed to be her fiancé, and she was supposed to listen to his opinion. What if these people discovered he hadn't been schooled in Boston? That he'd never set foot in the city? His masquerade with Natasha O'Sullivan would be over.

"A wife should back her husband," he said firmly.

"She will," she retorted, staring up at him, "when they actually wed."

"She should begin now," he insisted, "and certainly not contradict his word in front of strangers."

"I believe the question was posed to the would-be

bride first, so it is in fact the would-be groom who is doing the contradicting."

He groaned.

"Oh, hey, listen," said the gentleman. "We didn't mean—"

"Nonsense," Natasha replied, "we'd be happy to join you." She batted her eyes at Simon as if daring him to continue the battle.

Her stare was a feminine combination of ice mixed with heat. A tiger in skirts, indeed.

But if he continued arguing and insisted they walk away, she'd get her buns in a blister and may never trust him enough to confide her criminal desire to join him— as Ledbetter—in his crime sprees. It would surely take him days longer to get back to this point of trust with her.

Hell. What a situation.

The strangers broke the standoff. The woman, round and short, with a graying bun and wearing an expensively tailored bodice and long, pleated skirt, stepped forward toward Natasha. "We are so pleased to meet you. I'm Carolina Dooligan and this is my husband of thirty-seven years, Beuford."

Beuford tipped his fine bowler hat in greeting. He was even shorter and heavier than his wife. Dark and spry, like a leprechaun. "Meeting someone from home is a sweet pleasure after being on the road for two months." He held out his hand, and what else could Simon do but shake it?

He tried not to grumble as they finished their formal introductions.

"Now, Miss O'Sullivan," said Mrs. Dooligan, leaning closer in a conspiratorial gesture, "I'm on the look-out for some pretty gems set in gold."

"Let's try another shop, shall we?" Natasha suggested.

"Yes," Beuford muttered. "Preferably somewhere where I won't feel like punching the salesman."

"The West is wilder than you might imagine," Simon warned him. "You've got to be on your guard, especially when you're taking out your wallet and laying down a wad of money. You've got to watch for thieves from every angle."

"Humph," said Beuford as they made their way into sunshine again. In the far distance beyond the silhouette of the town's buildings, the Laramie Mountains sat outlined like the shadow of a huge sphinx. "Pretty as a postcard."

Simon ushered them two doors down into another shop, as crowded as he could find. If things were busy and noisy, and if all went according to his plan, it would be difficult to talk. Especially about Boston, possibly tripping up Simon on some fine detail about the city and exposing that he couldn't truly be Jarrod Ledbetter.

Natasha took Mrs. Dooligan by the arm, led her to a display and pointed to a brooch made of blue sapphires. Or so they looked.

Damn, he was impressed by Natasha's knowledge of gemstones and precious metals. She'd been around them her entire life. All the more reason that Ledbetter would've chosen her as his partner. It was surely what had attracted the criminal.

Beuford nudged him. "Where, Jarrod, were you born and raised in Boston?"

"Actually, I was born in Nebraska."

Natasha interjected from several steps away, "But he studied at Harvard for several years."

Beuford whistled in amazement at Simon. "Hot dang! A Harvard graduate! I've never met one. But I could tell, you know. I could tell by the way you carry yourself. All fine and mighty. And of course you are, with the size of your brains and the bushels of money it must've taken your folks to put you through. What did you study?"

"Economics. Business history."

"Ha-ha! Business! Mighty fine choice. What business are you in?"

Simon's lips went dry. This was getting too close for comfort. "Jewelry."

"Just our luck! I knew it! I knew you and your lady friend knew something more than the average flop." He darted to his wife's side. "Carolina! You hear that?"

Simon shook his head with annoyance as Beuford badgered his wife with the news. She seemed as equally impressed as her husband, raising her gray eyebrows in delight, grinning at Natasha and giving Simon a little wiggle of her fingers, as if she were saying hello all over again. Simon darted into a cluster of shoppers so that he wouldn't have to talk to Beuford anymore.

"Jarrod! Yo-ho! Got another question!"

Simon ignored him while he wove through display cases.

"Phew, it's hard to get your attention, sir," Beuford panted, finally catching up. "I say, where did you live while you went to college? Right in Cambridge? Or Boston?"

"Both," Simon replied vaguely. He'd looked at some maps when he was being drilled by the detectives and knew that Cambridge and Harvard College were on the other side of the river from Boston, but preferred not to elaborate.

Beuford frowned.

Mrs. Dooligan hailed them. "All finished! Look what we decided upon." She held up her wrist. Two black-and-gold bangles dangled from it. "And my locket to match." She patted the golden oval that hung from a golden chain above her high-collared blouse. "It's encrusted with a ring of blue sapphires."

Beuford squinted closer. "Get a good price?"

His wife nodded. "Natasha negotiated with him."

"Well, it's a lovely choice," said Simon, once again tipping his hat in goodbye. "Off we go, Natasha." He grasped the back of her arm, forgetting that he'd vowed to stay his distance. The heat of their contact rippled through his bare fingers.

"Shall we have breakfast together?" Natasha twisted within his grip to look around his shoulders and back at the Dooligans. "I'd like to hear about Boston."

"Don't worry, dear, we haven't left you," said Mrs. Dooligan, trudging up from behind and suddenly appearing to Simon's right.

Oh, joy.

Simon led them through the doors into the crowded street.

Beuford scoured the cafés and tents, packed with people coming and going. "Where do you recommend, Jarrod?"

Simon looked for the busiest, crammed eatery. He pointed two doors down to a tent that barely had standing position. "Grub's real good in that one."

Mrs. Dooligan's loose cheeks bunched in disappointment. "But...but it's so very..."

Crowded? thought Simon. So noisy that they wouldn't be able to do much talking? He grinned in self-satisfaction and led the way. Smoke billowed from the fires of outdoor hidden kitchens behind the tents and shacks.

"Table for four, please," he told the scruffy waiter, who was yawning.

They were led to a makeshift bar. Perfect. Now they had to sit in a row, which would make it doubly difficult to talk. He chose the farthest end stool. He held out the seat next to him for Natasha. Mrs. Dooligan sat next to her, and Beuford on the other end.

They read from cardboard menus. Round tables were squeezed in around them, filled with miners, travelers, ranch hands and gamblers. Simon had been distracted from Natasha for the past hour, but now they were pressed together so close their thighs touched.

It was unbelievably sensual sitting next to her: not wishing to inhale the scent of her fresh-scrubbed skin, but being forced to; not wishing to imagine what her sultry legs might look like beneath the fabric of her skirts, but wondering with every tug of her leg against his what sort of shape she had beneath all that clothing.

Instead of deciding on the menu, he was contemplating whether her corset clasped from the front or the back. How many ties it might have and how her ample breasts might feel in the palm of his hand.

"Coffee, Jarrod?" she whispered in his ear.

"Huh?" he asked, unbalanced by the feel of her warm hand on his wrist and her gentle breath next to his ear.

Natasha's face dipped next to his. She indicated the coffeepot the bartender was holding in front of him.

"Coffee? Oh. Yeah, sure."

While the bristly-faced man poured the steaming brown liquid, Simon tried to ignore the shape of her cleavage, which was nearly touching his biceps. If he leaned over just a couple of inches, they would brush.

Steady, he told himself. *You idiot. What are you doing?*

They placed their breakfast orders with the bartender.

Cheers rose behind them at the miners' table. A harmonica started up at another table, and a heated conversation in the corner was turning into an argument.

Fabulous. Too noisy to talk.

Natasha tapped his leg. He shivered from the vibrant charge that jolted through his skin and landed somewhere in the depths of his belly.

She raised her voice above the racket of the rambunctious crowd. "Mr. Dooligan is asking you something."

Simon leaned past Natasha's silky shape and pretended to be interested.

Beuford, too, was leaning forward against the bar. "What brings you to Cheyenne, all the way…"

Simon cupped his hand over his ear. "Can't hear you!"

"…the way from…"

Simon shook his head, pretending to be frustrated at the noise level. "Sorry. Don't understand!" He settled back into his seat and sipped his coffee, quite pleased at avoiding the question.

"I heard him." Natasha pressed close again. "He's asking what brought you to Cheyenne all the way from Boston."

She was going to translate, was she? Maybe sitting

next to her wasn't such a good idea. Her thigh kept brushing his, and the warmth of her breath lingered at his ear. It bristled the hairs on his neck and made him fantasize how lovely her breath would feel all over his naked body. Dammit, he was getting aroused.

Simon jerked his hand away from hers and took another sip of his black coffee. Hell, now he was in a fix. Anyone who looked at the lower part of his body could see how affected he was by the flirty woman next to him. He couldn't walk out of here like this.

He thought of old men and prune juice and pigs rolling in the mud…anything to rid himself of his fantasies of her bare body straddling his.

He inhaled sharply as it seemed to be working.

Beuford was asking what brought him all the way to Cheyenne from Boston.

"Ask him what he means," Simon said to Natasha.

He didn't look at Natasha when he said it, but he could tell from her hesitation that she was perplexed. The couple seemed easy to fool with double-talk, unlike Natasha, who was turning out to be very quick-minded.

She turned and shouted to Beuford, "What do you mean?"

"What do I mean?" Beuford repeated softly, as if stumped by the odd question. "I mean just what I said."

The bartender returned with platters of food. Simon was off the hook for several more minutes.

"More coffee, miss?" asked the bartender.

"More buns, please," Mrs. Dooligan requested, "and butter if you have it."

The food was good. An accordion now joined in with the harmonica. Pleased at the raucous turn of events, Simon cheerfully tapped his boot in time to the music.

Simon ripped through his meal, giving silent glances at Natasha's plate to speed her up. Finally, they were done and Simon rose to leave. He'd put his time in, and that was all that was needed. He pulled out his billfold to pay for the breakfasts, but Beuford snatched the ticket.

The sound of singing from the far corner of the tent rose to a loud level. Beuford shouted to be heard. "It's the least we could do!"

"Thank you kindly," said Simon, leading the way out of the tent near the cashier boy, who stood outside. "We hope you enjoy the rest of the day."

"But wait a sec—" Beuford began to say, holding his thick wallet open.

"We'd love to spend more time—" said his wife, loosely clutching her handbag and trying to regain Simon's attention.

"That'll be a buck twenty," said the cashier boy, insisting on payment.

Simon inhaled a sweet lungful of air. Ah, the smell of freedom. He strode away, pressing his firm hand on Natasha's shoulder to lead her along.

"Shouldn't we wait to say goodbye?" she asked. "We barely got a word in."

Simon distracted her the fastest way he knew how. "It would be a lot more enjoyable talking about our wedding plans alone."

"Why—why, yes, I suppose it would—"

They were stopped by a heart-piercing scream behind them.

Simon reacted. He ducked, pulled Natasha aside to instinctively protect her and pivoted to look at the commotion. He slid his hand into his jacket and planted it on the gun in his shoulder holster. He was ever so aware of the derringer digging into the back of his waist, also at hand if needed.

The Dooligans were getting *robbed*. Mrs. Dooligan was screaming, while Beuford stood dumbfounded at the cashier's table, looking after the fleeing man who'd stolen his wallet and the other one running in the opposite direction with his wife's handbag.

Simon leaped in alarm as he quickly assessed his next move.

Chapter Six

Simon rapidly calculated which bandit he should chase. Beuford likely had more money to lose in his wallet than his wife did in her handbag, so Simon focused on the runaway thief in the cowboy chaps and checkered shirt.

Simon sprang into a run. He called to Natasha, "Stay put with the people here!"

"Be careful—" she sputtered, but he was already racing in pursuit.

Revolver in hand, Simon dodged a team of oxen, ripped past a man hauling a large sign and jumped over two bales of hay. He turned at the livery.

The runaway thief caused a horse to rear. Women screamed.

The man at the reins hollered, "Stop! You low-lyin' troublemaker!"

But the skinny thief kept running. He turned his head, caught sight of Simon getting closer and panicked. He tumbled over a crate of ducks. They squawked. He flew over a tower of luggage at the railroad depot and dashed inside.

The depot was packed.

Panting, Simon surveyed the crowd. He looked over the heads of most people. He spotted the thief hopping onto a train that was rolling out of the station.

Simon lifted his revolver and took aim, but there were too many people crossing between him and the line of fire to shoot. Bystanders might be injured.

Damn. He lowered his revolver, but the crowd caught sight of it.

One man shouted, "Gun!"

People hollered and some screamed in panic. Someone yelled, "Don't shoot!"

Cursing at the commotion, Simon holstered his firearm back inside his jacket and watched the train pull away. Through a window, the thief gave Simon a nasty grin, tipped his hat goodbye and waved with Beuford Dooligan's wallet. Bastard.

Simon tried to calm the bystanders. "It's all right, folks. No harm done. Just trying to catch a thief."

"Did he get away?" asked a farmer leading a goat.

"Afraid so. On the train to San Francisco." He was as good as gone, Simon figured. But the thief would likely be jumping off that train before it got anyplace close to San Francisco.

With a fast clip, Simon made his way back to Natasha.

She was comforting Mrs. Dooligan, who was shaking and dabbing at her cheeks with a handkerchief. Beuford, pale and trembling, was reporting the incident to the local sheriff and his deputy.

Oh, great, thought Simon. The two lawmen were unaware that Simon was an undercover detective, and he could not blow his cover by admitting it. He hoped that the sheriff wouldn't prod.

Beuford let out a sob when he spotted Simon returning empty-handed.

"Nothing?" asked Beuford.

"Sorry."

"Did you see the whole thing?" The words *Sheriff Locke* were stitched into the man's shirt, below his shiny badge. He was middle-aged, with messy red hair and a ripe belly.

"I had my back turned to it, but I saw the thieves run," Simon explained. "The one I was chasing, who took Mr. Dooligan's wallet, got away on the train to San Francisco."

"Aw, hell," said the sheriff. "I'll have my men telegram the next stop, but he'll predict I'm going to do that. He may have hopped off already. Aikens," he said to his deputy, "why don't you go to the telegram office and do that?"

"Yes, sir." The deputy was no more than a freckle-faced kid. Maybe twenty. He turned and headed down the street.

Beuford offered an opinion. "Maybe the thieves started following us right from the jewelry shop."

Simon looked to Natasha, who stood sympathetically beside Mrs. Beuford for support.

Simon shook his head. "No. No one followed us. No one was watching us as we ate, either. It was someone who happened to notice you and your wallet at the cashier station." Simon's training, years of detective work, made him constantly aware of who might be following him.

Mrs. Dooligan handed her husband her hanky and Beuford sobbed into it. He mopped his tears. "They took all we got. Four hundred dollars."

"You carry that kind of money on you?" Sheriff Locke asked, incredulous. "Unarmed?"

Beuford sobbed. "I was on my way to find a bank to deposit it. It's half our life savings. I was only stopping to buy Carolina some jewelry because I promised her the world if she'd come to Cheyenne with me."

His wife patted him on the shoulder.

"What happened to the other thief?" Simon asked the group. His eyes met with Natasha's.

"He got away, too," she declared with a moan.

"What did you lose, Mrs. Dooligan, if you don't mind my asking?" Simon peered at her.

The heavy woman sighed. "I didn't carry any money. I had a few personal items—a hairbrush and pins. Old train tickets. Notes on where we've been. It was a very pretty handbag, though."

"I'll buy you a new one." Beuford's words were raw and rattled. He explained to the group, "We've got more funds in the bank in Boston. We've been scouting the West, looking for a place to open our shop, and that's why we were carrying all that money. Took us ten years of saving. Lanterns are my speciality. And Carolina, here, would like to sell cooking utensils. We do have more funds in Boston, but it'll take a few days to get it wired here. What're we supposed to do till then?"

Mrs. Dooligan ran a shaky hand over her cheek and looked to the sheriff. "Perhaps we can go with Sheriff Locke? You'll put us up, won't you?"

"Sorry, ma'am, we don't run a charity. That's just the way it is, plain and simple. You might try one of the churches." He pointed toward the tent beside the twenty-four-hour gambling house.

"Stay in a church tent?" she whimpered. "Sleep on the floor? With my bad knee?"

While they conversed, Natasha nudged Simon in the ribs. With a jolt, he looked down at her face. She looked to the Dooligans, then pleaded with Simon using only her pretty brown eyes.

"Now, come on," he whispered. "We can't put them up." There was no way in hell that his detective agency would cover the expenses of two unknown strangers who had nothing to do with his mission. And why would he personally jeopardize his situation by continuing a relationship with this couple?

They'd been nothing but a headache for him thus far. Beuford Dooligan had been careless with his wallet, flashing his wad of cash in front of a whole tent full of strangers. Especially after Simon had warned him about the wild nature of the town.

If Simon opened his billfold and simply gave them some cash to tide them over a few days, they'd be following him and Natasha around like long-lost puppies. He'd never be rid of them. What he had to do was make a clean break now.

Simon didn't wish to seem heartless, though, especially in front of his "beloved" bride-to-be. So he simply glanced down at Mrs. Dooligan's sapphire necklace, hoped she would subconsciously take note and waited for the idea to sink into her mind.

Her hand shot to her new locket. "My new jewels. We could return them and use the funds to survive."

Beuford sighed. "I don't want to do that. Besides, a sign in their window says somethin' about no refunds."

Mrs. Dooligan groaned. "Maybe another jewelry

exchange…" She scoured the street, reading the hand-painted signs above the row of businesses.

"Well," said Simon matter-of-factly with little emotion, "it's a mighty good thing you have that option. Take care, now."

He turned to leave, refusing to make eye contact with the Dooligans so he wouldn't succumb to pity. However, Natasha interrupted.

"Jarrod, I have an idea," she said loudly.

"Darlin', we've got a wedding to plan," he replied.

"A wedding?" Mrs. Dooligan gasped. "Dear me, here we've been going on and on about our own lives and troubles. Go ahead," she said, weeping again, and this time Simon couldn't tell if it was from the joy of the wedding or disappointment that they were leaving. "You young people don't need us burdening your lovely plans."

"Thank you," said Simon, trying to remain unaffected by the outburst. "Good luck with your lantern and cooking-supply business."

"Jarrod," Natasha called to him as she stepped to the shorter woman to console her. "There's no need to sell those lovely jewels, Mrs. Dooligan. And if you did, perhaps we could take them off your hands."

Simon's eyes widened. He froze for a second. What was this all about?

He didn't know what to make of her.

Was Natasha concocting a plan to go for the jewels?

What a sweet plan. Buy the jewels at a fraction of their cost and fleece these desperate people in their time of misfortune.

Hell, she was three steps ahead of him. She was a genius. Equal in deviousness to Ledbetter.

But Simon's personal disappointment in her stung like a whip to the back.

He had no reason to be disappointed in her. He didn't know this woman. He had no connection to her, no stake in whether she was a person of good character or bad; he simply had a mission to fulfill, and she just might be the one to lead him to the stolen cache of goods worth three hundred thousand dollars.

He clenched his jaw. What could he do now except go along with her plan? To turn her away, to seem as if he wasn't interested in any plan she might have to abscond with the Dooligans' jewels, would be alerting her to the fact that he wasn't the real Ledbetter.

"There, there," she consoled Mrs. Dooligan. "We'll come up with a plan where you don't have to sleep on anyone's floor."

Natasha, bold and decisive, looked up at him with those piercing brown eyes that shimmered like caramel and cocoa. Who was this woman? Who was she to affect him so much? Who was she that he'd lost such control last night and had kissed her as he'd never kissed any woman?

She was no one, he told himself.

Just another woman in the line of duty. Just another woman who'd be disappointed in him if she knew the truth. That he wasn't good enough, strong enough, loving enough to keep her. That he deserved only fleeting women in fleeting nights.

He didn't want her anyway. He hated her type—the type who could steal and cheat and lie.

He had an obligation to Eli and Clay. Even though he wasn't able to save their lives, he could damn well ensure anyone who'd been involved in Ledbetter's dirty schemes—including her—would pay.

"Yes," he said assertively to the Dooligans. "I've got a cabin on the outskirts of town. There's an adjoining one you can stay in. Along with Miss O'Sullivan."

Beuford teared up again and mopped his face. "Bless you."

His wife tried to compose herself. "Thank you so much, sir."

Natasha's lashes flickered, and then her expression warmed with a smile. Her face transformed. Her smooth cheeks lifted, her skin glowed, her pretty pink lips stretched over a fine row of sparkling white teeth. The black velvet ribbon that crossed the curvaceous hollow of her throat gleamed against dewy flesh. Her pink cameo with its dark profile of a young girl seemed too innocent of a picture for her to wear.

Brilliant actress, he told himself with disgust.

She was beguiling, and as dangerous as a jungle cat. One bite would be lethal.

However, he'd broken through in his assessment of her, hadn't he? This situation with the Dooligans had worked to his advantage. Natasha's knowledge of jewelry, the robbery, everything had brought him closer to revealing her true nature. She was a wicked liar, and he would get the information he wanted from her, maybe sooner than he thought. If he had them all together under one roof, he would have better control over the situation. And that was what it was all about for him. Control.

The new arrangements were only proper, thought Natasha. Thirty minutes later, she watched as her trunk was hauled up on a wagon by the hotel's bellboy, alongside Jarrod's bag and the Dooligans' from the hotel where they'd been staying. She would stay in a cabin with the older couple. They would act as chaperone to her and Jarrod. Natasha couldn't very well move in with her fiancé and two of his employees in their cabin, nor could she stay by herself in another.

It would be scandalous. A woman with morals and character wouldn't besmirch her reputation. Even though the more time she spent with Jarrod, the more she daydreamed of doing just that. She stepped into the front beside Jarrod in the awaiting four-seat leather buggy. The Dooligans squeezed into the backseat.

"We can't thank you enough," said Beuford, who'd recovered from his teary-eyed bout of shock from being robbed.

"Won't hear of it," said Jarrod, shifting his body coolly away from Natasha's in the driver's seat, making her wish he'd sit closer. "It's the least we can do to help."

The bellboy flicked the reins and they rolled down the dry, rutted street.

Natasha replayed the moment back in her mind at how quickly Jarrod had leaped to the Dooligans' rescue. He'd bravely tried to apprehend the thief all by himself, charging down the street like a trained bodyguard with a gun in his hand. She glanced at him. She'd heard him say that Cheyenne was a dangerous place, and she'd seen many men with guns slung across their hips, but she had no idea he was so capable with revolvers.

Obviously, he was prepared and knew how to handle himself.

Educated from Harvard, owned a chain of successful jewelry shops and willing to put his life on the line for strangers? How had she gotten so lucky?

"How many residences do you travel between?" she asked politely, wishing to get to know him better.

"Several. There's the cabin here. The one in Santa Fe. Two in Montana Territory. Plus Oregon."

"Gracious." She wasn't sure which town they would settle in primarily. "Are you partial to one place in particular?"

His eyes grazed her, and a slow, hot fuse seemed to burn between them. One look had the power to ignite her. It withered away her sensibilities and made her wonder how much adventure he would seek in bed.

She withdrew her pleated fan from her satchel and fanned her face.

Would he be a wild lover?

A daring one who preferred to try different positions in different places around the home? Just like the ladies of the boardinghouse had described? Mercy, it was difficult to believe some of the stories she'd heard from her female friends, but as she was getting to know Jarrod, she realized that something exciting was happening between them. It couldn't be just on her side. He must be feeling that heady pull of desire himself.

Judging by that feverish kiss they'd shared, she would guess that he *would* be daring. Would she be able to satiate his appetite?

She hated to admit it, but part of her was secretly glad that he was consciously slowing things between them. She wasn't sure if she was ready for nights with him.

"I enjoy the places all for different reasons," he answered.

"Such as?"

"This one here is busy with a lot of different people coming and going. Always full of action and a little bit dangerous." He rubbed his large hand on his knee. "Santa Fe's nestled in the hills. The stone architecture's beautiful." He tilted his head, and his dark blond hair brushed the top of his expansive shoulders. "Montana air is the purest. You've never breathed in anything so clean and fresh as when you step into the mountains. And Oregon, well, simply the color of the ocean is enough to seduce you."

The way he said *seduce* rippled off his tongue. When he raised an eyebrow at her, she was sure he was thinking of another type of seduction. One that might have her lying beneath him, lost in a bare embrace…

"Yes, well," she said tightly, pressing her knees together, "they all sound charming."

Was it her imagination, or did everything they speak about seem to have hidden meaning? Every word he said, every syllable, seemed to undress her.

They rolled through the busy streets, passing blocks of more shops, tents, makeshift canvas businesses, plank buildings and log cabins. Within ten blocks, the buggy drew to a stop.

She heard the driver of the wagon behind them tell his horses to stop, too.

She looked about as Jarrod and Mr. Dooligan slid out of the buggy to claim their baggage. The earth was dry and caked. Two cabins sat beneath a cluster of pine trees and cottonwoods. A creek rolled past an outer building, which looked to be a small barn.

Natasha jumped out of the conveyance and brushed at her long skirts. She was helping Mrs. Dooligan to her feet when Jarrod's two colleagues rushed out of the cabins.

Her heart jumped to her throat.

They were in neatly pressed white shirts, trousers and suspenders, still looking like educated business-men, but to her dismay, they barreled out of the cabin with guns in hand. The guns were pointed at her and the Dooligans!

Chapter Seven

"There's no need for guns." Simon could barely contain the fury in his voice. He stepped in front of Natasha and the Dooligans and confronted his two men, Fowler and McKern. What were they doing, raising their damn weapons?

"Sorry, boss." Fowler, tall and skinny, lowered his revolver and ran his hand along his shirt. He plucked at his suspenders.

McKern holstered his two guns—two! Several inches shorter than his cohort, he frowned. His lips smacked together beneath his thick mustache. "Thought your visitors were trouble. We weren't expectin' you for a few days."

On the outside, Simon shrugged it off as though it wasn't a big concern. On the inside, he was seething that he had so little control over these two well-educated apes. He didn't bother turning around to assess Natasha's reaction for fear of giving away his own, but instead tried to exude serenity.

The horses neighed, but the driver of the wagon and the bellboy soothed the animals with calming voices.

"Are you folks married yet?" McKern grinned at Simon and Natasha.

"Not yet," Simon answered quickly, wishing to bury the topic. "Still making plans."

"Please don't let us interfere," Mrs. Dooligan peeped.

"Not at all," Simon said with steadfast control. He turned back to his men. "We've run into a bit of a situation," Simon explained as he began to unload suitcases. Fowler and McKern jostled around the wagon to remove Natasha's trunk. "These two folks, Mr. and Mrs. Dooligan from Boston, were robbed. I've invited them to stay in the second cabin along with Miss O'Sullivan till the sheriff and deputy apprehend the culprits." *Which'll be never,* thought Simon. The two ruffians were long gone.

He glared at McKern and Fowler as if to say, *Keep your lips sealed around the sheriff.*

"Well, howdy, howdy," said the two apes as they welcomed the Dooligans and Natasha. They were quick to silently admire the new jewels around Mrs. Dooligan's throat. Heavyset McKern had the audacity to smirk at Simon, as if he understood that the jewels were up for grabs.

Simon nodded in pretend collusion. Then as they were shuffled into their respective cabin, he commanded beneath his breath, "Hands off until I say."

Fowler whispered with a grin, "Now you're bringing them straight to our door."

Natasha stood nervously in the center of the commotion, watching as her broken trunk with its mishmash of ropes was set carefully inside. Simon appraised her every movement, trying to assess who she was and what her intentions were. When she turned her face to the sunlight, it captured such a pretty angle of her cheeks and the curvature of her lips that the muscles in his throat tightened. When she ran a slender finger along the hollow of her throat, rubbing at an itch, his stomach wavered. When she stepped on a twig accidentally and it snapped beneath her boot, she startled and stepped back, her long skirt swinging about her hips as he stood and wondered whether that was the sun he could see cascading through the fabric and outlining the silhouette of her shapely legs, or just his imagination.

He forced himself to look away. She was not to be trusted. And with the outrageous thoughts he was having, neither was he!

"Thanks for the ride," Simon told the bellboy.

"Our pleasure, mister. If ya need us again for any travel, just holler. We got several horses for hire, too." He watched the other hired driver unload more bags.

"Are you fellas ready for a home-cooked meal?" Mrs. Dooligan planted her thick hands on her short hips and looked from Simon to Fowler to McKern. "In Boston, I was a chef at the best hotel in the city."

"Mrs. Dooligan," said Natasha, "I had no idea of your talents."

"Which hotel?" asked McKern.

"The Prince Regent," Mrs. Dooligan answered.

"I've eaten there." McKern beamed in genuine interest.

Beuford leaned in close to his wife and scratched his eyebrow. "Do tell, Mr. McKern. Whatever brought you to Boston?"

"Business. I just finished college in Michigan and was passing through on my way to New York City. There to meet up with Fowler. He was finishing a jewelry apprenticeship."

Beuford whistled. "I'm honored to meet you fine people. It isn't every day one comes across such a group of educated gentlemen."

Fowler gloated.

Simon turned away and headed for the wagon for the last bag. These men were responsible for how many armed robberies? Scaring the living daylights out of how many older couples, just like the Dooligans? People who'd finally earned and saved enough money in their lifetime to buy some fine pieces of gold or diamonds or sapphires to enjoy the finer things in life, only to have them snatched away at gunpoint.

Where had they been when Simon had had to burn his clothes from the shoot-out because the blood from Eli and Clay couldn't be washed out?

He swallowed hard and tried to temper his rage.

No matter what he thought of the two apes, the Dooligans would be safe here until Simon gave his orders. He'd been quick to mention to Fowler and McKern that the sheriff and deputy were investigating the Dooligans' robbery. The implication was that the law might be calling at any moment to ask more questions or deliver news of sightings, and none of them—Fowler, McKern or Simon, acting as Ledbetter—would be stupid enough to risk harming the Dooligans until all that business with the law was over.

Fowler and McKern followed Simon to the wagon. The bellboy and other driver were occupied with the horses.

Tall, skinny and clean-shaven, Fowler reached for the upholstered bag and spoke in a low hum so the drivers couldn't hear. "Say, boss, I take it the Dooligans won't be here week after next? Come Wednesday, when that shipment comes in on the nine forty-five?"

What shipment? thought Simon, but he didn't blink. He had no idea what Fowler was talking about, but he was too experienced, had too many years with the detective agency, to show his surprise. "Of course not. We'll proceed as planned."

McKern snickered as he slapped the boards of the wagon.

Simon's mind raced. The nine forty-five. It had to be a train. Or it could be a stagecoach. Hellfire. What had Ledbetter planned before his death? What setup was Simon walking into? He had to get rid of the Dooligans and Natasha O'Sullivan by then.

Today was Thursday. He had thirteen days to find the stolen goods.

Thirteen bloody days.

"Our contacts in San Francisco sent word this morning," McKern continued. "The rubies and diamonds are coming in, in a crate marked Chandeliers."

Simon grinned. "Smart decoy."

"Not smart enough for us," Fowler said with a chuckle.

Train or stagecoach? Simon wanted to shout the question, but he restrained himself. He was supposed to know the answer. "How many guards are coming with it?"

"We asked but couldn't get a definite number," said Fowler. "My guess is somewhere between two to ten."

Train, thought Simon. Ten men couldn't fit on a stage.

"If they don't want to attract attention," said McKern, his mustache gleaming in the sunshine, "they'll go with the lower number. But if they're scared of what they might lose, they'll go with the higher. Either way, we'll be ready for them."

Why would they be ready for the greater number? Three of them against ten? They weren't supposed to be sharpshooters but jewelers who committed crimes with the force of guns over innocent, usually unarmed victims, so how could three of them be enough to take down ten men? McKern's comment likely meant he was expecting more of Ledbetter's gang to show up to help them. This was a big heist and likely took months in planning. What else had Ledbetter set up?

Simon had no safe contacts here in Wyoming. His orders came from Montana Territory. He had no quick way to inform the authorities of anything. But he did have some time on his hands to send a message.

He nodded at his men and indicated they should shut up now, because the bellboy and driver were turning around.

Fowler and McKern straightened, said goodbye to the hotel employees and watched the buggy and wagon roll away.

That left them with no horses. But they didn't need horses because they traveled by train or stage wherever they went. It was easier to blend in and get lost in a crowd that way, too. Horses could be rented whenever the need arose.

Simon turned to face the two isolated cabins nestled in the cluster of trees, and with a jolt, noticed Natasha was watching him. What had she seen? She couldn't have overheard anything, he was certain. Did she know about the upcoming heist? Had Ledbetter told her in his letters?

Thirteen blasted days. Simon cursed in the wind.

* * *

"I can't eat another morsel," Natasha declared several hours later at the dinner table of their small cabin, so full she could barely move. "Everything was delicious, Mrs. Dooligan. What a feast."

Mr. Dooligan circled the table, offering coffee and tea. Natasha chose mint tea.

Mrs. Dooligan looked proudly upon the white table linen strewn with the finest Victorian crockery and silverware—which was why she had so much luggage—and urged the men to eat more. "Jarrod, please, if you'll finish the trifle—"

"Thank you, I must decline. The brazed pheasant and potato chowder were quite filling. You are a remarkable cook."

"Mr. Fowler, Mr. McKern," the kind woman suggested, "the cranberry scones and candied yams—"

"Don't mind if I do," said Mr. McKern, reaching for a cheese pastry. "This is the best meal I've had since landing in Wyoming."

Natasha was seated with her back to the blazing logs in the stone fireplace, across from Jarrod. They'd been avoiding each other's gaze since they sat down, but he caught hers now.

The slow burn up the back of her spine had nothing to do with the crackling fire, she confessed, but more to do with the boldness in his sharp green eyes, the clench of his jaw and the flickering artery at his temple. He was inches taller and much more muscled than any of the men here. In his crisp business shirt, offset by the unruly length of his dirty blond hair, his look was daunting. Unrelenting.

He was to be her husband, she thought. How would she handle such a man?

"Pardon me," she said, stumbling out of her chair. "I need to get some air."

The men quickly rose, exhibiting good manners, but Jarrod surprised her. "I'll go with you."

"No, no, please. I'll be fine." So much had happened today, and she wanted to be alone to think. She did wish to spend time with him, of course, but wished to gather her thoughts first so that she knew exactly how to proceed from here, what to ask him and how to voice her concerns.

"Dear," said Mr. Dooligan, clenching the coffeepot and looking up at Natasha's face as she passed, "you mustn't walk alone out there. You saw what happened to us today."

"Yes, yes," his wife clucked. "Do let Jarrod accompany you."

But Natasha was trying to get *away* from Jarrod.

He was already at the door, opening it for her, and she found it impossible to object. She would look silly and petty if she objected to her fiancé accompanying her for a stroll beneath the night sky.

They headed to the creek. It was almost pitch-black, for there was only a quarter moon. When she turned her back on the lights coming from the town's buildings and casinos and she peered up, thousands upon thousands of stars lit the sky like white buttons on black velvet.

"Aren't those the prettiest jewels you've ever seen?" she asked with a sigh.

He looked over at her, but not up. "Mmm-hmm," he murmured, making her shaky again. He had the ability to penetrate her veneer like no other man she'd ever met. One flicker from the side of his cheek, and she succumbed. What was he staring at? Her cameo necklace? Did he approve of what he saw in her? He certainly seemed to, she thought with a blush.

"The Dooligans took to the place with no problem." She glanced at the cabin they'd just exited. Her dangling earrings brushed her neck. Dim moonlight cast dark shadows on the grass. Dew had fallen. She could smell the sweet moisture and feel the heaviness of her skirts as they dampened.

She lifted one edge of her hemline and they continued to stroll toward the rushing water. The bubbling sound evoked a giddy sensation of pleasure. It was peaceful and sensual and throbbing within her.

"How about you, Natasha? Did you take to it?" His voice had deepened to a rich, husky intonation that reminded her of saxophones that she had heard spilling out of steamy nightspots in Chicago.

She swallowed hard, reminding herself they were talking about only innocent, surface things. Or were they? There always seemed to be a hidden agenda to his words.

He was a puzzle, this man of hers. His letters had been so cool and matter-of-fact, yet the man here in front of her was so vibrant and fiery, almost as if they were two different men.

"Yes, the cabin is very comfortable," she answered, finding her voice much stronger than she expected. She felt weak and vulnerable, totally at his beck and call, for whenever he deemed it timely to wed was when it would happen.

And suddenly that was an irritation to her. Why should he decide their marriage date? Weren't they in this together? Had they not already decided, by letter, that they would be husband and wife?

It was a blow to her pride to have to wait to plan a wedding she thought he would want to consummate as soon as he'd met her. And something about the travel here, something about all she'd been through in gaining her independence since her grandfather had died, made her speak her mind.

"Why are you waiting?" she asked softly.

"Excuse me?"

She drew up to the trunk of a large cottonwood and stopped beneath it. Overhead, leaves shimmered above his tall frame, playing peekaboo with the shadows and angles of his face. His hair—that maddening splotch of untamed blond—drew across his shoulders. He'd rolled up the sleeves of his shirt. His muscled forearms, lightly dusted with fine hairs, glistened in the pale moonlight.

"You're waiting," she repeated softly, "to set a wedding date. Taking your time. Maybe even stalling. Perhaps you're gauging the weather," she said. "Or are you gauging me, Jarrod?"

He flashed a look of surprise. She didn't usually see him at a loss for words. Everything he said and did always seemed timed and methodical, carefully thought through. But the rasp that escaped him spoke more than any words could. He was surprised because she'd aimed and hammered the nail precisely on target.

"I'm not stalling. I'm sorry I've given you cause to worry. It's been a long day for all of us, with the robbery and moving here with the Dooligans—"

"You see?" she interrupted. "You're changing the subject. My, how you dance so easily around the topic."

He was again taken aback. His neck turned color,

but as she studied him closely, she couldn't be sure in this weak lighting. Then as quickly as she'd noticed his embarrassment, it disappeared. Replaced by a more serious tone.

"Truly, Natasha, I would like to marry you as soon as we can plan it."

Yet he didn't come near her. There was no kind touch of his hand along her back, no clasp of his fingers over hers, not an inch of movement.

"I wish you would say it like you mean it."

"What?" He fumbled. "Why, I... You're putting me in a very... Of course I want you to be my... That's preposterous that you should think otherwise."

"Is it?"

"Didn't that kiss last night prove anything to you?"

And there it was. The kiss. She'd been thinking of it all day, every time she looked at him. All through dinner, even when he was simply asking her to pass the sugar bowl or whispering thank-you from across the table.

Every damn thing this man did affected her.

His breath, his rugged stance, the curve of his lying lips—yes, they were lying—even the sight of his large cowboy boots shuffling in the grass.

She sighed and looked over the streaming water beyond the grassy slopes in front of them.

How could she get it out of him? What was bothering him?

"What is it that's troubling you, then? You seem like a different man than you were in the letters."

His jaw slackened in surprise. His eyes widened. "There's no need to go accusing me—"

"I'm not accusing you of anything. I'm trying to

understand you." She snapped her shoulders toward him, feeling a button pop on her bodice as she did so. "Oh," she exclaimed, flattening her hand over the gaping fabric.

"You've lost something. I saw it go flying."

"My button." And suddenly she was more exposed than she'd ever felt with him. Her low-cut corset barely covered her breasts. She felt cool air whisper through the fabric and thereby knew her bare skin was visible. "Ugh," she muttered beneath her breath, irritated at not only the button, but at him and his elusive talk. "I've no thread and needle to fix it here. And where is the blasted thing?"

She bent to the grass, searching for the button on her knees. He did the same, yards away. They met on the cushiony slope, both empty-handed.

She glanced down at her bodice and cussed. It wasn't one button gone, but two! Lord, how embarrassing.

"Here's one." On one knee, he reached over to give it to her, and his gaze dropped to her treacherous bodice.

As a hand-me-down at the boardinghouse, the garment had been worn by several women many times over and the fabric couldn't take any more wear. She was dirt-poor. How could she explain that to a man she was trying to impress?

It was too late to cover up, for he'd gotten an eyeful.

The air fell silent, save for the rhythmic breathing between them. The dewy grass moistened her fingers. The stream smelled of clay and freshwater, and the cottonwood leaves above them swayed in the warm, gentle wind.

She took the button from his hand, their hot fingers touching. She pulled back as if his touch scorched. Then she turned and sat on the grassy slope, watching the stream ramble by. She'd find the other button tomorrow in the daylight. She wasn't sure whether the garment was worth repair, whether the fabric could take any more strain.

And now she was embarrassed by that fact. How little she had in the world. How it must seem to him that she was begging to be wed. She didn't need a man. She could survive on her own—and would—if only she knew if he planned on marrying her.

All pretense of trying to hold together her bodice left her. She let the thing gape. She turned away from him, so at least he couldn't see it.

"You don't see stars like this in Chicago," she murmured up at the sky, rising to her feet.

"I noticed the stars, too," he said, standing tall beside her once again, "when I first moved from Boston."

"You seem to notice a lot of things, yet ignore others."

"I notice everything," he said quietly, "even if you think I don't."

"Yes, well, maybe that's true." She knew something about him from his letters. Yet meeting him in person was almost as if they were starting over in getting to know each other. "It doesn't matter, Jarrod, if you don't wish to marry me," she said solemnly, trying to withhold the pain of rejection. "I would simply like to know, one way or the other—"

Her words were cut short when he moved in, spun her around and muffled her mouth with his.

Chapter Eight

Their lips locked in heated contact. Simon slid his mouth over Natasha's. He succumbed to her softness, her moist appeal, the scent of her skin. He reached up and tangled his fingers into her long hair. He felt pins collapse and barriers shatter.

The kiss seared right through him. It played with his resolve not to go near her, piqued his desires and damn well risked everything he believed was true about himself. He was better off alone. If you trusted someone, loved someone, then you'd always have to be watching out for them. How could he control every dangerous situation then? He wanted to make decisions for his own life, not be responsible for anyone else's happiness. He'd tried that as a kid and failed. Clay had tried it, and where had it gotten his young widow, Sarah, the girl he'd known all his life and married, or their young boy, Tucker?

Simon didn't want this woman. He *shouldn't* want this woman. He *couldn't* want this woman.

His brains, his duty as a detective and his honor to

his friends told him no, but dammit, his aching heart said yes.

At first, she seemed shocked by his advance, then responded. She slid her hot lips beneath his, tantalizing him with slow, luscious movements. He pressed harder, deeper, swirling his tongue and being thrilled when she touched her own to his.

With a rasp, he cupped her face, kissing past her mouth, over her lips, her cheek, her soft, sweet earlobes, down her creamy throat.

She groaned softly and he reveled in the sound as it echoed above the brook's babble. He pressed against her lovely body and she relented, relaxing backward until she lay on the grassy slope. They were safe here, beyond the visibility of the cabins.

An eagle soared somewhere high and screeched softly, horses clomped on a faraway street, banjos drummed and a church bell rang.

He continued kissing her throat, running his hands along the outside of her dress, wishing with all his male arousal that he could explore the expanse of gaping cleavage, but daring not.

They would never be married.

He knew it with every passing second. In the past half hour, she had produced doubts in him that perhaps she wasn't a knowing partner with Ledbetter, that she was truly caught in the middle of this storm just as he was.

There was a part of him that ached to please her, to wash away her fears, to tell her not to worry and that any reservations she may have sensed in him were false. That he was going to marry her.

But she was smart and observant and too hard to fool

for long. He'd better get on with his plan, finish what he came here for with the detective agency and leave her life as quickly and coldly as he'd entered.

But he was anything but cold toward her.

He kissed her throat, sucked at the flesh. His lips brushed across the black velvet of her cameo. She inhaled the air with another loud moan, pressing her fingers into his hair, torturing him with the seductive curl of her fingers, making him ache with a throbbing so big and so hard...

He cupped her ribs, ran his fingers along the ridge of one plump breast and wove his way to the gaping bodice. He lifted his head momentarily to take in the view. Her tender cleavage shimmered in the pale moonlight. Her pink shell cameo with its dark silhouette dipped above her cleavage.

He unfastened one button, and then another and another, until her clothing came undone and exposed her golden corset. The cloth was soft and pliable and melded to the mounds of her beautiful breasts. Lowering himself, he kissed the upper part of her right breast.

She inhaled sharply. He slipped her corset downward and exposed one very large and gorgeous areola. He plucked at a nipple. It hardened. His mouth came down and clamped softly over it. He flicked his tongue over the mound of flesh. The weight of her cameo shifted and planted itself to one side of her breasts.

Who was that groaning? Him?

With a hunger he didn't know he had, he grazed her flesh and ran his lips over the swell of one breast into the glistening, creamy valley between, then up to the other side. With a soft tug at her corset, the left breast became exposed, too.

He had to take in the view for just a moment.

He pressed up on one elbow. Breasts and pink, glistening nipples and skin so perfect and smooth and mesmerizing to watch. The weight of them shifted slightly. Everything jiggled to his right. Natasha shifted again and the mounds jiggled to the left, beckoning for his lips.

He whispered against her luscious flesh, "You are utterly breathtaking, Natasha."

He looked up at her face, at the fervent picture she made in the grass, sprawled out with her arms to her sides, her brunette tresses spilling about her half-naked shoulders.

"Someone up there," he said with tantalizing strokes, "made you for me."

She seemed pleased by that.

He was unsure why he said it. It had slipped out. But if he were truthful with himself, he would admit it was as though there was something spiritual between them, as if they had transcended their bodies in this moment in time and were more than the sum of their parts. They were more than a man and woman together. They were something better, something stronger, something more meaningful.

He kissed her breasts again. He worked his way up her throat, kissing where the strand of black velvet caught the nape of her sultry neck. Then he kissed her mouth while he stroked her breasts. They were firm, warm clay in his fingers. He played with her nipples, pulling them into longer shapes and enjoying sweet victory as she moaned into his mouth. He wanted all of her.

He wanted her now.

But in a flash of inner torture, he knew he would

never have her. How could he have Natasha O'Sullivan and still be true to his reasons for being here?

It was astounding to Natasha to be confronted with her sexual awakening.

Jarrod's touch evoked the promise of so much more. His fingers at her throat, his breath upon her lips, the raw look in his eyes and the long, smooth fingertip that blazed a trail down her breastbone to her nipple.

Was this what real passion was?

It was like a fire that had started somewhere low inside her, a match lit between them by his very first touch. The power of his touch made her pulses throb, her breasts ache and started her heart in such a mad rhythm she was sure he must see it pounding beneath her ribs.

And oh, the way he tugged at her nipples. The sensation went straight to her groin. How on earth could the two places on her body be connected?

She was breathing so heavily that it rippled through the air as he kissed her throat. His lips came around to her mouth again, his fingers delicately dancing around her bare breasts. When their mouths met, they nearly devoured each other.

He was a wild beast, running his hands everywhere—across her ribs, down her waistline, clamping over the fabric of her skirts to stroke her thigh.

What crazy things he did to her.

She found herself lifting her hips to meet with his, digging her head into the plush grasses beneath her, running her fingers through that wavy blond hair that made him look more like a fur trader who'd been out in the wilds for a year than a businessman with expertise in stones and precious metals.

Everything about him was delicious.

Did he want her forever?

She didn't know.

But he did want her *now.* In the heat of the night, beneath the glistening stars and the quarter moon.

As virginal as she was, untouched by any man, she knew that he wanted to make love to her.

She urged his fingers over her nipples, sucked his bottom lip, heard him moan and could only imagine what it might be like to be taken here in the open moonlight.

Would he be slow and gentle?

He caught his breath and seemed to come to some conclusion. He ripped his face away from hers. His fingers stilled on her breast.

"This isn't right," he whispered.

"What's not right?" she asked in tremulous reply. Her lips felt bruised at his roughness.

"I'm not right."

"We're to be married, Jarrod. The sooner the better, I think, after this."

"You've never…?" He peered at her with curiosity swirling in those deep green eyes.

"If you're asking if I'm a virgin…I think you know the answer."

He swore softly beneath his breath.

"Why does this anger you? I would've thought you'd understand—"

"Of course it doesn't make me angry—"

"But you're cursing—"

"At me! At myself! Dammit, I shouldn't be anywhere near you!"

"Jarrod, when you touch me like this, I can't wait for you to make love—"

"No!"

He pulled away from her and rose to a sitting position on the grass. Cool air brushed over her. She got a chill and instinctively gripped at her clothing.

"I'm not…" he began, stumbling through the words. "I'm not…"

She waited for him to finish, but he didn't. "What, Jarrod? What are you trying to tell me?"

That I'm not the man for you.

But how could Simon say those words?

"I don't wish to take advantage of you, Natasha."

He didn't for one moment think she was a virgin. She was coy one moment and teasing the next. No naive woman moved with her flare and sexuality. She was seasoned, he thought. Not that he held it against her; simply that he was acknowledging her practiced charm. And her vague response to the question of her virginity…that he should know the answer…

Indeed he did.

But despite how practiced she might be, he was outraged at himself for how far he'd let this rendezvous progress. She was not his to take.

He ran a rough hand through his hair and panted to catch his breath.

This damn woman. This damn situation.

He didn't want to take advantage of her, but what man could resist her?

With a groan, he rose to his feet. He turned toward

her, and without looking at her disheveled appearance for fear he might bed her here and now, he offered his hand.

She clasped it. Heat electrified between them. When she was on solid footing, he withdrew his hand and shoved it into his pocket.

She, too, fought to catch her breath. He heard the rustle of fabric, the shuffle of a corset, the fastening of buttons.

He dared not look.

He willed himself to gain control over his body and his mind.

I do not want this woman. It would complicate an already complicated situation. He could pretend to want her, pretend to want to love her, for that would let down her guard and help him solve this crime, but he could not actually love her.

After a moment had passed and her movements had stilled, she spoke. "If you truly don't wish to take advantage of me, Jarrod, then you know what you need to do."

What? What the hell did he have to do?

Her nostrils were gently flared, her lips full and red from his rough kisses. Her hair was a tangled mess, but oh, so starkly beautiful set against her smooth cheeks. "I began this conversation thinking you didn't want me. But that doesn't seem to be the case."

"And what is it that you think I must do to prove myself?"

"If you truly care about my honor, coming all the way from Chicago in response to your promises, then you must set a wedding date."

Her vulnerability pierced his heart. Marrying her

was the last thing he could do. He wasn't the man she believed him to be. He wasn't Jarrod Ledbetter. He was an imposter. Someone who'd kissed her throat and held her breast under false pretenses.

And yet, perhaps he should be the one angered at her. Maybe her scheming with Ledbetter had led to Clay's and Eli's deaths. Maybe she was responsible for creating a widow out of Clay's wife, Sarah.

If only his friends were here to advise him now, they'd talk well into the night about this assignment, about his next step. But everything was mixed up. *He* was mixed up.

Simon was a private detective. He'd gone into this line of work to catch the slime and vermin Natasha associated with, the underbelly of society who stole and killed at their leisure so they could have shiny baubles to wear. Baubles like the cameo necklace that dangled between her breasts at this very moment.

How could he be rid of her constant questioning, so that he could be free to continue his mission to uncover the whereabouts of the stolen three hundred thousand dollars and to bring Fowler and McKern—and possibly her—before the courts to stand trial?

Easy. He would use another lie.

If she was innocent, then his lie would do no harm.

"Let's marry Thursday after next," he said gruffly. Thursday would be the day after Wednesday's big heist. One way or another, a Thursday wedding would never be in the cards for her, but the thought of one would keep her appeased.

"Thursday?" Her eyes brightened. "Are you sure?"

"Absolutely. The minister, a friend of mine from one of the biggest churches in town, is away till then. I was hoping to surprise you upon his return, but obviously I can't leave you waiting forever." More lies. He didn't know the minister from the big church, but he'd read the headlines from yesterday's papers and had seen that the reverend was away.

"That's in two weeks," she said, her expression racing as though she was thinking of all the details that needed her attention.

"Will that give you enough time to settle in? Buy some things you need?"

She nodded. "You had this planned all along?" Her smile seemed gracious and sincere.

He shrugged.

"Jarrod, I'm sorry I doubted you. I thought you were stalling, and here you were planning something special."

"Perhaps keeping secrets from each other is a mistake." He was trying to coax her, to prod her into divulging all she knew.

She blinked and tugged nervously at the front of her bodice, which was still missing two buttons. She'd managed to align the fabric so that it no longer gaped, but had to keep her fingers there so it wouldn't come undone.

Now that he no longer had to look at her naked breasts, his pulse slowed and his breathing returned to normal.

She flexed her neck and puckered her lips as though she, too, had secrets she was keeping from him.

He was determined to discover every secret she had. Every little nugget of information about the stolen goods.

"There's one more thing." He grinned gently, fully

in control now and trying to melt her inhibitions. "Let's keep our wedding date a secret from the others for now. In case the minister doesn't return on that Thursday but needs a few more days out of town to conduct his business. Let's not tell the others until we've spoken to the minister ourselves."

"What's his name?"

Simon didn't miss a beat as he recalled the newspaper article. "Reverend Ericson."

"Where did Reverend Ericson go?"

"To the next town. He told me he had a baptism to conduct, and a burial. But once he gets there, there's often more church work that needs to be done."

Her face fell again in disappointment.

He rushed to reassure her. "On the other hand, he very well intends to return on Thursday. I believe that's what he'll do."

She relaxed again. "That sounds reasonable. I'll keep the date to myself. It would be less stressful for me, I suppose, if I didn't have anyone else's expectations weighing on my shoulders. In case it doesn't fall precisely on that Thursday." Her cheeks heightened. "May I do some shopping for the big day, though?"

"For a wedding gown?"

"I already have one packed in my trunk. I was thinking of a few other little necessities. Beeswax polish for my nails, and other little things that a woman needs."

"Please. Enjoy yourself. I'll foot the bill, of course."

She took a step closer and fidgeted with her bodice. "Shouldn't we seal the matter with a kiss?"

Sexually frustrated, but ever the picture of serenity, he leaned over and pressed his mouth to hers.

This time, he was very careful not to touch her else-where. She moved her mouth in such an enticing way under his that he couldn't help but respond. He lingered a moment longer, then abruptly pulled away.

Chapter Nine

I'm brilliant, thought Simon as he whisked Natasha back to her cabin. *She's happy that we've secretly set a date.*

It was a way to keep her quiet while giving him more time to solve his mission.

"Good night, Natasha," he said softly as he left her at the door. Her mouth dropped open in surprise, as if she'd been expecting another kiss, but he wasn't going anywhere near her again. Desperate to escape her loveliness, he added, "Have a good sleep. See you in the morning."

Mumbling to himself at how he'd managed to extricate himself from her sensual inclinations—he'd never met a woman who was so in need of affection—he pushed open the door of his cabin. This was what it would be like, he told himself, if she became even more of a burden than she already was.

McKern and Fowler looked up from their game of cards. They were gambling for the stack of coins in the middle of the table. The place reeked of cigars and whiskey and stale air. Simon opened a window and a fresh breeze tumbled in.

"Want a drink?" offered McKern. The greasy whiskers on his upper lip glistened in the lantern light.

Simon joined their table and watched them play cards. "I could use one."

McKern poured him a Scotch. "Tough night?"

"She talks too much, but she'll learn."

The men grumbled in sympathy.

Simon had to complain about Natasha to make himself believable. From what he knew about Ledbetter, the man was harsh and egotistical. Educated and light on the outside, but distrustful and hardened on the inside.

Could Simon describe himself with those same words? Distrustful and hardened?

He swallowed a shot of alcohol that numbed the inside of his throat, and tried to push the similarities out of his mind. He was not Ledbetter. Ledbetter had been an animal.

But they'd both come from harsh childhoods. Both had been orphaned young, yet Ledbetter had been whisked away to a life of privilege. Simon had lived hand-to-mouth, stealing scraps of food to eat, doing odd jobs.

When Simon was six, his father had walked out on him and his ma, and his ma had passed away from too much liquor right after his eighth birthday. Terrified that he'd be moved to a city he didn't know and placed in an orphanage with schoolmasters who carried whips and canes, Simon tore off for the railroad tracks. He jumped on the nearest train—leading to New Orleans, he soon discovered—and hadn't stopped running since.

You're no good. A leech. Bothersome to feed, bother-

some to talk to. That was what his father had said the night he left, those exact words.

There wasn't much Simon remembered from the age of six, but the words that had come spitting out of his father's mouth were forever seared into the black depths of his soul. Followed by his mother crying and pleading, then drinking herself to oblivion every single night afterward.

How many men had Simon himself shot, and left widows behind? Granted, those men had been outlaws wanted across the land, but Simon had done things he couldn't forget. Those were lean years of living on the road and depending on his gun for survival.

He wasn't good enough for Natasha O'Sullivan. Whether she was pure of heart or blackened, he'd never be good enough to remain true to one person for the rest of his life. He hadn't even been able to do it for his mother.

He hated to admit it, but when she had finally passed away, she had put him out of his misery. He'd been glad that he was finally free of the horrible memories of what she'd done to herself and her life, and how'd she'd deserted him, too, just as surely as his father had. She was still physically there with him biding her time and killing herself slowly, but it might've been easier if she'd walked away clean and abandoned Simon, too. The illnesses, the delirium, the thrashing, begging and convincing him to buy her more booze…

He'd bought his own mother her poison of choice. Eight years old and stupid.

He'd never be stupid like that again. He'd never be tricked. He was the one in control here. He was the one doing the tricking. All in the name of the law.

Simon shuddered. He peered at the golden liquid in his shot glass, thought of his mother's drinking and couldn't bear to take another sip. He turned to the apes.

"How would you fellas like a little diversion?" Simon was putting together something in his mind, trying to sense where the stolen cache was. He tapped the table and they dealt him in.

Fowler cracked his knuckles. "You mean get out of here?"

"Hell yeah," said Simon. "We need to top up our funds."

McKern's eyes lit up. "You'd like us to tap into the stash?"

"A celebration's in order, for a job well-done. It's always been me and the other men boarding the train, taking the loot and leaving it behind where you two conceal it." They would've concealed it precisely where Ledbetter would've directed them to. So, Simon could not pretend he did not know where that was. "Now that we've finally met in person, I reckon you don't have an aversion to spending some of it."

Fowler cackled. "Yee-haw."

"It's in the perfect spot," McKern rambled. "Just like you ordered."

"Of course." Simon coolly played a card. He didn't flinch.

McKern chomped on his cigar. "The ride up the mountains and back won't take more than a day. Four hours there, four hours back."

The mountains. The damn Laramie Mountains. That was where they'd stashed the loot!

"What route do you fellas usually take?" Simon prodded gently. "With the sheriff poking around, we've got to be careful."

"We could approach it from the south, but that Eastern Ridge road...nothing but cliffs and villages. I'd say we stick to the shortest route and head directly west." McKern withdrew his cigar. "I recommend we trip up the sheriff and leave separately. Want to meet at your cabin first?"

"Sure. Which one?" Simon didn't have a clue. "I've got so many of them."

Fowler chuckled with admiration. "So we hear."

McKern answered, "The cabin ten miles due west, just after the junction of those two valleys. The one right at the river."

Simon sat back and grinned. "Sounds good. We'll go early on Monday." That would give him more than three full days to get a message to his superiors where he was headed. "We'll take a nice ride in the country and leave the others behind. I was thinking we should shift the hiding spot before the next heist. Get the gems together, cut what we can. Appraise the gold pieces."

"Sure thing." Fowler blew a smoke ring into the air. A strange look seemed to pass between him and McKern. Fowler's lips curled into a thin line, as if he was trying to rein in a jolt of temper. What was he angry about?

McKern squinted. An artery pulsed in his throat. He seemed to be burning with resentment, too. "What about your bride?"

Simon tried to keep his voice cool. "What about her?"

"Don't mean to be sticking my nose in, but we noticed there's been no wedding yet. We heard from your other men last month—you know how some like to talk—that you were planning to get hitched the moment she stepped off that train. Is there something wrong with her?"

The other men they were referring to were likely the ones who died with Ledbetter in the gunfight. Confidently, Simon spewed another lie. "Turns out she's nervous. She's got cold feet and I don't want to push her. I thought I'd give her more time to get accustomed to Cheyenne."

"Don't see what she needs to get accustomed to…." McKern muttered.

"She's a woman. She should be told and not asked…." Fowler complained.

Simon shifted in his hard chair. He was dancing around a touchy subject. He had to give these men a reasonable explanation for the fact that there'd been no marriage yet, while at the same time pretending to be the eager groom. If he got into the same false explanation with them as he had with Natasha—about Reverend Ericson being out of town—they were likely to ask more questions in town, since they knew the place and the people. So saying that she had cold feet would be enough.

Simon poured them another drink and they seemed to settle. He'd accomplished a lot in the past half hour. The jackpot was sitting and waiting for him somewhere in the Laramie Mountains. He didn't know precisely what place, but he had a direction and a distance. It was roughly a three to four hours' ride away, for he wasn't sure if the four hours included time spent packing the stolen goods. And it was on a road called Eastern Ridge.

It was urgent that he send word to his contacts.

* * *

The next evening, Friday night, McKern chomped down on the stub of his cigar as he and Fowler, dressy in tailored gray suits, headed toward Cheyenne's finest gentlemen's club. They strode past the harsh lights of a gambling house. McKern bit down on the bile and rage that threatened to spill out of him. He patted one of the Colt revolvers slung around his hips, assuring himself that he was in control of his temper. But the smooth, warm wood in his palm only strengthened his mad desire to pull the trigger and make blood splatter. Nothing calmed him like a good fight.

"I'm going stir-crazy in that damn cabin," McKern spat. "Between the Dooligans and that uptight woman asking a thousand questions about Cheyenne, if I don't get out soon, I'm going to kill someone."

"Take it easy." Fowler tapped his bowler hat. "Think of the bonus we're about to get. You've got to mind your temper for two more days. At least while we're within the town limits and the wanted posters are tacked up at the jailhouse."

McKern snarled, "They don't even have a fair description of us. Idiots. They don't know who they're looking for."

"No sense getting yourself worked up." Fowler shook his head. "Big Rita will calm you down. Like she always does."

"It's the O'Sullivan woman who's getting to me, keeping the boss waiting like she is. She needs a good smackdown."

"It's not your place to give it to her."

"She keeps this up, and I will." McKern rubbed his throbbing temples. The headaches were becoming reg-

ular. "And what the hell is it with Ledbetter? I know
he intends to rattle those sapphires off the old lady's
throat, but how much patience does he expect from us?"

"He can't snatch them from her neck while the sheriff is still sniffin' around. Did you notice today when
the lawman came by asking more about the missing
wallet, Ledbetter was as cool as ice water? Be patient.
Ledbetter's remarkable. You don't get to be head of a
jewelry enterprise unless you keep focused."

They reached the gentlemen's club, a luxurious Victorian mansion. Fowler pushed open the side door. In
the smoky, candlelit room, they were immediately be-
sieged by a banquet of lovely, corseted ladies. One of
them was playing the piano, long legs stretched out
like a cat beneath the keys, wearing spiked black heels.

"Mr. McKern, Mr. Fowler," said Big Rita, the top of
her breasts wobbling over her black lace corset. "Welcome back." She winked at McKern, setting him at
ease, and he chuckled. She was the enterprising madam,
and she herself usually provided a good roll in the sack
and a good laugh. "Who's your pleasure this evening?"

McKern bellowed, "Bessy and Dora. And a little
bit o' you."

Big Rita purred as she joined him. She ran her hand
along his belly.

Across the room, Fowler made himself comfortable
with a pale, heavyset woman with a bountiful behind.

"Two educated gentlemen like yourselves," murmured Big Rita, "always get my finest ladies."

Men's suit jackets were hanging on pegs along the
wall. An old man in baggy clothes with sparse white
hair and a spine curled over from old age was seated

next to the coats, McKern noticed. And goddamn him, if his fingers weren't picking the pockets.

McKern's rage boiled over. He kicked the chairs. He slammed the wall. He lunged at the old man. "Rob us blind, will you, while we got our pants off?"

Women gasped. The piano-playing stopped.

McKern grabbed the old man's fingers and twisted hard.

"Ah," the old man whimpered, "I didn't…"

"Please," whispered one of the younger, well-dressed ladies as she stepped forward. "Please, he's one of our cooks."

McKern sneered at the sniveling cook. "You best find yourself another occupation." McKern held tight till he heard bones crack and the man suffered. Silver coins slipped from the crooked hand, and the man crumpled to the floor. A pitiful heap of greasy white hair and ill-fitting clothes.

Another customer, a stocky, middle-aged man with a scar near his right eye, shuffled out of a room, barefoot but clothed. "That's my coat. Much obliged, mister."

"Justice of the peace," one of the ladies whispered. "Justice Weatherton."

Fowler picked up the coins and returned them to the justice.

The tension eased from McKern's shoulders. Delivering fair punishment always did that to him. "Now, then," he said, turning around to Big Rita, "how's about we take the nice room next to the piano?"

Just past dawn the next morning, Simon watched Natasha with fascination.

She was target-shooting. It was everything he could

do to keep her occupied. Later this morning, he'd promised to take her to the market. Tomorrow the promise was to attend Sunday services with her and the Dooligans, in the church tent beside the market. McKern and Fowler had snickered at him when he'd agreed to Natasha's request, but had declined the offer themselves.

Simon knew the two men believed he had a false reputation to uphold as a prominent, church-abiding jeweler, but Simon was also pleased to divert Natasha's attention so that they wouldn't have to spend romantic time together.

He watched Natasha concentrate. She peered down the short barrel of her Remington double-loaded derringer, ignored the chirping of the birds around her, located the knot in the fence post and squeezed the trigger.

"Bull's-eye," said Simon, standing under the cottonwood beside her. "So tell me. How come your landlady taught you ladies how to shoot?"

"Mrs. Pepik's late husband was a policeman. He taught her, and she passed her skills to us. She believes every woman should be able to protect herself."

"Why'd you pick that gun? Because it's got a nickel-plated finish with a pearl grip?"

"It was very kind of you to send the money for it."

He didn't know he had. He went along with her and nodded.

"But looks are not the reason I bought it from her."

"Is it because it's small? Easily concealed in your handbag?"

"That is an advantage, I'll admit. But the gun chose me. Mrs. Pepik had me try several. This one fit well in my hand and therefore I'm a great shot with it. As I'm sure you know, accuracy is everything."

"There are lots of things I'm learning about you," said Simon. "I get the feeling you're a lot more experienced in certain areas than you let on."

Guns for one, thought Simon. *The bedroom for another.*

She smiled in that self-assured way, and he knew he was right.

No virgin that he'd ever been with moved as she did when they were alone, or seemed to be so self-aware of her sexuality. Not that he'd been with a lot of virgins, but in his youth when he'd started getting comfortable with girls, he'd come to recognize several. He usually steered clear of them. He'd made the mistake of getting close to one once, sleeping with her when she was eighteen and he sixteen and too young to know the consequences, but never again. He didn't care for the burden of training her, nor the burden of being saddled with a woman who would then expect a commitment to follow up on her training. All young women were starry-eyed when it came to their first lovers.

He preferred an experienced woman in bed.

Someone like Natasha.

She hadn't professed to be a virgin the other night; she'd danced around the topic.

Well, he could dance, too.

He told himself this was all a well-played game that would soon be over. They wouldn't see each other after Monday.

Yesterday morning, Simon had gone to the telegram office and had sent an urgent message to the town where his contact was waiting.

The message read: "Laramie Mountains. Eastern Ridge road. Three to four hours' ride from here Monday morning." The detectives would know what that meant—that the stolen goods were there. He gambled they had enough time to send backup.

Simon watched Natasha handle her gun. "I have to leave on a short trip on Monday," he said.

"You do? Where?"

"The mountains."

"Ah," she said, taking aim with her second bullet. "Going to check on your treasure?"

The admission startled him.

So she *did* know. She knew about the treasure, the stolen goods, Ledbetter.

He felt as though he'd just been punched in the gut.

Every time Simon thought she was innocent, she'd surprise him with another comment. Her hands were soiled in this. He wasn't sure exactly the level of her guilt, but she damn well wanted to be a participant.

Why was he so disappointed in her? Because he'd been holding out, hoping he'd misjudged her. Hoping she was innocent and caught in the middle of something she was unaware of.

"Exactly," he said calmly, watching another bullet imbed itself in the wood. "I'm going to check on my treasure."

He leaned back against the fence post, deliberating whether he would need to take her along on the trip. If she knew where the stolen cache was, would her presence be helpful?

Nah, she would be another complication.

McKern and Fowler were enough to lead him. He was hoping simply to locate the goods tomorrow and let the railroad authorities deal with it from there, but he also had to prepare for a shoot-out if the two got suspicious that he was not the real Ledbetter. So, it was better and safer for all involved if Simon kept her out of it.

"While I'm gone," he said, trying to create a distraction for her, "I'd like you to pick a place we might visit on our honeymoon."

She beamed at that. "A honeymoon? How wonderful." The morning sunshine cracked through the clouds and hit one side of her face, illuminating her high cheekbones and upturned mouth. She cupped a hand over her eyebrows to shield her eyes and squinted at him. "Such as?"

"The West Coast. New York. Maybe Paris."

"Paris?" Her entire body energized at the notion. She shifted her posture and her shoulders lifted. Her white blouse strained against her bosom. Her long skirts moved against her boots. "That's the sweetest thing…"

Why the hell did this woman have to be a criminal? Why couldn't she be the innocent woman she appeared to be to the outside world?

To his displeasure, she came over to kiss him.

She planted herself between his boots as he stood with his back against the fence. He cupped his hands behind her waist and allowed the kiss.

Her lips were gentle and warm. He played his role and kissed her firmly. He brought his hand up and thumbed her soft cheek. They lingered like that for a moment, he hoping she'd break free and release him.

He brought his hand off her face and they parted.

She kept her hand on his leg. *Dammit, woman,* he thought, *steer clear of that area.*

"How long will you be gone?" she asked.

"You tell me," he said with a firm smile. *Come on, Natasha, tell me what you know.*

"Hmm," she said, peering toward the mountains. "In your letters, you said it wasn't too far. Maybe three or four hours?"

He nodded, squaring his jaw. Distance confirmed. "Should be home by nightfall."

"What's the name of the village?" she asked. "You never mentioned it in your letters."

He swallowed and thought quickly. So Ledbetter hadn't disclosed the exact location. Smart man. Was she trying to outmaneuver him now? Did she want the name of the village so that she had reassurance she could find the goods herself, if need be?

"I'll tell you all about it when I get back." He patted her behind and released her.

She laughed at his gesture and reloaded her weapon.

McKern and Fowler said they'd leave unannounced tomorrow morning after him, telling no one where they were going, but secretly meeting him at his cabin. They'd ride together from there. They'd told him they had rented horses from the local "ladies" in town that they would collect in the morning, while Simon had rented a mare from the Mountain Hotel.

Once Simon located the treasure, he wouldn't need Natasha anymore. Tomorrow after he confirmed the stolen cache was there, he would ride away. The mission would go down one way or another. The railroad authorities and the detective agency would decide how and when to recapture the stolen property. Federal marshals would move in to arrest McKern and Fowler.

Simon would also tell the authorities what he knew about Natasha. They would detain her and send other detectives to interrogate her. Maybe she knew about Ledbetter's other scams and secrets that would be useful to authorities. By then, she would be out of Simon's hands, no longer his responsibility.

He wouldn't give a damn what happened to her.

He would be free.

At least, that was what he told himself as he watched her reload her double-barreled pocket pistol with .41 rimfire bullets.

He gritted his teeth at the mix of emotions churning through him.

Loss, sadness, loneliness. That empty hollow in his heart.

He'd come to like her. There, he'd admitted it. She was easy on the eyes and charming. She was friendly and helpful to the Dooligans, cheerful when she arose in the morning, liked to hum when she did the dishes, was extremely alluring when she talked about jewelry, talked about her grandfather with great love and joy, and was optimistic about the future.

But Simon wouldn't lose a moment's sleep over her.

He was leaving tomorrow and she would be a memory long forgotten. Like every other person he'd ever cared about.

Natasha pulled the trigger again, very much aware that Jarrod was carefully watching her. She should be happy, she told herself. She should be pleased they were getting married in less than two weeks.

Yet something was troubling her. Although she was trying to appear very self-assured in front of Jarrod, she was more terrified than ever that she'd never be able to live up to his expectations as a wife. It was all talk, wasn't it? All the conversations she'd had with Valentina and the other experienced women at the boardinghouse.

Natasha didn't know anything about men. She might pretend she did, she might go along with Jarrod's kisses and pats of affection, but she was terrified that he'd always feel like a stranger to her. What did she know about the bedroom or how to please a man? In all her conversations with Jarrod, things had never gotten more intimate than talk about surface things. What sort of derringer she preferred, what sort of jewelry pleased him most, how long he'd been in business and what his homes were like.

What about talk between two people who were truly in love?

She realized she had to give love time to grow, but it had to develop from something.

What about letting down her guard and asking him about things that truly mattered, such as children and what he thought was important in life, who his friends had been while growing up and what his grandparents had been like?

Nothing between them rang deeper than conversations like these about target practice. It was partially her fault, she knew, but she didn't know how to go beyond that stumbling block of feeling as though he was a stranger, that she'd made a mistake coming West on her own and what a silly notion she had that she could divulge her innermost feelings to a man she'd barely met. Truth was, she'd never been able to divulge her sentiments to any man. She was inexperienced, shy and ever careful of being hurt. It had taken many years to come to terms with the excruciating pain of losing her parents, wondering if there wasn't more she could have done to prevent their passing. Being their caregiver at the age of fourteen and barely knowing how to wash their clothes. Maybe she could have given them more soup, more water, more medicine… And then losing her grandfather.

At least she wanted to try again, loving Jarrod.

But she still sensed it in him, too, the detachment, the teetering of indecision.

He was going away on Monday and had never asked if she'd like to come along. What was she supposed to think of that? Didn't he want to open up to her? Wouldn't he allow her the opportunity of trying to do so?

"Do you have room for one more on your trip?" she asked with a flare of confidence she wasn't feeling.

Jarrod's green eyes flashed. His mouth pulled into a grin. "You like adventures, do you?"

"Especially with my husband-to-be."

He shrugged, his blond hair brushing his wide shoulders. "We'd need a chaperone, then, and the business trip would turn into something more difficult than it needs to be."

Difficult? Her company would be a nuisance? She tried to bite her tongue, but he never wanted to compromise. "How does a woman convince a man to see the light?"

"A woman bides her time and lets the man make the decisions."

"Sometimes a woman can see the truth better than a man."

"No man likes to be pushed on anything."

"Then men are stubborn mules." With a flounce, she took her derringer and stalked back to the cabin, trying to ignore the meaning of the wall of silence behind her.

Chapter Ten

"I'm getting damn suspicious of this whole situation." McKern slammed the boards as he and Fowler strode inside the barn that belonged to the gentlemen's club. It was early Monday morning and they were following Big Rita, who was ten yards ahead and out of earshot. She was leading them to the mares they had rented. A dozen horses around them shuffled on straw and munched on oats that were being fed to them by two young stable hands.

"Suspicious of what?"

"Of *him* and *her,*" McKern growled. "Why are they putting off the wedding?"

Fowler eyed the horses Big Rita was now patting. Real beauties—two roan mares. "Ledbetter explained it already. We've known him long enough to realize—"

"That's just it. How long have we known him?"

"Over four years."

McKern shook his head. "No, that's how long we've been working for him. How long have we *known* him?"

"I suppose we only met him in person last week."

Fowler squinted in the early-morning light. "You don't trust him? Why, his reputation—"

"I'm not talking about his reputation. I'm talking about the man we've known for one week."

"Hellfire," said Fowler. "If you're thinking—"

McKern indicated that he shut up. Big Rita had turned and was now within earshot.

"Do you have two more horses we can rent?" McKern asked her.

"Why?" asked Fowler, but McKern shot him an order of silence.

Big Rita, dressed in an impeccably tailored blouse and skirt—although McKern enjoyed her better naked—patted the withers of one reddish-brown mare. "Certainly."

While she went to tell her stable hand, Fowler whispered, "Ledbetter said he's renting a horse from the Mountain Hotel, remember? He doesn't need us to arrange one."

"It's not for him," growled McKern.

"You're getting horses for two more riders? Who are we taking?"

"It's time we put Ledbetter to the test. If he's who he says he is, he won't blink. But if he's not…" McKern finished his ominous train of thought by patting the Colt in his holster.

No matter how many years Simon had put in as a detective, this was always the part he hated most. Waiting. He waited by the narrow river. He'd been here nearly two hours already, but there was no sign of McKern or Fowler. His black mare slurped water at the grassy incline. From the distance where the two rivers converged, the loud gush of a waterfall added to the tranquility.

Tranquility was the other thing that always made him nervous.

He rarely heard it in the towns that he passed through. He was more accustomed to the sound of train whistles, galloping hooves, the rattle of an old piano, the holler of men or the blast of gunfire.

It wasn't easy to be still and calm. His ma had always reminded him that, as a child, he could never sit quietly. *Do you always need to be jumpin' and climbin' and racing the neighbor boys? Honestly, Simon, watch your neck.*

Those were the happier memories he had of his ma.

"Hey, girl," he said to the mare as he walked over and patted her soft shoulder. The fringes of his black suede jacket shimmered in the sun. Denim jeans clung to his legs.

The mare whinnied. Light sparkled off her glistening black coat. He marveled at the length of her neck and her elegant, sloping shoulders—both great attributes for speed. He'd done well to pick her from his choices at the hotel's livery.

The animal stopped for a moment, lips poised above the water. He looked to see what had mesmerized her, and he, too, saw them—trout swimming through the crystal clear water. If only he had a fishing rod.

The crackling of a faraway branch made him reach for his guns. This time, he wore his revolvers at his hips. No sense hiding the fact that he was armed as he rode through the wilderness. Sometimes the simplest way to ward off trouble from passing strangers, if he should meet any, was to make it known that he could protect himself. He still had his hidden dagger strapped to his right ankle, and the derringer tucked into the back of his shirtwaist, hidden by his jacket.

The earth thudded softly on the trail a hundred yards or so away while he watched for the approaching horses to appear. It sounded as if there were more than two riders, which confused him. Three men, maybe four, getting closer.

Hang tight, he told himself. He stepped out into the trail to make himself, and his revolvers, visible. Startling someone was never a good idea on the trail.

"Jarrod!" Fowler came through first, followed by McKern.

So it *was* them. They were both in suits. A bit formal for a ride, wasn't it?

"Hope we didn't make you wait too long." McKern, thick as a bull, swung off his horse.

"I figured you'd be coming along soon," said Simon, watching with impatience to see who else they'd brought.

A middle-aged man dressed in black, neatly trimmed white beard with a scar on his temple beside his right eye, appeared and stopped next to McKern.

"Who's this?" asked Simon. What the hell were McKern and Fowler thinking, bringing along a third party on their trip to the stolen goods?

"This here is the justice of the peace." McKern introduced him with a clearing of his throat. "Justice Weatherton."

The man with the scarred temple grinned and slid off his horse. "Pleased to meet you, Mr. Ledbetter."

"Justice of the peace? What's this all about?"

And then the fourth rider appeared.

Simon looked up into familiar brown eyes.

Natasha.

His mind raced as he put the pieces together. A justice of the peace? He paused. Holy crow. A wedding? Dammit, whose idea was this? Hers or his men's?

They wanted a marriage ceremony? *Right now?*

What the hell were his options? He should be the one in control of this situation, as he always was! But he shouldn't reveal how angry he was.

He tried hard to focus on her pleasantly, as any groom would. He noted her shiny brown hair, swept up at the back to reveal the sultry curve of her neck, the bonnet with the artificial grapes and cherries, the prim Sunday-best jacket with its worn elbows and matching blue skirts. She was one pushy lady. If this was her way of forcing his hand...

"Good morning, Jarrod," she cooed.

On the other hand, the detective in him reasoned, if this was McKern and Fowler's idea, why would they arrange such a thing? Was it a test?

"Hello, Natasha," he greeted warmly. "What a lovely sight." He moved to her horse to help her dismount.

Jarrod placed his hands at Natasha's waist and easily lifted her off the mare and set her in her high-heeled boots onto the pebbly trail. She enjoyed his strength and his embrace, and was completely flustered at seeing him. Who would've known that he would plan this? She'd misjudged him terribly. She'd thought he was trying to squirm *out* of the marriage. He'd made it clear that he didn't wish to bring her along on his trip. This man could certainly keep a secret!

"I can't believe the surprise you planned," she told

him, breathless to see him as she slid her body down his. The heat of his proximity sent her blood rushing.

He smiled at her intimately, as though they were the only two here. As though he could sense that she was thinking ahead to the wondrous day he had arranged.

"You're in agreement, then?" he asked.

She nodded, still with her hand on his forearm.

He looked to the bags strapped at the back of her saddle, complete with wedding gown neatly folded inside, and toiletries. The others carried food that Mrs. Dooligan had prepared. There were four of them riding, so they could handle more bags than they might otherwise bring on the trail, adjusting for the weight on the horses. They'd kindly allotted Natasha the space on theirs.

"I admit," she said, "I thought it rather unorthodox when Mr. McKern first told me this morning. Your calling for the justice of the peace and hoping that today would be our wedding day." She tried to make sense of why he would keep this to himself. "You never said anything about it yesterday. And this morning when I arose, you were already gone."

"I didn't wish to mention it because I was afraid you would refuse me today. There being no minister available."

That would've been nicer, she thought, but good things sometimes never turned out the way a person planned. The justice had the jurisdiction to marry them, and she was thrilled to know that Jarrod held fast to his faithful intention.

"I would be honored to marry you today, Jarrod."

He gave her a tilt of his handsome face and turned to Justice Weatherton. "Sir, if you might accompany her to the cabin and help her with the preparations?"

The justice squinted at Jarrod's sweaty temple. She'd noticed it, too.

"There's nothin' to be nervous about, lad," the justice informed him. "Why, I've married more couples in the last year than there are buffalo on the range." He turned to her. She was also getting uptight, now that the moment was here.

She'd been wanting this all along, hadn't she? Jarrod wasn't exactly a stranger anymore. She was growing to care for him a great deal.

Simon tried to mask his agitation as the justice directed Natasha to the cabin. "Right this way, miss."

They were helped by Fowler carrying her bags. While the other three were gone, Simon concentrated on taking deep, calming breaths. He turned around to face off with McKern. Before he could say a word, McKern started talking.

"I recalled what you said about her having cold feet," McKern explained, "and so thought we might help you speed things up."

"Did you, now?" Fury and resentment seeped into Simon. How dare this imbecile force Simon's hand. There had to be more to it. This was a bold move by an underling. "What made you think I needed your goddamn help?"

McKern's nostrils twitched. For the first time since they'd met, Simon sensed deep agitation in the other man. McKern's gaze penetrated the cool, sunny air.

"Seems to me," said the cutthroat, "everyone's a touch jittery about this wedding. Why do you think that might be?"

Simon noticed the sly fingers reaching for the guns,

the way the man stood ready, bracing for a fight. Hell, this man *yearned* for a fight.

And Simon knew, deep inside his soul, that this bloodthirsty animal would shoot him in the back if Simon gave him any inkling that he wasn't Ledbetter. That was what this was truly about. This bastard suspected something was amiss between Simon and Natasha, and he was on a hunting expedition.

Damn him. Simon wasn't going to give him anything. "I already told you. She was getting cold feet."

"Seemed pretty hot to me. All I had to do was tell her that this was your idea, and she obeyed. Like she should."

"Let me make one thing clear." Simon came over and stood a head taller and inches away from the ugly face. "I don't need your help with women."

The artery in McKern's jaw throbbed. "Understood." He deflected his rage by looking away, but sent a shiver of warning cascading up Simon's spine when he took out his revolver and spun the barrel as though he was offhandedly checking to see if it was fully loaded.

Those bullets were meant for Simon or Natasha. Likely both.

He did a quick assessment of his choices.

Now that she had eagerly accepted the invitation, if Simon refused, it would contradict his reasoning that she was the one who was hesitating. The result: bullets to the head.

His other option was to marry her today. Surely it wouldn't be legal. He would be taking the name of a dead man! A false name wouldn't hold any weight on a marriage document. All he had to do was say a simple "I do." An annulment before a judge—or more likely,

a simple agreement that it never happened legally—
would erase the stupid memory.

It was either that or dying in any number of ways
that McKern was notorious for. Slashed throat, thrown
under a moving train, dynamite, point-blank gunshot
to the head.

Simon shuddered that he might be responsible for
Natasha's painful death. She might be a thief, but she
was not a violent person. Faced with the sudden possibility of her demise, he believed that she was not a
lot of things he'd assumed she was. In a flash, her true
persona came shining through.

These were the facts:

She hadn't asked for this wedding today; the scum
in front of him had.

She wasn't trying to be forceful or nasty or greedy;
the scum in front of him was.

Simon believed now that her character was a lot
clearer and truer than he'd given her credit for. Perhaps she had some knowledge of Ledbetter's criminal
activities, but Simon had a feeling she'd come across
those innocently. In any case, the authorities would need
her alive in order to question her, and her safety was
up to him. Now, having to make a life-and-death decision for her head, Simon believed he'd been wrong
about her all along, and that she would cooperate with
the authorities and not run from them.

God, he'd been so stupid.

How could he have misjudged her so terribly?

Simon knew if he were alone and he had only himself to look after, he could survive. He could jump on
his horse and charge through the river and over the crest

before McKern and Fowler even got into their saddles. But he wasn't alone.

Simon could escape, but two other people would be dead. Natasha and the justice.

If Simon took out his gun and shot at McKern and Fowler, there would likely be a gunfight, and still Natasha and the justice might be harmed. And Simon's orders were to keep McKern and Fowler alive until they recovered the railroad's property and the two men were apprehended for murder.

Thus, there was only one answer here.

"We'll do the wedding first," Simon declared calmly. "Then we'll put Natasha and the justice back on their horses and send them home. Then the three of us, as planned, will ride into the mountains to recover the goods. If there's one thing you know about me, you know that pleasure never gets in the way of business."

McKern stared at Simon, then grinned and holstered his gun. "The justice plans on going back to town as soon as it's done. But the lady thinks she's spending the night. I imagine you'd want her to."

Simon bit down on his impulse to thrash the man. "Nothing I'd like more. I suppose we can conduct our business without letting her interfere." How could he refuse to spend his wedding night with his new bride? He was cornered. "You and Fowler bunk out here tonight. We'll take the cabin. First thing in the morning, the four of us will ride out to get the goods."

Could Simon take the chance and confide in her who he was? She would have questions and disbelief about who the real Jarrod Ledbetter was, things that McKern and Fowler would overhear. Hell, Simon thought, she might even bolt or panic, and still be shot dead by Mc-Kern. So he'd keep quiet for now.

This plan wasn't so bad, except for the wedding-night arrangements, but he'd take that a step at a time.

McKern seemed to calm down. "Yes. We'll hit the trail come morning."

Simon looked to the horses, laden down with saddle-bags and packs. "I'm surprised you didn't bring the Dooligans," he said with sarcasm.

"Oh, they wanted to come," said McKern. "The missus sent a large spread of food. Says her rheumatism prevents her from riding. She sends her regrets."

"What a shame," Simon said lightly, knowing that McKern didn't like her, and trying to get back on friendly footing no matter how agitated he was inside.

McKern snickered at the sarcasm.

Fowler came out of the cabin and Simon motioned to him. He made his way to the horses. "Let's unload this stuff. We're about to have a party."

He bristled with discontent and anger and fear for the two people inside. He wasn't for a moment appeased that he'd headed off trouble by agreeing to this ceremony. He knew there'd be a gun trained on his back the entire time.

He'd been in life-threatening situations like this before in the line of duty, but never felt as though he had much to lose. But this time…

Hell. And in his mind, he had already said goodbye to Natasha O'Sullivan.

Chapter Eleven

Excitement and anxiety for what the day and future with Jarrod might bring had been building in Natasha all morning. What if they never tore down the uneasy wall that sometimes sprang between them? What if she continued to treat him as if he was a stranger and not to be trusted with her deepest feelings? To his credit, he'd arranged for this day quietly and had called for her. And she'd been so surprised to hear that he owned this cabin. The scenery was breathtaking and the sunshine added to the day.

Why was she so worried? This was her wedding day! She hummed cheerfully in the cabin as she lifted her clothing bag off the table. The men were now setting up the food tables outdoors. Mr. McKern had told her on the trail that he'd packed Jarrod's suit for him in a separate pack, as he'd requested.

Justice Weatherton, seated on the dusty bench by the fireplace, shuffled through his papers.

Natasha reached for the buckle on her bag and noticed a wet, burgundy stain on the outside of the canvas cloth. "Oh, no."

"What is it?" Justice Weatherton looked over.

"Oh, no, no, no," she repeated, quickly unbuckling the straps of the bag to have a look at her wedding gown folded neatly inside. To her horror, the folds of the gown contained a red wine stain the size of her fist.

Frantic, she looked to the food bag that had been resting on top of hers. Mrs. Dooligan had packed it, and this food bag obviously held a bottle of red wine, for it was soaked clear through with burgundy liquid that had obviously caused the stain on her gown.

"Miss O'Sullivan?" the gent with the whitish beard asked again from the unlit fireplace. "May I help?"

She gasped, choking up inside as she pulled out the gown to assess the damage. The stain was two feet long! Smack in the middle of the front!

She stood gaping at the horrid mess, motionless in disbelief. She opened her mouth to respond but couldn't utter a word. What was she to do? Red wine on white lace and satin!

The justice had already jumped up and was barreling out the front door, hollering, "Mr. Ledbetter! Better come quick!"

She was still holding the gown when Jarrod rushed in with a canteen of water, in jeans and work shirt. He took one look at the stain, then her face, and carefully offered her the canteen.

She set her gown on the table—well away from the wine bag—and feeling herself still pale and reeling from the awful surprise, dabbed water on it. It only smeared and spread the stain farther in lighter, pinker rings.

Fighting back a well of emotions that wobbled in her throat, she set the whole mess down and simply stared.

"We could take it to the river," Jarrod said gently. "Dunk the whole half of it in clear water. There must be a cake of soap here somewhere and I could scrub the stain against the boulders."

Knock her beautiful gown against the rocks? "It's ruined."

"I think we should try."

"I handled this gown so carefully from Chicago. My dearest friend, Cassandra, bought it and shipped it all the way from California. It's the most beautiful gown I've ever owned."

"But it's just a—" Jarrod started to say, then stopped himself.

Men didn't understand. It was the meaning behind the gown.

"Let's try to wash it in the river," he suggested again.

Another deep voice boomed from the doorway. It was McKern. "There's not enough time for it to dry. And Justice Weatherton needs to move on with his day."

From her peripheral vision, she caught looks and signals passing between Jarrod and McKern, but when she looked up, Jarrod was looking calmly at her, and dare she say, his expression was emotionless. He didn't care!

"It's bad luck," she rambled in a panic, trying to make it clear what was happening here. "A ruined dress is bad luck for our wedding."

"It's not bad luck. It was just an accident," Jarrod replied. He unbuckled the food bag and lifted out the wine bottle, then searched for the cork. "The gown got wet with wine. Mr. and Mrs. Dooligan were trying to be generous in helping with the preparations and…and they should have been a tad more careful."

Fowler muttered from the doorway, "Fools. Who

would pack red wine and not check to make sure the cork was tight?"

McKern must've nudged him, for Fowler—both men in pressed trousers and dress shirts—declared, "Well, how do you expect me to feel? It's her wedding gown! Everyone knows what it means to a girl—" There was a silence followed by an "Oomph."

"It's bad luck," she repeated to Jarrod as she stared at the mess. She felt like weeping. "I can't marry you now. Not like *this*."

McKern cleared his throat.

Jarrod fell silent. "Please, gentlemen, may I have a word alone with my bride?"

"Remember," McKern warned, "the justice has to move on with his day."

Why was everyone being pushy? This was supposed to be their special day!

"The ride here was so peaceful," she told Jarrod as the others cleared out. "I was so touched by your romantic surprise. Getting married in a beautiful, secluded spot by the river. The whole ride here, I was imagining what sort of a home we would make together and how many children we might have. And now it's turned upside down."

Jarrod took a deep breath and turned away to study the gown, but not before she caught an odd glimmer of guilt in his eyes.

What did he have to feel guilty about? The wine stain was no more his fault than it was hers.

He touched her hand in a gentle caress. His words were moving and honest. "It's the day, isn't it, that makes it special, Natasha? Not the fabric, not the jewelry, not the promise of a fancy honeymoon, but the vows we say to each other and the promise of love between us."

When he turned his face to hers again, there was no guilt there anymore, but lots of unspoken sentiment. He seemed to genuinely feel and understand the moment.

"I wanted to look beautiful for you," she whispered.

He cupped the falling hair back from her shoulder. "You're beautiful the way you are. From the moment you stepped off that train, I couldn't believe you were sent to me."

His words were lovely, but... "You don't feel that it's bad luck?"

"I'm afraid it would be worse luck if we don't marry right now."

His manner and his voice soothed her ruffled spirits.

"Stay right here," he said. "I'll be right back."

Curiously, he tore out of the cabin and came back a moment later. He held out a beautiful bouquet of wildflowers. They were made of pretty pinks and yellows and whites, with green ferns and wild grasses.

She sent him a tremulous smile and took the bouquet from him. Their fingers touched and sent a tingle of anticipation through her again.

He was right. Why let something like this ruin her day? It was Jarrod she cared about and not the fabric.

Simon had never been to a wedding before. It was strange that his first time should be his own, and a pretend one at that. Sometime very soon, he would have to explain to Natasha that he was doing this to spare her life.

The gods would surely rain down hard on him.

He'd changed into a clean white shirt, blue trousers

and matching blue jacket to join Justice Weatherton and McKern and Fowler at the river's edge.

Simon wanted to wear his guns but knew it would look odd to Natasha and distrustful to the two cutthroats who were eagerly watching and waiting for a misstep.

Surrounded by nature, cocooned by tall cottonwoods and elders and spruce and pine, listening to the flow of the running river and the waterfall behind the cabin, Simon inhaled sharply when she exited the cabin. She turned to walk toward him with her bouquet of wild-flowers, as though she were walking down the aisle of a church.

Despite the fact that she wasn't wearing her intended gown, she'd made the most of what she had. She'd pinned her long hair off her face so that it streamed down her shoulders, and she was wearing a pretty net-ted veil at the back of her head. She'd parted her white blouse at her throat to reveal a double string of pearls nestled against her throat. Her dangling earrings, which looked to be a combination of pearls and rubies, glis-tened beneath her silky hair.

She'd smoothed out the pleats of her blue skirts and had polished her high-heeled black boots, which shuf-fled through the wild grasses leading to the path to him.

Simon was struck by her beauty. By the smooth glow of her skin, the tender smile, the look of sensitivity and intellect in her hopeful brown eyes. She had been so disappointed seeing her gown ruined. Some women, he supposed, might have collapsed in tears or anger, yet he had been impressed that she'd overcome her dismay and made the best of it.

Guilt pummeled his gut. She was being open and

believing in him as a husband, and he was being closed and deceptive.

She didn't deserve this. Even if she'd accidentally aided the real Ledbetter—which Simon wouldn't discover until she was thoroughly questioned—no woman deserved unkindness on her wedding day. She might be a thief or a want-to-be thief, but she wasn't a killer like Ledbetter. Simon was certain of that. She might be holding secrets of her own, but was not capable of underhanded deals and shady jewelry practices, and not murder.

Natasha didn't even realize she was attending a shotgun wedding.

In the future when she discovered his treachery, he would be a disappointment to her in every way. She'd be disappointed that he'd lied, that he didn't love her, that she could no more trust him than she could a weasel in a chicken coop.

That saddened him more than he had imagined it ever could. He was a disappointment, just as his father had always told him he was. He could never hope to please any woman, let alone on her wedding day.

Yet for some inexplicable reason, he wanted to make Natasha happy today. He wanted to show her that he was capable of it. That he was larger and mightier than his father's harsh, demeaning words ever would be.

Simon, in this moment of watching her walk down the aisle of this church, nature's blissful retreat of sunshine and clear water surrounded by the scent of moist vegetation, could for the first time in his life place himself in another man's shoes. He could understand—truly understand—how it might feel to be marrying for all the right reasons.

What were those reasons that God intended? Kindness, love, the desire to make the other person's burdens in life lighter, to share in the joy of living, to perhaps bring babies into the world that he and his wife might love together and protect.

What, truly, was more important in life than love and respect for another soul?

He heard McKern move beside him and realized there was something more important right now. That was survival.

If Simon slipped up during the ceremony, he'd get the first bullet to the temple, Natasha the second, Justice Weatherton the third.

Natasha stepped up beside Simon. He didn't fake his smile. He was truly touched by her beauty and had meant every word of what he'd said to her back in the cabin. Her gown meant nothing to him; she was a gorgeous woman with or without it. And when she'd first stepped off that train, he couldn't believe that he'd been sent to meet her, and that in the end, he would have to send her away.

"You look beautiful," Simon whispered.

He was rewarded with a shimmering smile.

Soon, he knew he would be rewarded with a smack to the face. But there would be time to think of that later. His mission came first.

"Dearly beloved," the justice began.

Natasha and Simon turned to the magistrate.

Simon tried not to dwell on the words. They made him uncomfortable, knowing that he was pretending through the vows and that she wasn't.

"We are here today to witness the joining of this man and woman…" the reading began "…in a state of matrimony in the eyes of God and the law..." Simon focused on the chirping of the chickadees in the branches, the caw of a cardinal, the sharp hoot of a lonely owl as the man continued. "...let no man put asunder..."

A bead of perspiration dripped down his temple, the only outward sign that he was bothered by any of this. He would make McKern and Fowler pay dearly for what they were doing, forcing his hand like this, making a fool out of him and Natasha—and for her painful discovery that was sure to come.

"And so, by the sanctity afforded to me by the Territory of Wyoming and the legal courts of the land, I now pronounce you man and wife."

Fowler whistled in celebration.

Simon turned to Natasha and, trying to do what he figured he should, lowered his lips and brushed her mouth. She went to return his kiss with fervor, but he pulled back hastily, which caused a clumsy moment between them. She wanted a bigger kiss, and he a smaller.

"Mr. and Mrs. Jarrod Ledbetter," said the justice, "congratulations. Now, if you don't mind signing the legal documents, I've got them right here."

"Absolutely," said Simon, grateful to get it over with. He barely read the words as he scrawled his false signature on the paper, one that he'd studied before he'd left on the mission so he'd get it right. Ha. If he only knew when he'd practiced forging the name that the first time he'd be using it would be his own marriage certificate.

Simon smiled with great show at his new bride and handed her the pen and ink.

With a contented sigh that pulled at his guilty heart, Natasha signed her name.

* * *

The feast lasted two hours.

Simon saw to it that they moved the long plank table outdoors in the shade, where they enjoyed the chicken and ribs, and pecan-and-raisin pie that doubled as a wedding cake.

Justice Weatherton ate the most and was the first to rise and leave. "I really must be getting back. I'm due for a meeting late this evening."

"Thank you for your services," Simon told him as the heavy man eased into his saddle. He was returning with some of the excess bags, to be deposited at Simon's cabin in Cheyenne, such as the ones containing the empty food tins and wine bottles. It left Natasha only with the light clothing pack containing her wedding gown, which for some reason she refused to part with, another small pack for light clothing and her handbag.

"You made it a very special day, sir." Natasha brushed the hair back from her soft shoulder. The netting of her veil fell along her back. Her cheeks were reddened from pleasure, or perhaps the wine. There was plenty of wine.

Simon tried to engage McKern and Fowler in conversation for the next few hours, so that he and Natasha wouldn't be caught alone. He didn't know what she had in mind for her wedding night, but he was certain of what he had in mind for his.

Nothing.

They collected firewood. They removed the saddles from the horses. They arranged baggage in the cabin.

When the two brutes drank more wine, Simon joined in all the toasts. He poured for Natasha, too. With a frown at perhaps how loud and tipsy the men were getting, she sipped hers more slowly.

Darkness fell. They drank more.

Simon cleared the table of leftover food and platters by a lit lantern. Natasha jumped to start at the other end, with a look to McKern and Fowler, who'd now started a campfire close to the trees where they'd already positioned their bedrolls. It was blazing and they were laughing.

"Please," said Simon, uncomfortable at how cozy it was with her here, the lighting setting off pretty shadows in her high cheekbones. "Let me do this. Why don't you go on into the cabin and relax? You're still wearing your veil."

"I suppose I should remove it. It's just that I've enjoyed the day so much." She pressed her lips together in a look of unabashed sweetness.

How long did he have to continue to lie to her? How long did he have to continue looking into those big brown eyes that seemed to demand so much from him?

Ah, hell. The overabundance of wine was making him stupidly sentimental. Why had he allowed the others to pour him so much drink?

He chafed at the double meaning in his next words. "It's been a day to remember." *And Lord, will you remember it.*

She was too affected by the wine herself to be whisked out of here quietly now. There'd be arguments from her and demands of explanation, and sure as the devil, McKern and Fowler would attack. Besides, now that they were "married," they were not in immediate danger if they stayed put.

That left him with three options.

As soon as they hit the trail tomorrow, he'd devise an excuse to send her safely back to Cheyenne. She looked to be a good rider, and he knew she was a good shot, so she'd be safe in daylight. The second option was to gallop away *with* her tomorrow and forget about his mission. But he was so close to finding the stolen goods and avenging the deaths of Eli and Clay that if he could do it safely, he'd damn well see it to the end. If all else failed and he couldn't send her on her own or get away with her, then he believed that once they hit the Eastern Ridge road, agents, lawmen and backup from the railroad would be there to help. Simon had sent the telegram; they *had* to be there. He'd order them to take her into their custody while he completed the job.

The most likely option was the first. Send her on her way tomorrow on some made-up excuse why she had to return to Cheyenne on her own.

She lifted the last of the wine in her goblet to her lips. She brushed past him toward the cabin, but stumbled over the collection of dried firewood.

His hands shot out. "Careful."

He braced her with firm hands digging into her upper arms.

She tilted her face up at him in the soft Wyoming moonlight and smiled softly. Was she tipsy, too? The swell of her lips rose to a perfect semicircle, jutting so beautifully against the black velvet sky. The pearls at her ears accentuated the whiteness of her teeth and the youthful energy in her expression.

He dropped his hands abruptly from her body.

He might be loaded, but he still knew he had no right to touch her.

He was not her husband.

He was not anything to her.

"I'll go water and settle the horses," he said in a cool clip, wishing to get as far away from his new wife as possible.

Chapter Twelve

They needed to discuss the bed. Natasha swayed in the darkness, still affected by the wine. She set down her glass on the rough nightstand and gave the straw mattress a good pat. Dust swirled into the air. She sneezed.

Jarrod was tending to the fireplace in the other room.

"Sweetheart?" she called out. "Are you coming?"

He hollered from the other room, "I have to wait for the fire to die out before I can join you. The embers need to be cold."

"Do you need to be that careful?"

"We don't want any mishaps while we're sleeping. Go on without me and I'll join you as soon as I can."

She grumbled at his answer. Mr. McKern and Mr. Fowler were spending the night outside by the campfire, which left her and Jarrod alone with the entire romantic cabin to themselves. She couldn't wait for him to kiss her. She was nervous and didn't know what she should do next, but believed he would be gentle.

She was disappointed that she had to wait for him, but at least it would give her time to prepare herself for her new husband.

My new husband.

She liked the sound of that and smiled as she patted the other side of the bed, making everything clean and fresh. She went to open the window slightly, tugging on the upper portion. A gush of fresh air rolled in and settled on her bare toes.

By the light of one lit candle on her nightstand, Natasha peered at the bed and called his name. "Jarrod?"

"Yes, honey?" he answered from beyond the walls.

"Which side would you like?"

There was a long pause. "I'll sleep by the door."

She smiled to herself. Such a protector.

There were clean sheets in the armoire, which she flattened on the mattress, and pillows that had seen better days but would do for tonight.

Jarrod had already poured clean water into the night pitcher on the washstand and had added fresh towels. She used them now to scrub her face and brush her teeth.

Then she stripped out of her wedding clothes—the veil, the white blouse, the skirts and petticoats—until she was wearing only her pearls and corset.

"Jarrod," she called again. She scratched her wrist. Why was it so itchy?

"Yes, darlin'?"

"I'm ready when you are." Anticipating what the night might bring, she looked down at her attire. She'd never worn anything so revealing and daring. Feeling shy, she reached for one of his pressed white shirts and tugged it over her corset and pearls. She had no robe with her, so this would have to do.

As anxious as she was—she could barely control the

jitters in her stomach—she would try to be pleasing and open to his suggestions.

How many other women had he had?

Plenty, she suspected.

And she herself had never been with a man before.

She frowned because there was no response from Jarrod.

"Jarrod?"

"Go on ahead, honey. Someone put an awful lot of logs on the fire, unfortunately. It's going to take a while to die out. Just rest your head on the pillow and before you know it, I'll be there."

She picked up her wine goblet and took a sip. Was there no other way to solve this? This was their wedding night.

Natasha came out of the bedroom carrying a candlestick and a glass of red wine, wearing nothing but his white shirt and a double strand of pearls. She clutched at the opening of the shirt to hold it together, but hadn't fastened the buttons. Beneath the pull of the white cotton, he saw the outline of a lacy white corset. It seemed to fall only to her waist. Was she naked from the crotch down?

Dear God in heaven, Simon couldn't bring himself to look away.

She certainly knew how to entice a man. Those long, smooth legs and glimmer of bosom between the buttons of his shirt brought him to full attention.

Swaying in rhythm to her walk, the pearls at her throat shifted over her throat. With an expression of delight and experienced sexual innuendo, Natasha came to stand beside him as he lay on a pillow, surrounded by fox pelts strewn on the floor. He, in contrast to her, was still fully dressed in the shirt and blue jeans he'd changed into an hour ago.

Her bare ankles were at his eye level, her pretty toenails buffed with a waxy polish, her calves smooth.

He gulped and followed the outline of her slender legs, over the gorgeous dips and curves of her feminine knees, up the muscles of her thighs.

"Let me see," he murmured, unable to help himself, and tugged at her shirt.

She let it slowly part open.

She was beautiful. He moaned in torture. How far was he going to let this go?

She wasn't wearing any bottom, just a corset on top. His searing gaze rolled up her long, naked legs, past the glimpse of escaping hair at the juncture of her beautiful legs, her lower half enticingly naked. His gaze slowly rose up her whalebone-crushed waistline, his heart beating in time to the wind at the back window thrashing a branch against the glass. He followed the soft, perfect, white lacy cups of her breasts, the creamy hollow of her neckline, and settled on her full lips.

She kneeled on the reddish soft pelts beside him. When she did, one of her naked breasts tugged out of her corset, followed immediately by the other. The double strand of pearls swayed over them.

"Oh, dear," she whispered, her hands occupied by the candlestick and wineglass in the other, so that she was unable to tug the fabric back up. "I'm afraid I've had too much to drink. I'll get that as soon as I sit…"

"Leave it," he mumbled, feeling the rise of heat within him and the deep throbbing need that spread throughout his limbs.

She lowered herself farther, and in response her bare breasts pointed to the ceiling. He flinched and watched. The rich areolae, dusty-pink and ever so smooth, perfectly outlined the flattened nipples. She was a walking oil painting, an artist's dream that should be admired from every angle and forever etched into his brain.

When her naked bottom reached the fox furs, she planted her candle and wine on the planks to the side of the fireplace. One strand of pearls shifted over her right breast, glossy ivory beads shimmering over plump nipples.

He supposed he could help her with the things she had in her hands, but then he wouldn't be able to admire the slightly off-balance way she was maneuvering.

He was already rock-hard.

How the hell did he get himself into this situation?

In the name of duty and honor, he had to keep his hands off this?

She was a temptress, and she knew what she was doing to him. She was experienced with men; there was no shyness in her posture, simply a woman who was aware of her effect on the opposite sex. Whatever experience with men she'd had in Chicago, she'd learned her craft well. The pearls alone against her skin caused an uproar in the beating of his pulse. The soft, flickering candlelight over her breasts and thighs and the dark triangle between her legs caused his mouth to go dry.

Damned beauty.

She took a sip of wine and replaced her glass on the plank floor.

"You're not drinking any more?" Her voice was husky, cutting through the darkness. The warm fireplace beside them crackled with flames.

Hell, he was guilty of stoking the fire with more wood when she hadn't been watching just to keep it burning and give him an excuse to keep himself out of the bedroom. But she was guilty, too, of stoking a fire even more dangerous.

"I wanted to keep my head clear," he murmured. Ha. As if he could think clearly sitting beside a naked work of art.

She shifted to lie at an angle across the pelts, moving her long legs on top of one another and nudging her dainty toes together.

Oh, to be between those legs, nestled by those toes.

She closed her eyes for a moment, lying in front of the fire as if she were contemplating something or perhaps simply enjoying the heat, which gave him the opportunity to study her face. Golden light skimmed her thick black lashes. It cast a warm glow over her cheeks and her full bottom lip. The pearls dangling from her earlobes glimmered from behind her long, glossy brown hair.

He reached out and stroked the side of her face. She nuzzled against it like a lazy cat and inhaled, sucking air into her throat, then flashed those gorgeous brown eyes open at him.

She did something insane to him. She stirred his restlessness, made him feel a hunger for intimacy.

With a tug of guilt and restraint, he was determined to finish this mission tomorrow in the name of the two closest friends he'd ever had—either as a kid or an adult—and so he dropped his hand from her face and pulled away. He still had his life, but Eli and Clay were dead because he wasn't able to save them.

This moment with her was crazy. He was crazy.

She reached out to him then. She took his face between her hands and leaned in close to kiss him.

Her mouth was succulent. Warm, moist, tender, evocative.

He couldn't help himself. He buried his fingers in her rich chestnut locks.

She was every bit as erotic as he thought she would be.

Battling his inner war of emotion, he slid his hand from her silky hair to her soft upper arm. He moved his thumb over and stroked her nipple.

"Mmm." The moan came from the back of her throat.

He deepened his kiss, putting pressure on her mouth and pulling her closer. When he gently explored her lip with his tongue, he was surprised to find her matching his gentle swirling motion with her own.

He pressed on top of her, pinning her to the pelts. His mouth caressed and wooed her as his gentle hands fondled her breasts. Her corset was pushing everything up and out, exaggerating her curves and the glory of her magnificent breasts. He ran his fingertip along her cleavage, marveling at the dip. She made the mistake of reaching out to run her hands into his hair. Mistake because it ignited the deep fire within him and pushed him over the edge.

He cupped her jaw, kissed her like mad, ravished her body with his migrating hands. In a fever pitch, he undid the drawstrings at the front of her corset. Her jutting breasts rested on her rib cage.

He lowered his head, his blond hair trailing her skin, as he kissed her breasts and sent little swirling motions along her skin.

"You are the most gorgeous thing I've ever seen,"

he rasped, trying to control himself but knowing that he was off the deep end. How much wine had it taken for him to lose his control? Or was it simply the sight of his beautiful Natasha?

"Jarrod...please...take off your shirt."

It rankled him that she was calling him Jarrod. Why couldn't he be Simon, just for tonight? He felt like himself in every way, not the villainous stranger she thought he was.

Simon. Call me Simon.

But he never dared to say the words.

He rose off her, never for a moment taking his eyes off the splendor. Flames from the fire rose and spat behind him, their silhouette dancing across her skin in mesmerizing flashes.

He unfastened his buttons and tugged out of his sleeves.

Natasha, with heated expectation in her eyes, ran her hands along his muscled forearms and up his biceps. Her body lifted off the fox pelts as she rose to meet him. Now she was totally naked except for her pearls. The shorter strand had tightened against her throat, the longer one framing both pointy breasts. Such fascinating nipples.

He cupped both breasts and lost himself in her touch.

Her fingers were attentive to the curves of his muscles, trailing along his flesh, down his throat, his breastbone, across the rigid lines of his chest.

She didn't stop there.

With a half smile and a groan of surrender, he basked in the pleasure of her fingertips. She blazed a hot trail down his stomach, along the midline of his abdomen and then lower.

Oh, yes.

Her experienced fingers circled above the denim of his crotch, outlining the huge swell of his manhood, sending shivers down his spine.

He throbbed, his heart racing like a Thoroughbred's, his emotions trapped in a jumble of confusion that he refused to explore at this moment. He wanted this woman, this beautiful woman who beckoned to him like a tempting siren from the sea. He didn't wish to examine why or what drove them; it simply was inevitable.

He was glad she wasn't a virgin. It would make it easier for him and more enjoyable for her.

He unbuckled his belt, unfastened the buttons of his denims and sprang to glorious attention. She gave a little gasp of wonder, which made him feel pretty damn proud.

"I'd like to make you feel good, Natasha."

"You're doing a good job already."

"What do you like in bed?"

"I like your touch. Surprise me."

He laughed softly as he came down to kiss her. Naked body against naked body.

She moved her arms up around him and hugged him. Her voluptuous curves pressed against him, breasts, hips, mouth against his.

Why did her kiss penetrate to his heart?

She had the power to move him. Uplift and tease and send him thinking about things he'd rather leave dormant; thoughts of future possibilities, of what he wanted out of life, if he could ever be enough for Natasha.

His large hand drifted down her rib cage, thumbing the curvature beneath her breast. It was such an intimate spot, and he loved exploring it.

With a moan of pleasure, she lifted her legs over his waist, arching beneath him, telling him in unspoken words that she was ready.

He was at her command.

He dipped his hard shaft along the slit of her hot, moist body. Still kissing, she pressed her mouth harder against his in response, signaling how much she wanted this. He pressed himself along her ridge to make entry easier, marveling at how wet she was for him. He glided his shaft along the path that was sure to be bliss.

She was breathing heavily. He panted alongside her and broke his mouth away to kiss her throat.

"Are you ready?" he asked gently.

"Yes, I'm ready for you, Jarrod."

It's Simon, please...

But her words sent him reeling into another world.

He slid and stroked the outside of her until she seemed to be tumbling into an abyss, breathing harder and faster and moving her body up and down in a rhythm to his fingers that were cupping the outside of her mound. He pulled his shaft away and used only his fingers. Her hands moved along his back, gripping more firmly, clenching and digging in until she suddenly froze. She burst into an orgasm that was sweeter than words for him. He kissed her jaw, her throat, her shoulder.

He'd done it. He'd made her come simply with his hands.

His erection was so hard for her that he could barely contain his own needs. But he held back. Seeing her in such a tantalizing position, a woman with commanding experience in the bedroom, yet so vulnerable and soft beneath his touch, made him want her all the more.

Her muscles seemed to loosen as she relaxed and gave a soft sigh of contentment.

He gently removed his hand. Now it was his turn. He wanted nothing more than to make love to Natasha. Nothing could stop him.

He pressed his rock-hard shaft along the slickness and, with a quick thrust, entered.

He didn't get what he was expecting.

She let out a soft moan of pain, and he realized to his shock that he was wrong about her. Confused and dismayed, he frowned and stopped moving.

She *was* a virgin.

Chapter Thirteen

"What is it, Jarrod?"

Natasha noticed that everything had changed in a matter of seconds. His hands on her rib cage froze, he stopped kissing her throat, and he stopped moving on top of her. There'd been a jarring of pain when he'd broken through her virginity, and she wished he'd continue for she was still extremely sore and speed would help matters, but something was definitely wrong.

"Are you all right?" she asked. Lord, he hadn't had a physical attack of some kind, had he? An infliction of the heart?

"I'm sorry," he whispered and rolled off her. He seemed to be breathing fine, thank goodness.

She rose on an elbow in the soft furs. The pain left her, but she felt a trickle of blood escape onto the pelt. No time to worry about that now; she'd deal with it later. She was concerned about Jarrod.

"What are you sorry for?" she asked tenderly.

"The pain I've caused you. I should not have done this."

"But the pain's to be expected. My friends…other

women at the boardinghouse…they explained to me what it's like the first time."

"But I didn't know you were a virgin."

"Pardon me?" She frowned, now completely confused. He'd rolled away from her not because he was feeling ill, but because he hadn't expected her to be a virgin? "You thought I came into this with… But I told you I was."

"Not precisely. You said that I should know the answer to that when we discussed it."

"Well, of course you should know the answer," she said. "What did you think I was? When you had asked, I told you of my virtue in our letters!"

"Well," he stumbled, "you seemed so experienced, the way you moved…and where you placed your hands…and how unabashed you are in your nakedness…"

She glanced at his torso and caught sight of his withering erection. He was no longer interested in her.

He looked to where she was gazing on the lower part of his body and scrambled for a response. "It's not what you think, Natasha—"

"I don't have to think anything. I can see how put off you are by me."

"I'm not put off. I'm extremely impassioned—"

"I think your body speaks better than your tongue."

"Damn my body," he cursed. "I didn't think you were a virgin."

"And that should explain your—" she looked to his falling manhood "—your declining interest?" She couldn't control the hurt and confusion she felt. "You don't want a virgin, obviously. You were more enthralled when you were anticipating a harlot."

"Any woman who enjoys the pleasure of a man is not a harlot—she's exercising her right," he said firmly. "The same as any man."

"And you find those type of women much more exciting than *me*."

"*No.*"

"*Yes.*"

He tried to explain. "I appreciate the fact that you're a virgin."

"*Was* one."

He groaned, collapsed on the fox pelts and stared glumly up at the ceiling.

"So that's to be the way of it? On our wedding night? You expected someone different from what you got." She could see his disappointment in every movement of his body, every twitch of his expression.

Jarrod closed his eyes and sighed again. Speechless.

She crossed her arms over her breasts, suddenly feeling cold and exposed.

"How was I to know?" he mumbled to himself, staring at the rafters. "Who saw this one coming?"

"What precisely are you saying?"

He peered at her, then to the outer door, where the two other men were camping, then back to her. If he was intending to explain himself, he changed his mind. "I'm sorry the night was a disappointment to you. That *I'm* a disappointment."

She rose from the pelts and turned her back on him, not wishing to expose herself further, and not as unabashed in her sexuality and her nakedness as he assumed. She was feeling rather insecure and unwanted. Why wasn't she good enough for him the way she was?

His sexual excitement had withered on the vine, right before her eyes.

She scooped her corset off the floor and made her way back to the bedroom, all the while feeling the burning heat of his gaze on her body. If he wanted to look, let him look. If he thought she was secure in her sensuality, let him think it.

But when she got to the room, she closed the door behind her and fell onto the bed in a hopeless mess.

"Just one kiss," Simon mumbled to himself on the pelts when Natasha left. "All I wanted was one kiss, and now look."

What an idiot.

The more time he spent with her, the deeper he was falling.

She'd lost her virginity to a man who wasn't even her husband.

He'd had no right to take that from her. He was liar, a traitor, a selfish beast who deserved to be hanged from the nearest tree.

Absently, he scratched an itch on his right palm.

With a string of curses, he rose and tried to pull on his jeans. Still slightly affected by the alcohol, he lost his balance and tried again. He'd been drinking too much; he needed air.

He grabbed his shirt—and a towel, for he intended on bathing in the river—when Natasha burst out of the bedroom door. She was loosely covered in a towel. Her face was scrunched up as though she was going to blast him again.

"You don't need to say any more. I'm truly sorry for—"

"Jarrod, look." She held out her hands, rubbing the sides of her palms as if to relieve their itchiness. Her voice rose, as though in a panic. "What is this?"

The crackling fire cast light onto the tops of her hands. They were covered with thin red streaks. She turned her hands over and her palms were reddened, too.

"What is that?" he asked. "Are they blistered?"

She shook her head. Her loose hair fell in a thick tent around her shoulders. "Just streaky."

He went to cup her hand for a closer look, when she exclaimed, "You've got them, too."

He examined his hands. Sure enough, the red streaks were there. No skin abrasions or cuts or blisters. Just strange red lines. And damn it, itchy. He brought his fingers over the red parts and rubbed.

"What do you think it might be?" she asked again.

They'd chosen to forget their earlier harsh words at each other and concentrated on the mysterious rash.

"Did you touch anything odd?" he asked.

"No. Did you?"

He shook his head. "Just the dinner and the wine." He took a quick inventory of the room. "What did I touch? The firewood. The poker. The fox pelts."

"But as far as I can see," she argued, "my body is clear. It's just my hands, so it can't be the pelts. And I didn't touch the firewood."

He stole a glance at her long, bare legs and her bare shoulders. He didn't dare examine her further, for he was getting heated glances from just that bit.

"Trust me," she snapped. "My body isn't affected."

"Okay, okay. No need to get your knickers twisted. If

you're wearing any." He thought some more about what he'd touched. "I handled the horses earlier."

"That might be it, I suppose...."

"Maybe it's from the perfume in the cake of soap, or water from the river?"

"I washed my face with the soap and the water, and it's not affected."

And then it dawned on him. "Oh, no."

Her lashes flashed upward. "What?"

He whistled. "Nah. It can't be."

"Tell me."

He shook his head, thinking about it some more. "It can't be what I'm thinking. That would be too cruel a joke."

"What? Something the others did to us?"

"No, no. It's...aw, hell, Natasha. What did you do with the bouquet of flowers I cut for you?"

"The flowers? I put them in a jar in the bedroom." She paused. "Don't tell me. You picked poison ivy for my wedding bouquet?"

"*No,* I'm no fool. I know what poison ivy and poison oak look like."

"Evidently something's affected us."

He sighed. "It could be that I shuffled through a patch of it while I was picking the flowers, and it rubbed off on them. That would explain why it seems to be a mild case and no blisters—"

"For heaven's sake, Jarrod, how could you be so careless?"

"You think I did it on purpose?"

"First the spilled wine on my wedding gown. Then my husband is not able to perform his husbandly duties. And now this?"

"For hell's sake, I can perform any and all husbandly duties—"

"This is the most bad-luck wedding! I never should've married you today. I should've stopped when I saw that red wine stain and listened to my instincts, but no, I had to—"

"Shh," he whispered, looking to the door. If McKern and Fowler arose and found them arguing, they'd know something was amiss. Simon was sobering up quickly. He still had two lives to protect. Hers and his.

She grumbled and wiggled her fingers in frustration as though the sting was becoming unbearable. His were starting to sting, too.

"We need to soak our hands in cool water," he suggested. "That'll help with the sting."

She nodded to the bedroom. "I don't have any more clean water in there."

"Let's go down to the river."

She agreed. They took some fresh towels, she pulled her blouse and skirt over her head, and they left by the back door. He wore his unbuttoned shirt, trousers and guns.

The night was dark and still. The moon hung overhead, casting everything in a silky glow.

Natasha muttered beside him, "Let's hope we don't get bitten by a rabid raccoon. That would be a topper for our wedding day."

"Lighten up."

"Don't you tell me to lighten up. You have no idea—"

"Shh."

"And don't shush me! That's the second time you've—"

"Please, Natasha, don't wake them. You won't get privacy for your bath then."

She grumbled in complaint, but she quieted.

"And for your information, I *can* perform my husbandly duties."

"Oh, I'm sure."

Was that sarcasm? he wondered with annoyance.

Frustrated, he felt the need to explain again why he'd malfunctioned. "There are reasons why I couldn't…"

"Lighten up," she said with a smile.

That really corked him. How could *she* tell *him* to— Oh, what was the use of trying to explain himself? It was hard to be truthful when truth wasn't on your side. He couldn't perform because he—he probably felt awful and guilty that he was taking her virginity away under false pretenses. He couldn't possibly explain that to her, so decided not to fight.

"Thank you for the good advice," he said lightly, equally sarcastic.

She raised an eyebrow as if surprised that he was being civil.

The river appeared to their right. Shrubs and trees lined the edges. The moon played on the shoreline, gilding the rippling current in soft tones of gold. They strode through field grasses as high as their knees.

They grew quiet but kept walking along the river's edge; he wasn't sure why. Perhaps it was the distant sound of a waterfall that drew them. Night birds fluttered their wings in the branches of tall ash trees, scattered maples, birch and pine. The scent of dew and moist earth filled the air.

"Here," Simon said, leading her through an opening

in the trees that dipped gradually to the pebbly shore-line. "We've got privacy here."

She sighed, as if grateful for the solitude. They stepped beside the lapping water. Moonlight glistened off the deep blue waters. To their left, a very high water-fall came into view. At the top of a rocky cliff, the wa-terfall was narrow, only about ten feet across, so the force of the water seemed rather gentle.

"It's got to be thirty feet high," Natasha said in breathless wonder. Then she scratched at her hands. "They're getting unbearably itchy."

"Be careful not to cut the skin with your finger-nails. We don't want any festering wounds. We've still got a long ride in the morning." He wasn't sure what time it was. Ten o'clock? Eleven? He was too worked up to be tired.

He rubbed the back of his tingling hands together and kept rubbing. It helped.

Natasha looked up at him with newfound shyness.

Shy? he thought. After all they'd been through to-gether?

With a grumble, he took off his shirt, guns and pants. He dived into the circular pool of water at the base of the waterfall.

"My," he said in surprise.

"What is it?" her voice echoed over the water. "It's not snakes, is it? I hate snakes."

He laughed gently in her direction. "It's warm, Nata-sha. The temperature of a warm bath. It's fed by some sort of underground spring." He turned to peer into the waters. "Look, there, it's bubbling."

"Did you know the water would be warm up here?"

"No. But that's likely why..." He stopped himself.

He was going to say that was likely why Ledbetter had chosen this location for his cabin, but he should know that, considering he was supposed to be Ledbetter.

"Why what?" She was still fully clothed, but her boots were off and she was lifting her skirts and touching the water with bare toes.

"Likely what'll make this a great swim. Come on in. The water does help with the discomfort."

"Then turn away."

"What do you mean, turn away?" he said. "I've already seen you without a stitch of clothes."

"That was before…when you…we failed at…couldn't perform. And we both know what a disaster that was. The only reason I'm here is to clean up and soak my poison-ivy hands."

With a huff of frustration, he circled in the water, floating above the surface and staring off into the dark shadows of the trees.

Was she trying to stab at him on purpose, talking about his failure to perform, or did the insults fly naturally for her? For Pete's sake, something like that had never happened to him before. It happened this time only because of…he wasn't sure what. Probably a combination of things. Surprise that he'd been caught off guard, not knowing she was a virgin. Feeling doubly guilty that not only was he lying to her about being her betrothed, but sleeping with her when he shouldn't be. And maybe even a bit of fear that he could never live up to her expectations of a husband.

But hell, the way she went on and on about it, he had half a mind to prove to her that he could damn well *out*-perform any man.

He paused for a moment. What was he thinking?

This wasn't about him or his problems or what he needed to do to prove himself. This was about the mission that the agency was paying him for. This was about recovering the stolen goods that belonged to the railroad and its passengers. This was about delivering justice for the murder of his friends in the line of duty.

Simon was reminded that Clay had a boy around seven or eight. When Clay was alive, he never stopped talking about his son. *Tucker likes to swim. Tucker can outrun a deer. Tucker says the smartest things.*

For some inexplicable reason, Simon had always enjoyed hearing about the boy. Maybe it was because Simon had always wished his father had talked about him like that. Now Simon wondered who it was that had knocked on Clay's door to tell his widow and his boy that Clay would never come home again.

It caused a stab to Simon's heart.

And what about Eli? He'd been a loner, like Simon, but he had an ailing mother he was looking after. How had she taken that knock on her door?

Simon tried not to let it get to him. At least *he* was single and unattached and cared for no one, and would never put someone through that kind of loss.

He turned away from Natasha and dunked his head in the water.

Chapter Fourteen

The instant Natasha removed her clothes and hit the water, she forgot about the itchy streaks on her hands. Instead, the shocking cold made her gasp.

"You said it was warm!"

"It is," Jarrod answered at a distance. "Over here. Come over here!"

Her skin felt as if it had puckered from all her goose bumps. Her blood was pounding, and her breath came in gulps. Frantic to warm up, she swam toward him in the circular pool of water that shimmered to the side of the falls. The water began to feel less frigid, then grew lukewarm, then as she reached Jarrod, as warm as the tub water back at the Mountain Hotel.

"Are you all right?" Jarrod asked with concern.

She eased into it, relaxing now that she was in safer waters. "Better now. It is lovely, isn't it?"

"For a moment there, I was worried you'd seen a serpent."

"I wouldn't be surprised after everything else that's happened today." Her wedding had gone nothing like what she'd hoped for or planned.

"True enough," he said, going along with her sentiment, "or a canoe might come tumbling over the falls at any minute and squash us to death."

She tried to suppress a laugh, but their horrendous day *was* funny, and laughter escaped her. Who would ever believe it?

Jarrod, still frowning, softened and soon joined in the laughter. His wet hair was slicked back and his face looked renewed with energy and strength. His muscular arms cut the water with little effort. They were upright in the warm water, circling their arms to keep their balance.

"You look like an otter," she said, her breath catching at how handsome he truly was.

"An otter? That doesn't sound very appealing."

"I mean you're sleek and energetic and seem so at home in the water."

He smiled. "I learned how to swim when I was four."

"Four? That's awful early. Wherever did you learn that?"

The glimmer in his dark eyes strengthened. "My mother taught me in the local creek. She used to be a great swimmer. At some of the local fairs, she always placed first in the children's round. She had the ribbons tacked up in the house for a long time before she took them down."

"I'm sorry you lost her."

"So am I," he said with a husky note of emotion.

"And your father?" she asked. "What are some of the things he liked to do?"

Jarrod's face turned serious, almost cautious. "He liked to whittle wood. He could whittle the prettiest birds. He carved me this little bluebird once…. I kept it on my windowsill for so long…. Years in fact…"

"After he died, you mean?" she asked gently. She knew he'd lost his parents, but in his letters, Jarrod hadn't gone into much detail.

He nodded. "When he disappeared from my life." She took that to mean yes, after his death.

"Maybe you thought the bluebird might bring him back."

His jaw twisted, and the pain that flitted across his face indicated how much he missed his father. "It's what little kids do when they don't know what else to," he said. "They put signs out on their windows and think impossible dreams."

"I was an adult when I lost Granddad, but if he'd given me a little bluebird, I would *still* put it on my windowsill. So it's not the age that matters. It's the love."

"I'm…I'm not sure that I loved my father."

His admission caused her to go still. There was a deep pain inside him, something that he was truly trying to run from. There had to be a cause.

"Was he awfully mean to you?" she asked, kicking her feet gently beneath the water again, scared that Jarrod would say yes, but feeling the need to ask. "Beat you?"

"Yeah," he said softly, almost as though he didn't wish to admit it.

A knot clung to her throat like a ball of porridge. She sensed more. "Did he make you feel worthless?"

Jarrod nodded, too choked up to speak.

Her heart ached for him, thinking of how awful he still felt, the suffering he was still going through from the memories. "Then I think maybe as an adult looking back, you no longer love him. Because you know what he did to you, and your heart is protecting you by keeping his memory at a distance. But I think as a kid, you always loved him. That's how kids are. I understand your keeping the bluebird on the windowsill, Jarrod."

Something about what she said made him wince. His eyes misted. He was deeply affected, trying to retain his composure, but perhaps what she had said was painfully close to the truth.

"Natasha, I…I really wish… When this is over, promise you'll listen to my explanation."

"When what's over?"

He sucked in a breath so loud it rippled over the water. The falls gushed behind them. "When this trip is over, promise me…that you'll listen to my explanation. Promise me that you'll believe me when I say that this is the real me with you here. That I mean what I'm saying—"

"Well, of course, Jarrod."

"Jarrod." He repeated his name in an oddly strained voice.

She wasn't sure she understood. He wanted her to believe the explanation of what had happened back at the cabin? He seemed terribly perturbed about it. Even now his face had fallen, his eyes piercing hers as if it meant the world for him to clarify their wedding night fiasco. Maybe he wished to gain some time, till tomorrow, so he could better understand it himself.

"You're worried about what happened between us?" she asked timidly.

He moved closer in the warm pool, two feet away, looking as though he was begging for forgiveness. "Promise me," he whispered.

"I promise." She was feeling stronger and had a yearning to show him how sensitive she could be. "But there is only one way we can resolve this." She moved closer. "You know it and I know it." To get over the failure of their earlier try, they had to try again.

It was simple. She needed this in order to feel better about herself, as well as trying to make him whole again.

His gaze dropped to her bare shoulders, then to the waterline and her breasts, which she felt certain were visible just beneath the surface of the warm liquid.

She felt wanted. She could see in his eyes how much he wanted her. It was more of a burning ache she witnessed in the tremulous glistening of his dark green eyes, the tender expression in his cheeks, the solemn lips.

Yet he made no move toward her. He held back, the muscles in his jaw tightening, his biceps rippling as he stayed his distance.

It was up to her, just as Valentina had told her many times at the boardinghouse. It was usually up to the woman to help a man through his sentimental pain.

Even if Valentina hadn't told her, Natasha would simply sense it. She wanted to help Jarrod through everything.

She kicked her bare leg in the heavenly heated water and then she was an inch away, breathing his air, invading his space, her heart tripping in time to his own. He seemed to be holding his breath. She wrapped her arm about his neck, nestled in beside his naked chest, the tips of her floating breasts touching his skin, and kissed him.

Whatever indecision he may have been feeling, left.

His mouth melted against hers. With a soft splash, she heard his arms come out of the pool and felt them wrap around her, one at her waist and the other at her shoulder.

He kissed her urgently, as though his life depended on her.

No words could explain the multitude of emotions that churned through Simon. Sheer pounding excitement, a bout of nerves of where this was leading and a desire to make love to Natasha.

She'd touched something so deep and painful inside him tonight, something he'd never shared with anyone before, that it penetrated his reluctance and made him *want* to open up to her.

Who would've thought that he could actually find a *good* memory about each of his parents? Natasha had brought that out in him. And then her tender understanding about his mixture of emotions when it came to his father...

Natasha was like no other woman he'd ever been with. She moved him.

He kissed her mouth and pressed his tongue against hers, all the while balancing upright in the warm springs. They lost themselves in their embrace.

Somehow, he found the strength to pull away from her kiss. Although he felt he was being himself tonight, revealing his true self, she didn't know it. She thought he was Jarrod Ledbetter.

"Natasha," he murmured, trying to break free of her spell, his forehead pressed against hers. "Maybe this isn't what we need to do at this moment."

"It's exactly what I need. I feel like a failure, like

I wasn't enough for you. I did something wrong back there."

"You did nothing wrong," he snapped, angry at himself but never at her.

"Then show me." She wrapped her legs around him in the water. His erection bobbed upward, brushed the base of her buttocks. He moaned in torture—he so wanted her, yet he shouldn't touch her.

She moved slightly downward. Suddenly, his erection was at the opening of her body. He groaned, moved himself to rub against her, feeling the slick heat of her center. She beckoned for him.

They moved backward, wrapped in each other, until he found a set of smooth, flat boulders in the water behind them. She was still on top while he turned and rested on the warm stone.

It was comfortable. The rocks had dulled to smoothness from the waterfall's erosion over the decades. The water itself was clear and warm. So clear he could see the outline of her beautiful body nestled over his. Her breasts floated in the warmth, the pink nipples protruding toward him.

He moved upward and pushed. His shaft was enveloped by splendid heat. They were united beneath the warm current.

He'd never made love in a river before.

She moved on top of him and gently rode him. "Like this, Jarrod? Do you like this?"

Please call me Simon....

"I like it all. Whatever you do…"

She was excruciatingly gentle, teasing him with her up-and-down movements, bringing bliss and sexual fervor. She was likely taking her time because she was still aching from the first time.

"Are you sore?"

"A little. Not too much. Not enough to stop."

The smooth rocks beneath his backside remained firm and gave them stability. He cupped her breasts, savoring the sensual feel of her body, the turn of her hips, the curvy bones and hollows of her throat and shoulders as she twisted herself forward. Her long, loose hair floated in wet strands about the water.

He loved looking at Natasha, the concentration lines on her forehead, the determination in the way her mouth was set, the giving nature of her posture and her actions. His pulse and breath quickened at every change in her expression.

He didn't want this moment to end. He wanted this feeling of joy to last forever.

"Natasha, I want to pleasure you again, but we better stop before it's too late for me."

"My pleasure comes in seeing you. Please, Jarrod, do it for me."

He wished it was his name she was calling, but could she have said anything more pleasing to the ear? Her sexy tone in begging for his body…

He was almost there. His muscles tensed, his breathing heaved, his heart drummed inside his chest and pounded through his body.

With swift hands, he grabbed her by the waist and turned her in the water, still connected at their thighs, so that she was now resting on the smooth, warm rocks and facing him. Now he had control over the rhythm and the speed. He moved deeper inside her, savoring the heat and friction on his shaft, the perfect encapsulation of male and female.

Leaning back, she watched him under the lazy upturn of her dark lashes, the slight smile on her face so entrancing he believed he would remember it always. When she reached out and secured his waist with her slender hands and tugged him closer, he lost it.

His orgasm pounded deep inside her, inside him. It reverberated through his muscles with uncontrollable fury. He released and tensed, released and tensed. Wave after wave came crashing down on him, diluting his strength, absolving him of rational thought. He wanted Natasha. He cared for Natasha.

It subsided. The waves softened, the crescendo eased. He opened his eyes.

Natasha's hazy smile greeted him. He leaned down to kiss her throat.

"I was able to please you," she whispered into his wet chest. "Wasn't I?"

"You're incredible, Natasha. I've never been so pleased. I didn't think it was possible to experience something like this underwater."

"Me, neither." She kissed his chest several times with soft, butterfly lips. He'd never felt so connected to a woman before.

He pulled himself out of her, much as he hated to leave that heavenly spot. He tugged her off the rocks so that they could float in the warm water again.

"Are you all right? Still sore?"

Moonlight captured the serenity on her face. "I'm fine."

"Shall we wash up?" he asked gently.

She nodded.

"Wait here. I'll get our things."

He swam through the warm springs, entered the cold waters of the river and reached their towels and soap. He picked up those necessary things and made his way back to her and the rocks not by water, but along the grassy shoreline, totally buff in the moonlight. The feeling of freedom buoyed from the inner depths of his spirit.

He placed the towels and soap on the rocks, then dived headfirst into the water. He heard her yelp softly at the splash. When he came back up, she was laughing and reaching for the soap.

They lathered each other. He washed her hair.

He helped her out and toweled her. After the splendid warmth of the water, the cool air rippled over them, but it was energizing.

With more laughter, they flung off their towels to dress. He stopped her for a moment, reached out and took her hand so that he might study her in the moon's golden rays. They needn't say a word. They understood that something deep was happening here, something more than a union of bodies.

"Quickly now, wench," he said with amusement, lightly tapping her naked rump. For a moment, he allowed himself to believe they were a normal couple. "Before you get a chill." He tossed her skirt to her.

They dressed quickly in the cool Wyoming air. When she picked up her final items from the riverbank, he surprised her by swooping her up into his arms.

With physical ease, he carried her through the grasses in which they'd come, back the quarter mile to the cabin.

"You're a very light package," he said.

"You're my very own strongman." She wrapped her arms tighter around his neck, and he enjoyed the feeling of security it gave him. But as they neared the cabin again, his uncertainties returned.

How would she react to know he was not Jarrod Ledbetter?

She was just and kind, of that he was certain. But how deeply had she been involved with Ledbetter and his criminal activities? She had yet to confess what she knew about his stash in the mountains, but she had known something.

It was all so complicated.

Since she'd never met Ledbetter, only Simon in his place, then wasn't their relationship more real than not?

But, he argued in his mind, she'd started that relationship with the real Ledbetter in her letters, and Simon had stepped in to lie to her.

She would never forgive him.

He braced himself for the fallout that would surely bring. Everything they'd shared tonight might be irreparably damaged. But what exactly was he expecting? He was used to roaming from one end of the country to the other, so what could he possibly give her in return? Certainly not a life with him.

"Here we are." He set her down gently by the back door.

Should he confess? He had to tell her something. Should he wait until tomorrow, after he'd secured the stolen property? Then he'd give her a chance to explain herself and her involvement with Ledbetter.

Or should he confess now, as she was looking up at him, still misty-eyed and impressed with the night of wonder they'd shared? If he told her the truth now, he wouldn't be able to control what she might do. Control meant everything to him; it had since the age of eight, when he'd learned to depend only on himself. Their two horses were secured next to the sleeping men, so escape on horse would be impossible without being detected. Therefore, it would still be safest if they got a few hours of sleep, and he sent her away tomorrow.

Chapter Fifteen

"Now *that* was a wedding night to remember," whispered Natasha as Jarrod set her on her feet by the cabin's back door. Her heart was exploding with all the wonderful feelings they'd shared tonight. She'd pleased him and was proud of her accomplishment.

He didn't say anything, simply looked down at her freshly scrubbed face. There seemed to be a lot on his mind, for his expression wavered.

"How are your hands?" he finally asked.

She looked down at the mild streaks. "The swim helped a lot. The redness is coming back, but it doesn't seem to be getting worse."

"There's oatmeal in the cabin. I'll make a paste and we can apply it to the welts."

They listened for a moment in the stillness, but heard no sounds of the sleeping men on the other side of the cabin. Jarrod opened the door for her and then indicated he was going around to check on the campfire. She slipped inside.

What an incredible evening. It had started on the wrong foot, but ended in happiness. He'd disclosed what his childhood had been like, opening up to her in vulnerable ways. All would be right between her husband and herself, she thought.

The fire had died down to embers. She didn't bother prodding it back to life. She lit a lantern.

She rubbed the wetness from her hair with a towel and searched the bedroom for her nightgown. It was the only new article of clothing she'd invested in before her trip. It was made of simple soft white cotton with lace along the low-cut neckline, and lace straps.

She stripped out of her clothes and tugged it on. It fell to the floor in a pretty swirl. The hemline was also trimmed in lace, and her bare, waterlogged toes peeked out beneath the virginal fabric.

Tonight had been both exhausting and exhilarating. As any wedding night should be, she thought with a smile.

She prepared the sheets and fluffed up the pillows. When she heard the back door open, she went out to the great room to meet her husband.

Husband. The word had such a pleasing ring.

He was carrying two large canteens of water that he'd filled from the river.

"The horses are fine," he said in the dim lighting of the lantern. She set it down on the kitchen table among their supplies, as he continued to explain, "The fire's out, and McKern and Fowler are asleep in their bedrolls."

"That's good. We didn't disturb them."

His lashes flickered over her, assessing her. "That's a pretty nightgown."

She twirled around in it, wondering if the shape of her body could be seen through the cotton. She didn't mind; in fact, she enjoyed the flicker of excitement it brought to his eyes.

"Keep that up and we'll never get any sleep."

She basked in the newfound sexual power she had over him. Just one look at her and he could be aroused? The experience was new to her, but thrilling.

He strode to the table to set down his canteens, ignoring her to search for the oatmeal sack, but just when she thought he was no longer interested, he snatched her up with one arm and kissed her cheek.

His grip was lovely. Her clean, smooth skin beneath the gown slid so nicely against the soft cotton and then against Jarrod.

With a soft caress, he turned back to the table. "Aha! Here it is."

He took water from the canteen and mixed the oatmeal into a thin goo. "Hold out your hands."

He spread the stuff in a very light layer on her skin. The burn was instantly dulled.

"Feels good," she said.

"Take a towel with you to bed to avoid a mess."

"Yes, sir," she said dutifully. "And you? You'll need some on your hands, too."

He frowned for a second and looked to the bedroom.

"I've already set the bed," she told him. "You're sleeping by the door, as requested."

With an appreciative glance, he lowered his face and kissed her on the mouth. She trembled from his touch, and those flickers of butterflies began again.

He broke the kiss and handed her a canteen. "Fresh water for the bedroom."

She was getting sleepy. She took the glowing lantern and walked in front of him, getting the distinct impression that he was again staring at her behind through the soft cotton.

"That is the sexiest piece of material I've ever been witness to."

"Glad you like it," she said. "I bought it for you in Chicago."

When she turned around again, he seemed unsettled by her words. But perhaps she'd only imagined it, for his expression turned back to amusement. "Fill the pitcher with fresh water, wench."

She giggled, turned to the pitcher and basin on the corner stand, and did as she was told. Behind her, he was undressing, for she heard the sound of holsters being slung over headboards, denim falling to the floor, shirtsleeves coming off.

She could hardly wait to turn around.

He didn't sleep in the nude, did he?

She turned around.

He certainly did.

She took a deep breath, walked to him with drying oatmeal on her hands and gave him a long kiss, pressing her body against his, loving the feel of his growing shaft.

"We must sleep," he insisted with amusement. "You've got a long ride ahead of you tomorrow."

"Me?"

"We. We've got a long ride ahead."

"Then hop into bed and I'll fix your hands."

He dutifully slid beneath the sheets and blanket. His torso was beautifully tanned in contrast to the white covers. He was solid muscle. His windswept blond hair framed the strength of his jawline and tanned cheeks.

She knelt on the rug beside him and applied the

paste. There was something so pleasing about tending to her husband. "Does that feel better?"

He leaned back on his pillow and stared at her. "It does. Now get into bed beside me." He patted her space.

Gladly, she thought, but there was just one more thing. She brought the lantern to her side, set it on the nightstand and rummaged through her bag. "I should have looked for this before I put this paste on my hands...."

"What is it?"

She found the special gift, heaved onto the bed and brought it over to him in her oatmeal-covered hands. "A gift to you for our wedding."

"Natasha, I'm... You're too generous.... This is totally unexpected. And I'm so sorry. I didn't get anything for you."

"I don't need anything. And this wasn't something I bought. It was something I had."

She presented him with a gold pocket watch. It was slightly scratched from all its years of wear. He turned it over gently in his pasty hands, opened it and read the time. "Ten minutes past midnight."

"It keeps perfect time. It was left to me by my grandfather. He wore it every day. I wanted you to have it."

He didn't speak for a moment. "You shouldn't have done this, Natasha. You should keep it for yourself."

"I want you to have it. I think my grandfather would like you a great deal."

Jarrod swallowed hard and blinked away emotion.

She was delighted that he appreciated it so much. It was a gesture of her respect, admiration and anticipation of things to come.

"Thank you," he said, his voice deep with emotion,

and set the timepiece on his nightstand. He didn't turn her way again, and she sensed that perhaps he was as tired as she was. He needed to rest.

"Good night, Jarrod." She turned around, extinguished the lantern and settled into bed beside her new husband.

"Good night," he said softly. She detected a sense of melancholy in his voice, but chalked it up to exhaustion. It had been a big day for both of them.

Smiling, she wiggled in next to Jarrod. How odd to be sleeping with another person. She'd never done it before. It felt so strange and yet so right.

The guilt was intolerable.

Simon awoke the next morning shortly after dawn. He slid out of the bedroom without spending too much time gazing at Natasha, for that would've been unbearable, staring at her innocent face lying on the pillow.

He'd bedded Natasha O'Sullivan and he was neither her husband nor her friend.

At least, that was what she would think when she discovered the truth.

He pushed it out of his mind. He had other matters to attend to, for today was the day this farce would end. He'd get the goods, he'd take in McKern and Fowler, and he'd reveal himself to the woman he'd made love to in the middle of the night.

Was he *hoping* she was culpable herself in some way?

Would that make it easier for him?

It would.

He groaned at another whack of guilt.

How could he wish that she was corrupt in some

way, in cahoots with Ledbetter, simply because it would ease his own conscience? Wasn't that extremely self-ish of him?

He should be ashamed for even letting it linger in his mind.

Besides, he knew in his gut she wasn't. He'd been so intent to see her through dirty lenses that he'd judged her harshly at first. Now that he'd come to know her, he saw her for the honest and dependable person she was.

He grabbed his guns and clothes, dressed, took his towel and left the cabin.

Crisp morning air greeted him when he reached the river. The breeze was refreshing, the sky clear.

He crouched and rinsed his face. His jaw was bristly and needed a shave, but his supplies were in the cabin and he didn't wish to wake Natasha. His hands, now clean from any remnant of oatmeal, had improved from last night. The red streaks had faded to soft pink and the sting was gone.

He tossed the towel over his shoulder, sauntered to the horses and gave them a pat. He strode to the sleeping men. The logs had hours ago burned to ashes.

He kicked Fowler's boot, which was splayed out from underneath his gray wool blanket. "Hey. Time to rise."

The man grumbled.

Simon turned around and nudged McKern's dirty boot. "We've got a long ride ahead. I'd like to get back to Cheyenne by the afternoon." *To jail you filthy slugs.*

McKern growled, "What the hell? Leave me alone. Oh, Jesus, my head." He grabbed hold of his noggin with both hands. "Feels like there's an elephant stompin' on my brain."

They'd overdone it with the alcohol. Why'd they

drink so much? An empty bottle of whiskey lay near the fire, and another one that was a quarter full.

"Go rinse your face. You'll feel better."

McKern, oily-faced and scruffy in his clothes, squinted up at Simon, who was standing in the sun. "What about the wife?"

"What about her?" asked Simon.

"She ready for a ride?"

"She will be."

Fowler was already up and stretching. The foul odor of sweat rose from his tailored clothing.

"You can change behind the horses," Simon told him.

"I didn't bring a change of clothes," Fowler declared. "There's nothing wrong with these. Only been worn once."

Simon shook his head. Yards away, McKern was swishing out his mouth with leftover whiskey.

McKern spit. "That's better." He was no longer clutching his head. "I'll take the rest of this with me. To clear my head on the ride."

Anything to keep them settled and quiet on the ride there. Plus, if they were a bit tipsy, it would slow their reaction time.

"Sure," said Simon, "I'll go wake my...my wife." He stumbled over the word. He couldn't let his demeanor slip. Everything rested on his shoulders today.

Simon, his mind as sharp as a whistle, heard soft footsteps behind him. Neither Fowler nor McKern seemed aware, but Simon pivoted in what he felt sure was Natasha's direction.

"Did I hear my name called?" she asked, freshly dressed in a blue blouse and brown skirt. She held several tin cups and a steaming coffeepot. She smiled at

Simon in a particularly pleasing and private manner, and he bristled from the shame of his deceit. She turned her palm to indicate that her rash was nearly gone. He nodded, grateful.

"Ah, my lady," called McKern. "May we beg you for some of that brew?"

She went over, sat on a log and poured.

"I need to go in and shave," said Simon.

"Do what you need to, dear husband," she replied with a smile.

Simon tried to stifle a moan. She was smitten by her new role.

"So we're all agreed?" he asked. "We aim to leave here in one hour?"

"Fine," said Fowler, circling back from the horses to get some coffee.

"Absolutely," said Natasha.

"Sure thing," McKern mumbled. He patted his head again and moaned. "Now, tell me, Mrs. Ledbetter, may I beg you to cook us some eggs? Mrs. Dooligan insisted on packing some."

"Surely. And if you gentlemen would like to clean up, there's a lovely spot by the falls, if you follow this path. There's a natural spring, gushes up into a pool. The water's incredibly warm. Its temperature even surprised Jarrod."

McKern's eyes flickered over his tin cup. He took a sip. "You were there, boss?"

Simon nodded.

"And you discovered it together, Mrs. Ledbetter?"

She nodded, but Simon blinked and jumped in to clarify. He supposedly owned this property. He should know the springs were there. "I showed it to her this morning. It's always been a favorite spot of mine. We went for an early walk. Just the birds and us."

She seemed a bit flustered, but went along with his explanation. Perhaps she thought he was trying to protect her privacy by not mentioning last night and was calling for discretion. She nodded at McKern. "You'll need to rush, Mr. McKern, if we're to pack and leave within an hour."

"I think I'll pass on the swim," said the cutthroat. "Just need to wash my face and tidy up. I would be much obliged for those eggs, though."

Simon knew for a fact that neither man had seen him last night with Natasha. Simon had been a tracker and a detective for many years, and he'd bet his life that he and Natasha were alone last night.

And even if McKern or Fowler somehow knew about the rendezvous, so what? As far as these two men were concerned, he and Natasha were married. There would be nothing unusual in Simon wanting to spend a romantic night with his wife under the crest of a waterfall. In fact, he thought with another wave of guilt, Simon had played his role to perfection.

He strode into the cabin to shave and pack, but he still felt a shiver of unease. His pulse picked up its pace. His vision and acuity sharpened.

He checked his guns, made sure the barrels were loaded and vowed to be extra attentive today. His life, and possibly Natasha's, depended on his ability to lie and weasel and outshoot and outplay the other two men here.

Chapter Sixteen

Kale McKern's temples throbbed with jabbing pain. Hell, so did his forehead. He cradled his head as he sat on the logs by the morning campfire. Ledbetter and his wife had gone inside the cabin to finish packing. The eggs were done, the plates cleaned by the river, the horses watered. Ledbetter had already saddled up his horse and his wife's; their two animals were grazing up by the cabin. All McKern and Fowler had left to do was pack their bedrolls, douse the fire they'd used to cook breakfast and saddle up their two horses.

Except McKern couldn't move without feeling as if his brains were about to spill. Was it the wine? Or another bout of those god-awful headaches?

He leaned over and gazed at the hard ground, rubbing his temples.

Fowler's boots shuffled into view on the ground in front of McKern, so he looked up.

"Head still sore?" Fowler adjusted the bowler hat on his head.

"Shut your blasted mouth," growled McKern, his

thick middle shaking. "You keep asking and making me feel like a weak old lady."

Fowler shut his stupid mouth, kneeled and rolled up his blankets. His tall, thin body made sharp shadows on the ground.

"Toss me my guns!" McKern blasted.

Fowler reached over to McKern's bedroll and handed him his holsters.

With another wince of pain, McKern stood and buckled the revolvers on his hips.

A crow squawked real loud in the tree above and startled him.

He cursed, whipped out a gun and blasted the damn thing out of the branches. Except the bullet zinged the branch instead. The bird cawed and batted its wings the hell out of there.

Up on the hill, the cabin door kicked open. Ledbetter eased out with two guns cocked. "What is it?"

Fowler shouted, "Just shooting at some birds!"

Ledbetter nodded, lowered his guns and stepped back inside.

Fowler continued tying his bedroll with leather straps. "Want me to roll yours for you?"

"What the hell do you think?"

Fowler shook out the blankets, kneeled again and rolled. McKern still had the Colt in his hand. He raised it and aimed at the back of Fowler's greasy head. It would serve him right. Annoying idiot.

Ultimately, McKern lowered his weapon and holstered it. The real person he was frustrated at was Ledbetter. What kind of game was he playing?

If McKern could get a break from the pounding in

his skull and the flashing ache behind his eyes, he'd figure it out.

"What do you think of the new Mrs. Ledbetter?" McKern asked the idiot.

Fowler turned on his haunches, tied the leather straps around the bedroll and was careful with his answer. "She seems all right to me. They got married yesterday and passed the test. Right?"

"They haven't passed anything."

"How do you mean?"

"Are you really that stupid?" McKern snarled. It was dawning on him—what was wrong with this situation and what was wrong with Ledbetter and his new wife—and he had a damn headache the size of Wyoming. Fowler at least should be more clearheaded. "Didn't you hear what she said when she brought the coffee around? She was all excited that she discovered the hot springs this morning."

"What's wrong with that? We all marvel at it the first time we see it."

"Yeah, but this is Ledbetter's cabin. He's had it for a number of years. How the hell could he not know about the hot springs?"

Fowler wasn't catching on. McKern, frustrated as hell, spoke slowly as he would to a child. "She said the warm water surprised even Jarrod. And he didn't jump in right away to correct her. Only when I asked did he seem to notice the blunder and *then* he corrected her by saying he led her there."

"Ohhh..." Fowler's posture changed.

"And remember in Cheyenne when we said we'd meet him at this cabin?"

Fowler interjected, "We had to give him directions.... He said he had too many properties and he couldn't keep track.... Strange." He grabbed his jaw and rubbed. "Hellfire. What are you thinking?"

"You know what I'm thinking," McKern snapped.

Fowler said it aloud real slowly, as if he shouldn't even dare to say it. "That's not Ledbetter in there."

McKern was decisive. Rage increased the bolts of light behind his aching eyes. "I don't know who that son of a bitch is, but he's not our boss."

"He's after the payload."

McKern smirked. "Gotta be."

"What about the woman? Who is she?"

"Haven't figured that out yet. But looks to me like they're planning this together. Did you see her target-shooting in Cheyenne?"

"Yeah. Damn good shot." Fowler spotted her handbag resting on the other saddlebag she'd already packed. He grinned at it, finally thinking, thought McKern. Fowler opened her handbag. He pointed to her derringer and removed it.

McKern snickered. "She can't shoot without a gun."

Fowler threw it into the river. It made a nice splash. "What do you want to do?"

McKern wished his blasted headache would clear. It was affecting his vision. He'd missed a bird ten feet away. But people were bigger targets, and he had Fowler, a very keen shot, to help. "Keep your guns handy and wait for my signal. Don't kill him. Not until he tells us where the real Ledbetter is."

"What about her?"

A rush of excitement pounded through McKern. "Slit her throat."

* * *

Simon peered out of the front window to watch Mc-Kern and Fowler. They seemed innocent enough, using canteens to douse the remaining flames of the campfire. But they seemed to be in heated discussion over something.

Simon's instincts were on high alert ever since he'd heard the gunshot. Sure, they'd fired at the birds, but that wasn't normal. No calm man took out his revolver and wasted bullets and time shooting at feathers. Which meant that McKern was in one of his nasty moods.

Why?

Could be he was suffering from the adverse effects of too much alcohol. Or could be he was getting suspicious of Simon. He'd swooped in quickly to explain Natasha's unknowing blunder about the falls, but whether they bought it or not was the question.

Natasha came out of the bedroom with another saddlebag, cheerful and somewhat shy now that they were alone again. His blood was pumping in anticipation of McKern's next move and how Simon might protect himself and Natasha.

He had to tell her who he was. Now was the time to come clean.

Her rich brown hair was pulled back into a single braid, her toffee-colored eyes sharp and clear. She was dressed in her soft blue jacket and matching skirt.

"What are you looking at?" she asked as he peered through the window.

"Checking on the horses."

"Did you saddle them already? If not, I'm pretty good with a saddle—"

"They're fine. All ready to go." In fact, they were

grazing behind the right wall of the cabin this very moment, halfway between the front and back door. He was careful to notice, for they were his emergency means of escape.

She placed her saddlebag on the table, stuffing her lace nightgown into it and buckling up. Foodstuff lay scattered on the table. Earlier, he'd carried out the saddlebag that contained her wedding gown. He noticed it was still there beneath the tree, along with her handbag.

"We'll leave the extra food bags behind today and pick them up on our way back this afternoon." Another lie told in the name of seeking justice. He likely wouldn't be back anywhere near the cabin, but he had to convince her otherwise. He didn't want any extra weight in case they needed to fly on the horses.

"All right," she said.

She came up behind him as he turned back to the window to see McKern and Fowler call for their horses. The saddles lay strewn on the grass.

Natasha slipped her arms around Simon's waist.

For a moment, he closed his eyes and inhaled. She had the ability to stir his soul with her embrace. His eyes flashed open at the window, studying McKern and Fowler as they reached for their gear on the ground.

Last night may have been the biggest mistake of Simon's life. Of his career. He'd mixed the call of business with a side order of pleasure, and thereby jeopardized not only his life but hers, too, and put the outcome of the mission in danger.

This morning, he'd seen all too clearly how much backtracking he'd had to do when she'd let it slip that they'd been to the waterfall.

And he'd been blown over speechless when she'd

given him her grandfather's pocket watch. He didn't deserve it.

"I think you worry too much," she whispered into his shoulder and then kissed him there. "You're always frowning. Did you know that?"

He caught himself doing it. Which only made him frown deeper. His muscles were knotted.

"Jarrod, what was that this morning? What you were saying about the hot springs?"

He stirred, his cowboy boots shuffling on the planks. "How so?"

She let go of his waist and he turned toward her. Her smooth, dark eyebrows twisted with curiosity. "You told Mr. McKern and Mr. Fowler that you knew all along about the hot springs. Why would you say that?"

"Did I give you the impression that it was a surprise to me?" he fibbed. "I knew all along that—"

"Come on, Jarrod," she said, frustrated. "That warm water was as much of a surprise to you as it was to me." Her expression was insistent.

Staring into the depths of her morning-fresh eyes and her trusting expression, he grappled with a reply. This was it. Now was the time to tell her everything.

"There is something I need to tell you," he said softly. He strode to his saddlebag on the table to remove some dollar bills from the leather pocket. He put on his black hat and tugged into his black suede jacket, its fringes shifting at the sleeves.

"Jarrod? Are you going to answer me?"

"Listen, I need you to ride back to Cheyenne on your own."

"On my own? What are you talking about? Did you or did you not know about those falls?"

"I… No, I didn't know about the falls." It was a relief not to lie to her.

She furrowed her forehead. "But I thought you owned this cabin."

"Jarrod Ledbetter owns this cabin."

"Yes?" Her gentle features, the soft cheeks and rosy lips, skewered upward as though she was trying to make sense of it.

"Please, keep packing. It's imperative that you follow my directions." He would explain everything, nice and slow.

"What are you talking about? Where's my handbag?"

"Outside already. I put it with the others. But I'm not concerned about your handbag. Where's your gun?"

"You're scaring me, Jarrod. My gun is in my handbag." She spun around to look out the window. "There," she said, pointing outside.

"Blazes." He swore loudly, and she lifted her eyebrows in surprise. He continued, "I thought it was in *there,* in the night bag you kept by your bedside. I saw it in there last night." He pointed to her saddlebag on the table.

"Yes, and I put it in my handbag this morning. Why do you care where I keep my gun?" she asked softly. She opened the front door latch to go get it.

He grabbed her shoulder. "Hold on."

"Why? You're acting so strange this morning."

"Your handbag's not where I put it outside."

She swung to peer out the front window beside him, her skirts flowing around her boots.

He explained, "It's two feet over from where I placed it. It was directly on top of that saddlebag. Now it's to the side."

"So?"

"So they touched it. Now, why would they handle a lady's handbag and leave all the others untouched? Because they looked inside it, searching for something, and saw your derringer."

"What are you talking about? You're not making any sense."

His gut recoiled. They were in severe danger. He no longer had any time to explain anything. "They no longer trust us." Every cell in his body pounded.

Natasha grew pale. "Jarrod, you're scaring me. What's going on with you?"

"I'm not Jarrod Ledbetter."

"What?" She recoiled, visibly shaken. Then she lunged for the door.

Thinking fast, he grabbed her. He desperately hoped she would forgive him for what he was about to do. However, there was no other way for him to gain control of this situation except take it. And that was what he needed most. *He* had to be in charge of the next move. No one else.

"Sorry, darlin'," he said. Then with a sharp yelp from her, he cupped his big hand over her mouth and growled, "You're coming with me."

Eyes wide with shock, she tried to bite his hand. They struggled, she tried to kick him, but he maneuvered around her legs and held tight to muffle her screams.

She was a fighter. She batted his torso with clenched fists but it was no use. He was overpowering, ten times stronger than her, muscled from years of fighting and running. As silently as possible, he walked her, still struggling and thrashing, to the back door.

Heaven help him. He was kidnapping his own wife.

Chapter Seventeen

Natasha, horrified at the violent nature of her husband, raised her boot again and this time managed to hit him in the calf. What did he mean, he wasn't Jarrod?

"Ugh," he rasped in her ear, his large hand still clamped over her mouth. "Natasha, please…hold still if you want to stay alive." He pushed her out the back door of the cabin into sunshine and grass.

Stay alive? Her heart thumped at lightning speed. He was contemplating killing her?

What kind of man was he?

She felt like vomiting.

Granddad was right. He never would've approved of her as a mail-order bride. What on earth had possessed her to find a husband she didn't know?

This was what she wound up with—a lunatic madman capable of kidnap and murder!

She bit down hard on his finger.

"Damn!" He let his hand slide off for only a moment and then was upon her again. "I'll let you go as soon as we get on the horses, but your life is in danger. Follow my instructions!"

Her life was in danger? Why?

He muffled her moan. She felt as though she was on one of those carousel rides at the fair, only it had sped up to breaking point and she could barely hold on for dear life.

Last night they had been lovers.

Today at each other's throats.

Good Lord in heaven, she prayed, *help me.*

She stopped struggling as they approached her mare. The animals were almost at the back of the cabin, clearly out of sight from the other two men.

Should she try to make noise and call for help?

"Don't try to call for help," he whispered in her ear, almost as though he could read her mind. "It's not me you should be afraid of. It's them. They're murderers and cutthroats. They've killed thirteen people between them. Maybe more." He squeezed hard on her mouth but relaxed his hold on her wrists. "It's all up to you now, live or die." He slowly released his hold altogether. Then gently let go of her mouth, as if testing whether she was going to scream or not.

Confused about what was happening and who the hell he was, Natasha spun around to face him. She was panting, out of breath, so terrified that her hands were shaking.

She desperately wanted to believe him that it was the other two she should fear. But he'd shocked her with his violent behavior, dragging her out of the cabin.

"Natasha?" he whispered. His face was a mix of emotions.

She struggled to understand him. Why were his green eyes flickering at her in hesitation? Why did he plant his palms in the air in a gesture of momentary surrender?

"Who—who are you?" she stammered. She cupped her hand to her cheek.

He tapped his hat, exhaled at the big blue sky and planted one large hand on his holster. "What you need to know is—" he swallowed hard "—I'm not Jarrod Ledbetter. My name is Simon Garr."

She gulped, her mouth as dry as dust. "Are you the man I wrote to?"

He shook his head. "Awfully sorry. No."

She stepped back, trying to sort out her mass confusion. And then outrage. This bastard had tricked her!

"Where is Jarrod Ledbetter?" she demanded with fury.

With a startle, she heard Mr. McKern call out from below, "Boss?"

Simon Garr swore, terrifying her even more, then before she knew what was happening, he flung her onto the nearby horse. "Start on the trail. I'll catch up. Head toward the treasure! There's help there!"

Before she had time to object, he gave the horse a loud slap on the rear and the animal lunged forward. Natasha ducked beneath oncoming trees, found the reins and pressed her legs to the horse as it galloped away.

She heard a gunshot behind her that made her insides shriek and sweat pour down her temples. "Hee-ya!" she urged her horse. "Hee-ya!"

"Now, hold on," Simon snapped at the two grizzly men facing him. Sweat drizzled down his spine. McKern, the bastard, had shot after Natasha but thankfully missed.

Simon, furious, tried to hold them off. McKern's gun was now squarely aimed at him. Simon's horse had bolted at the sound of the gunshot, out of reach, so he had to talk his way through this disaster until he could secure the animal. His mare had startled and cantered to a stop beside the two other horses beneath the trees. They were in the midst of being saddled. Simon did a quick appraisal. The saddles were double-rigged— they each had two cinches, one forward and one flank. None of the cinches were done up yet. Only his horse was securely saddled.

Simon still held a gun lowered at his side. Fowler, thin and lanky in his bowler hat, paced nervously behind McKern, who was aiming his barrel right at Simon.

"What the hell do you think you're doing?" Simon marched to McKern to face him down. "Do you know how hard I worked to get that woman on my side?"

"Huh?" McKern fidgeted, finger on the trigger.

"Don't you ever aim a goddamn gun at me again." Simon reached out and pushed the barrel away.

McKern seemed rather shocked by the command. Unshaven and beady-eyed, he nervously appraised Simon.

"I said," Simon bellowed, "why the hell did you shoot at her?"

McKern blinked and seemed to lose his nerve. "She had a gun in her handbag. She's a liar. Not to be trusted."

"*I* know that. Son of a bitch! She comes from a long line of wealth in Chicago. Didn't you see the pearls she was wearing yesterday? Goddamn it, marrying her is the biggest heist I'll ever make! Her grandfather left her a whole store full of jewels," he lied. "When she sends for the rest of her possessions, she's not going to know what hit her!"

"Aw, hell," muttered Fowler. "We didn't know, boss, we didn't know."

Simon walked over to the thinner man, who was standing by the horses. Simon's mare was now only ten feet away. "Whose idea was this?"

"His." Fowler gulped. "But we both thought you might need our help with her."

"Help?" Simon shouted. "You think I need help with a goddamn woman?"

"Well, then," said McKern, still looking doubtful and measuring Simon second by second. The man clutched his firearm. An artery throbbed at his ear. "Where'd she go? Why'd she leave?"

"Hell if I know what's going through her goddamn feeble mind. She suspected something. Said you made her nervous. Next thing I know, she's on a horse and you're shooting bullets!" Simon spat on the ground and took another step closer to his mare.

McKern nervously tapped his finger on the trigger of his lowered weapon.

Simon's nostrils flared as he waited for the man to holster his gun. But he was taking his time. They stared at each other beneath the morning sun, the crows cawing overhead, the river rushing by.

"If she's so rich with all this jewelry," said McKern with great deliberation, "why doesn't she wear better clothes?"

"She left most of her belongings in Chicago. I told you."

McKern squinted. A bead of perspiration dribbled down his eyebrow. He seemed to come to some sort of conclusion and again raised his weapon. "Who the hell are you? What'd you do with Jarrod Ledbetter?"

Simon scowled and took another step toward his mare. "What the hell are you talking about? You make no sense."

But McKern was ready. He cocked his gun and fired. Simon dived to the ground in the nick of time.

To the other side, Fowler cursed and rolled from the path of bullets.

Simon didn't waste time trying to shoot back but jumped to his feet, ran to the men's horses, toppled their unsecured saddles, then leaped onto his once-again startled mare.

McKern shouted expletives. Bullets zinged past Simon's head. He ducked while his horse whinnied in fear, then reared. He held tight to the reins and patted her neck. "Run, girl, run!"

The horse bolted.

"Son of a bitch!" McKern shouted. "Tie the saddles!"

Two more shots rang out as Simon cleared the top of the hill. One grazed his right elbow but he kept racing. As he galloped over the other side of the hill out of view, he glanced back. Fowler was running to his fallen saddle to hoist it back onto his horse, but McKern decided to leap onto his mount bareback. The horse didn't seem to like that and bucked him off.

Simon looked ahead. He ignored the blood running down his arm and the wicked pain that seared it, and rode as if the devil himself was in pursuit.

An hour later, Natasha could barely catch her breath.

She pressed her wobbly thighs against her mare and curled forward in the saddle to maintain her speed. The dark mare jumped over puddles, surged over grassy slopes and weaved around pine and elder trees. Natasha was fighting for her life as well as wrestling with the horrible truths that faced her.

Who was Simon Garr?

Dear God, what had happened to her Jarrod?

How could this man pretend to be someone he wasn't?

He'd married her!

The marriage couldn't be valid, she desperately hoped.

And then the marriage night… She whimpered in anguish. He was a bastard for doing what he'd done to her. For lying to her so completely that she'd fallen into his arms and given herself to a stranger!

She'd heard a few gunshots when she left the scene and wondered if anyone had been shot. Who were the bad men here? Whom should she be running from?

As far as she was concerned, they were all criminally bent.

She trusted no one.

Where should she head? Perhaps she should turn around, go a different way. Simon Garr would be expecting her to forge ahead toward the "treasure," but she wasn't sure where it was. Why would he want her to go toward the treasure? She wasn't sure they were talking about the same treasure that the real Jarrod Ledbetter had mentioned in his letters.

Besides, she never wanted to lay eyes on that damn liar again.

She was going to head in any direction *but* the treasure.

She had to mask her tracks. She slowed her horse to

a trot and urged it to cross the oncoming stream. When she'd ridden another five hundred yards, she urged it to cross back again. Then she rode *in* the stream for another quarter mile.

Her methods didn't work. Soon she heard the gallop of hooves behind her on the hilltop. Her heart seized in fear. What would the person do to her? Why did anyone want anything from her at all? She had nothing!

Except the pearls at her throat and the precious jewelry she'd left back in Cheyenne. But if they wanted that, why hadn't they simply robbed her as soon as they could, back at the Cheyenne cabin?

What did these vicious men want?

She smacked her dry lips together. She'd lost her handbag and therefore her gun. She had a canteen of water, but little else.

She crossed the stream to the other bank, opposite to the oncoming horse and rider, and hid behind a clump of trees and thick brushes.

"Easy," she whispered to her mare, patting the animal's shoulder. The mare was panting loudly from the run, but the sound of the trickling stream would surely mask the heavy breathing.

Natasha crouched in absolute stillness as the unknown rider galloped past the other bank. He was a small figure in the distance, but as he drew nearer, she recognized the broad shoulders and long legs bending forward in the saddle.

It was the stranger, Simon Garr.

She held her breath. A combination of sadness and fear took hold of her heart.

Every moment she'd spent with him had been a careful lie, deceit so deep she couldn't fathom. He might as well have taken out a dagger and stabbed her heart to ribbons. Every kiss, every brush against her naked breast, every moment of lovemaking they'd shared last night was meant to deceive her.

She fought back tears as he rode past, hoping and praying she would never lay eyes on this cruel stranger again.

Had everything he said been a lie?

She tried to still her beating heart and the runaway terror that he might spot her and hurt her. Her thoughts raced with the implications of their night together.

She was an utterly ruined woman. Even if she became involved with the real Jarrod Ledbetter, how could she possibly broach the subject that she was no longer a virgin? He would have questions and she would have to explain how stupidly gullible she'd been.

Where was the real Jarrod? Had they harmed him?

She tried to block the lies Simon Garr had told her and concentrate on survival.

He galloped past and slumped, then straightened again. Was he hurt? Perhaps he was only turning to survey the trail. He never once twisted in her direction, seemingly unaware of her. She turned her eyes away from his painful image.

When she turned back, she saw him riding west toward the cliffs. She tugged the reins of her mare and headed north into the wilderness to the next town, away from Cheyenne and everyone she knew there.

Good riddance, she thought with a sob.

Chapter Eighteen

Approximately an hour later, after another epic strain of galloping through the foothills, Natasha finally stopped to rest. Simon Garr and the other two men seemed to be playing a violent game; she had pulled out of it by heading in another direction.

She watered her horse in a shallow river, and then as her mare was grazing at the grasses in a thicket of trees, Natasha anchored herself among the trunks. The river gurgled behind her, but she had a good view of the clear hillside ahead so that she could spot anyone who might be following her.

The muscles in her legs ached. Her lower back had been curled forward in riding position for so long that it was a heavenly release to relax. Her eyes darted back and forth across the green gulches and valleys, looking for signs of riders.

Nothing.

She had to think about how she could contact the real Jarrod Ledbetter, and the law to get help. She lifted her canteen to her lips. Water dribbled down her chin, spilling like a spring along her heated skin.

She was formulating options for her next move. She could continue to Cheyenne in a roundabout manner so that it would be difficult to track her—if anyone was following. Although she had no food with her, breakfast had been plentiful and she could go for hours more without nutrition. If she did return to Cheyenne, in as early as two or three hours, perhaps she would survey the cabins where the Dooligans were staying, and if it was safe she'd go in to quickly pack her jewelry pieces. They were the only thing of value she had to sell for her return ticket home to Chicago. Back in the safety of the Chicago boardinghouse, she would try to write to Jarrod. Perhaps she could locate him in one of the other towns in which he owned property, or through his business. Or should she move on to Montana and try to locate him from there? Talking to the sheriff would likely be her best option. He could then escort her back to the cabin to pack her things. She'd been shot at, and the men responsible would not get away with it!

She pressed her head against her knees and trembled at the thought.

Where exactly did Simon Garr fit into all of this? What laws had he broken that she could also report to the sheriff?

"Blazes," she muttered.

She'd given that man her grandfather's pocket watch last night. It was worth a fair penny and would've easily paid for her ticket home. But despite the monetary value, it held a place in her heart that no other watch could replace. Granddad had woken up with it at his bedside every morning, read the morning paper with it on the table, helped her with her studies late at night and kept time with it in church when the minister was giving a particularly long-winded sermon and Granddad was counting the minutes to escape. He'd often taken her to church as a little girl when her parents were still alive.

Natasha, he'd say, leaning above her in the pew, *if you could please sit still till the services are over, I'll bring you to Duncan's for a fine Sunday breakfast.*

"Oh, Granddad," she whispered now. "If you can hear me from heaven above, please help me."

Nothing worthwhile is ever easy came the reply.

"But this is extraordinarily difficult," she said.

You can do whatever you set your mind to.

That was it, wasn't it? It was what he used to tell her at Duncan's while she swung her legs over the wooden bench and they ate their eggs and ham. All she had to do was make up her mind what she wanted to do, then put one foot in front of the other.

"All right, then." She capped her canteen, rose and brushed off her skirts.

"Who are you talking to?" a deep voice called to her from behind.

With a jolt of alarm, she whirled around.

Simon Garr. Her heart gave a kick. Damn him. He was sitting on his horse as it stood in the river. He'd come up from behind and tracked her after all. When he tilted back his black hat to get a better look at her, sweat trickled down his hair. Well, at least he'd had to gallop like a devil to catch her.

"You think you're smart?" she snapped in a livid tone. "You think it's quite a feat to sneak up on a woman and scare her?" She pointed down the valley, thrusting her finger in the air. "Why don't you keep riding till you fall off the edge of the nearest cliff? Maybe you'll even wind up at that waterfall."

His expression softened. "I know I've hurt you."

"Shut up. Just go."

"I'd like to explain."

"Who cares what you'd like?"

He winced.

She could barely stomach looking at him. "You're a thief of the highest magnitude. You stole something from me I can never get back."

His voice quivered with deference. "You promised me, though. Remember? I asked you to promise me when this was over that you'd give me a chance to explain."

The nerve! "Is that what that double-talk was about? You were giving yourself an out while you were lying through your teeth? Well, you promised me you'd love and protect me till death do us part. Remember that bit? You son of a bitch!"

"A tiger in skirts," he murmured.

She tried to slow her rapid breathing. "The more you move your lips, the worse off I seem to get. It's best if you stop talking."

She strapped her canteen over her shoulder and called to her horse.

He removed his hat and swiped his dripping forehead with his shirtsleeve. "Where are you headed?"

"Home. Goodbye, good riddance and go to hell."

Her horse drew nearer and she reached out to touch her saddle, trying to hide her tears. They were coming just as much from anger as…as utter despair. She'd believed in him. She'd thought she was about to spend a lifetime with Jarrod Ledbetter.

She drew herself together, willed herself to gain control, drew a scraggy breath and turned to face him. "All

right, there is one thing you can do for me. You can answer my questions truthfully, and only my questions,
without embellishment."

He nodded. "I can do that, but it might be hard for
you to hear some of my answers without an explanation."

"Direct answers are all I want."

He stared at her. "Up until yesterday, Natasha, I
wasn't sure if you were part of this whole scam. I've
been tracking you. I know you're not headed to the
mountains, to the treasure. You say you're going home
and I believe you."

It only confused her more. He thought she was involved in a scam? She shook her head, standing there
in the grass beside her horse, refusing to be distracted
by anything that came out of his mouth. She raised her
voice. "I said straight answers."

"Okay," he said gently.

"Where is Jarrod Ledbetter?"

The pretender blinked and looked to the mountains,
then back at her. From the expression on his face, she
feared the news was bad. "He's dead, Natasha. I'm
sorry."

Stunned, she rubbed her forehead and tried to imagine how and why. Sorrow took root. The poor man.

"Did he—he write those letters to me?"

"Yes, he did."

"What happened to him? Why did he die?"

The pretender sighed. "He was the leader of the Ledbetter gang. Specialized in jewelry heists on the railroad. Those two men back there are his accomplices.
Ledbetter was wanted for armed robbery and murder."

A hardened criminal. Her heart thudded. She shook

her head, trying to grasp the story. She could choose to disbelieve it, but something about the tone of Simon Garr's voice, and his manner, gave her the impression it was true.

How could she have been so gullible to be tricked by Jarrod Ledbetter, too?

"He fooled a lot of people," said Simon, as if understanding what she was thinking. "Not only you."

The hurt, the anguish, the humiliation lumped in her throat. She talked past it but her voice reverberated with emotion. "I seem to be a pawn in a lot of people's games."

"I'm sorry."

"I don't care." She rubbed her forehead. "So he died during a robbery?"

"No. He was shot by lawmen who were after him for a long time. It happened only last week."

She steeled herself and stood ramrod straight in the sunlight. "All right. If Jarrod Ledbetter is dead, then who the hell are you?"

The hot sun beat into Simon's back as he stared at Natasha across the river. His lips crackled with dryness and his temples were slick with perspiration. His mare dipped her head and slurped water as he shifted his hips in the saddle to maintain his balance. His wounded right forearm, wrapped in a strip of cloth from the bottom of his shirt, throbbed.

"My name is Simon Garr. I was hired by a detective agency to recover the goods he stole on his last robbery on the Union Pacific. Loot worth three hundred thousand dollars."

"Detective agency?" she repeated, stunned.

"I'm a detective, Natasha."

She was quiet for a moment, her eyes darting across his face, his hands, his horse, the situation. "So all's fair in love and war?"

"*No.* That was not my intent. McKern and Fowler didn't know that Ledbetter had been killed. They always got their instructions through notes and secondary messengers, so they'd never met him in person. The game plan was for me to impersonate him, infiltrate the gang, find out where they stashed the three hundred thousand, recover it and arrest them. But then you came along."

"How inconvenient."

His gaze was all-encompassing. She stood alone on the patch of grass, defiant and strong. He'd never admired her more. "I had fully intended to send you home as soon as you stepped off the train. But then McKern and Fowler appeared, and I reckoned if I did try to send you home, my cover would be blown and you and I would be dead."

"You have an explanation for everything." Her gaze was measured. "You must've had a good laugh at how stupid I was."

His throat constricted with shame. "It wasn't like that at any time."

"Yes, it was. It was like that when you met me at the railroad depot. It was like that when we dined at the Mountain Hotel. You thanked the stars that I was falling for your lies."

He shook his head weakly but knew there was truth to what she said. "I'm sorry, Natasha. I didn't know what to make of you when we first met. I was trying to decode your intentions and your involvement."

"How could you carry it through to a wedding? How could you be so cruel to a woman on—on that day?"

He knew the depth of pain he'd caused her was immeasurable. "McKern and Fowler brought you, remember? I had left you behind in Cheyenne, and believe it or not, in my mind, the separation was supposed to be permanent. I didn't expect to ever see you again. But when they brought you, I truly believed that if I said no, then you, Justice Weatherton and I would've been shot on the spot."

"It escalated to the point of no return."

He nodded.

"Tell me," she said, "was there any such person as a Reverend Ericson who was supposed to marry us?"

He shook his head with shame. "I read his name from the newspaper, but never met him."

Her mouth trembled. "Why wait till now to tell me all this? Why didn't you tell me earlier who you were? Sometime after our first meeting at the depot?"

"Because I wasn't sure of your involvement with Ledbetter and your knowledge of the heist."

"*You* didn't trust *me?*"

He shrugged, wishing to cushion the anguish he'd caused her but not able to, apparently. Her expression was a giveaway—twisted, tortured, pained.

He continued to explain, "If I told you who I was, you would've blown my cover."

She stared at him boldly. "I didn't sign up to be a detective. You did."

"True enough. I wouldn't have drawn you in, except that I started to believe that you were in on it with Ledbetter. And then I had to keep you around to find out everything you knew."

"In on it?" Her mouth skewed with indignation. "That's ludicrous."

"I see that now. But you were so insistent in joining Ledbetter in his jewelry business, remember? So knowledgeable with jewels yourself. You took an interest in the Dooligans and said if she wanted to sell her necklace, you'd be interested—"

"Not to steal it off her throat!"

"I thought maybe…and then as we were heading out to find the stolen cache, you said you knew where Ledbetter had hidden the treasure."

She rubbed her forehead. "You keep saying that, but I said no such thing."

"You mentioned knowledge of the treasure—"

"I don't care about any treasure—"

"But he wrote something to you in those letters and I need to know—"

"You're still *working* me? Still want *more* from me?"

"It's my duty." *And my honor,* he thought, *to prevent the loss of any more innocent lives.*

"I told you I don't care to answer anything more about a stupid treasure. He never mentioned anything about stolen goods or hidden money…or stashed jewels, so we're not talking about the same thing, all right? But I do have one more question, and then I'm going to ride out of here and you're not going to stop me. Understand?"

He sighed, unsure how to handle her. If she were a man, he could strong-arm her into cooperation. Find a means to sort out their differences or simply battle it out. But he was through fighting with Natasha O'Sullivan. She was an innocent bystander who'd gotten caught in his tornado.

Now he had to back off and leave her alone. He couldn't force her to answer any more questions. His grazed arm started to throb again. Somehow he'd forgotten about it.

Her horse, standing beside her, was getting restless. Natasha reached out to calm the mare. "Do you get paid on salary or by the hour, Mr. Garr?"

He blinked. This was her last question? The shadow of his brim afforded him the luxury of a clear shot of her face. Her jaw tightened and her posture stiffened.

Her words stung. The chilly tone, the formal address. He shook his head, not understanding where this was leading.

"When we spent that time together in the river," she explained, "were you paid by the hour? Perhaps you got a bonus for bedding the dead man's woman?"

He withered. So that was what she was getting at. How could he explain the depth of his apology? His attraction to her had happened more quickly and more intensely than he'd ever fathomed possible.

"That wasn't Jarrod Ledbetter with you," he said hoarsely. "That was me."

She clamped her lips together as though she was holding back emotion, flicked her moist eyelashes and looked away.

"I guess we'll never know," she said with a shaky breath. "I have trouble telling the two of you apart. Criminal or detective? Seems you carry both blood types. And if I'm confused by your behavior and who you really are, then I can only imagine what hell you put yourself through, Mr. Simon Garr."

Her words were a punch to the gut. Raw, unhinged and barbed.

It was over. Whatever feelings she might have had for him, he had irreparably damaged.

The only truth he had left was the ice-cold realization that they might be former lovers, but they were no longer friends. After harrowing days of deceit and calculation, secretly planning and scheming beneath the noses of McKern and Fowler, Simon had come to an impasse. The woman he'd thought he could use to help him with his mission was through with him in every way.

Natasha O'Sullivan was disgusted and repulsed by his presence.

She hoisted one foot into her stirrups and heaved herself into the saddle. She tore off down the valley and didn't bother looking back.

Sadly, Simon didn't blame her.

Chapter Nineteen

Damn it all to hell, thought Simon when Natasha faded from sight, he had a mission to finish, if it was the last thing he accomplished here from this miserable situation. He owed it to Clay and Eli and their remaining family to see it through to the end.

Simon knew he'd caused Natasha immense distress. He wasn't feeling so hot himself. But the detective in him took over as it had countless times before when he'd faced human misery. He did what he did best—buried his inner grief and reacted outwardly. He steeled himself, mounted his horse and galloped after her.

The sun streaked the early-morning clouds and filtered down on the trees as he caught up with her.

"Go away!" she shouted from her saddle, digging in her thighs, accelerating. She cut through the wind and jumped a creek.

He did the same and gained on her. "You asked me a final question! Now I'd like to ask you one!"

She slowed to a canter. "I don't owe you anything."

"It's about your grandfather."

"Leave him out of this," she blasted.

"Here's my question. If I return your grandfather's pocket watch, would you consider helping my cause?"

Her dark hair had blown out from her pins. Snatched by the wind, it trailed down her back. He enjoyed looking at her, the way she planted her hips, the way her bosom was silhouetted in her tailored blue suit.

He braced himself and got to the meat of the problem. "We don't have a lot of time. McKern and Fowler are ahead of us, likely trying to recover the treasure before we get there. However, I know these trails from another case I had two years ago. We could cut back a different way to intersect them or possibly gain some distance in front of them, but the trouble is, Natasha, I don't know exactly where they're headed. I think you do."

She gritted her teeth, picked up her blue skirts and pressed forward to urge her mare through a gulley. He followed at her side.

"I told you what I know," she insisted. "Nothing."

Exasperated, he moaned. "Ledbetter wasn't the only man who died at the shoot-out, Natasha. Good men died, too. My two greatest friends, Clay Holborne and Eli Remington. Good men my age. One was shot in the throat and the other in the heart. I saw them die, and I'll never forget the scene. I blame myself. Clay left behind a widow and a young boy. I keep thinking how hard it must've been for Clay's kid when he found out his father wasn't coming home."

She remained impassive, but her lips twitched.

"Eli was a bachelor," Simon continued, "just like me. We used to always joke that we wouldn't get attached to any woman better than ourselves, for fear of what trouble we'd bring her." His voice quivered. "I should've listened to my own advice when it came to you, Natasha. I should not have let you get involved with me."

Her cheeks flickered. "Why should I care about your personal history? I'm through with you, remember?"

"You should care," he said, thinking carefully, "because McKern and Fowler are still out there. They're looking for answers to where Ledbetter is. If nothing more, they'll want revenge for his death. They might think—no, they *do* think—that you're responsible in some way for his disappearance. You're the link, Natasha."

"But you said yourself they were headed to the treasure."

"I'm not sure. That was a guess. And look at it this way. They already shot at you once. If we split up here, and they don't go after me but they go after you, their next bullet might hit its target."

She groaned. "Congratulations. If you're trying to terrorize me, you've succeeded."

"It's not that, Natasha. I'm trying to protect you. I think we should stick together until we get to safety. Look, I'm a good shot. Years of experience. And I'll help you get back your grandfather's watch if you help me locate the treasure."

"Where is the watch?"

"Back at the cabin. In my saddlebag, left pocket. It could get lost in this whole situation once the authorities step in, or if McKern or Fowler double back and take it, but I'll make sure to track it down and get it back to you."

She frowned.

"We're losing time," he urged. "If you promise to help me, I'll retrieve the watch and send it to you. In

Chicago, San Francisco, hell, in England if that's where you decide to go."

"It's a big decision, and I don't like you."

He sighed. "Yeah."

She tugged on her reins. Her mare stopped.

He circled his horse back around to face her. His right hand, the injured side, was losing strength in his grip. "I should tell you that I notified my superiors that we were headed to the Eastern Ridge road."

"When did you do that?"

"I sent a telegram from Cheyenne a few days ago."

"How did they respond?"

"Well…I didn't get a reply. But they operate on discretion. I've got to assume that I'll get help in some way, that they'll send other detectives—"

"What if they don't?"

"I don't want to put you in any more danger. So if we spot McKern or Fowler on the trail as we're looking for the treasure, then you're to break with me and make a run for safety."

She squinted in the sun, deliberating. "You'll return my granddad's watch and leave me alone?"

"I promise."

She raised an eyebrow at his choice of words.

"All right, so my promises aren't worth anything. But I will return that watch to you."

"Jarrod Ledbetter didn't write about a treasure in the sense you mean. It wasn't about money or jewelry or gold. He said he often visited the mountains to visit his family treasure."

"How exactly did he word it?"

"He said his parents were buried in the mountains. That they were his greatest treasure. They died when he was a boy, but he often stopped by the church where their funerals were held."

"Barn fire," Simon recalled. "They died in a barn fire." But her words weren't what Simon wanted to hear. He was hoping for more direction from Ledbetter's letters. He swiped his mouth with his hand. His lips were parched. He was feeling light-headed. He should drink something soon. The right side of his shirt was feeling damp. "Did he mention the name of the village? Any names at all?"

"Let's see…he often mentioned Cheyenne."

"Keep going."

"Montana Territory."

"Too far away."

"He mentioned a place once that gave me pause… Rattler's Nest? Rattler's Cove? No, no, it was Rattler Peak."

"Yeah, that's got to be it," he said. "I recognize the name. Rattler Peak. It's on the eastern ridge. Maybe he hid the stolen treasure somewhere in that village."

"But for goodness' sake, we can't go knocking from door to door. How would we find it?"

"Maybe the church is there. We could start by looking for it. Maybe someone who works at the church knew Ledbetter. He had to have had a contact in that village. I bet McKern and Fowler know that contact, whoever he is. So we're looking for a person, Natasha. Someone older, maybe, who knew Ledbetter's parents. Maybe even a distant relative who helped him hide the loot."

Simon grew light-headed again. He gathered his wits and slid down the saddle till he touched ground. He removed the canteen that was slung over his saddlebag and guzzled. When did he get so thirsty?

She dismounted and came around beside him. "You're awfully sweaty. It's not that hot out today." She was drip-dry.

"You lost your derringer back at the cabin," he told her.

She nodded.

"Sorry about that." He removed a Smith & Wesson from his holster and handed it to her. "Keep this for protection. I've got the other one."

"But I don't plan on riding with you for long."

"That's fine."

"Just as soon as we hit the village and I take a look around, see if it triggers anything else he said, I'll be gone."

"Good. Good plan."

He was tipsy. She watched in bewilderment. "I'll return your weapon before I go."

"You keep it for the ride back. I won't be able to use it."

"Why not?"

He parted his black suede jacket to reveal the blood soaking through his sleeve. It surprised him to see that the blood had soaked clear through to the bottom of his torn shirt. "I've only got one good arm to shoot with."

"Oh, no," she uttered in dread. "What did you do?"

It didn't appear to be a life-threatening injury, thought Natasha, fear rolling through her as she assessed Simon Garr. She tried not to disclose how affected she was by the sight of all this blood. She was angry with him, yes, but he was wounded and clenching his jaw in pain, and she couldn't very well turn her back on him.

He was breathing fast, but drinking water seemed to help him. He was sweaty but his eyes were clear.

"If you think you're going to get sympathy from me, you're wrong." She was trying to convince herself more than she was trying to convince him. She slid her hands up her skirt and quickly removed her petticoat, sliding it over her legs.

"I wouldn't think of it."

She kneeled beside him in the grass. Gripping her white petticoat, she yanked hard and tore off a strip she could use as a bandage. She tore another one to soak with water and clean his wound.

She leaned her face in next to the flesh and winced. It looked awful grisly. "The bullet tore out half an inch of flesh. It didn't hit your elbow, so the bones seem intact."

"I figured it wasn't serious. I can move my joint."

"Must hurt."

"I imagine that makes you happy," he said with wry humor.

Yes and no, she thought.

She worked quietly, tying the bandage around his arm. Being this close to him, his warm breath grazing her neck, her lips inches from the clean sweat of his brow, her knees tucked beside his leg, reminded her of the intimacy they'd shared last night. Splashing naked in the water, rocking against him, allowing her heart and her soul to be invaded by a man she thought was her husband.

Who was he to her?

No one.

Her heart trembled. Loneliness seeped in. She was

more despondent now, it seemed, than when she'd lost her granddad.

Last night, Simon Garr knew the marriage wasn't real. He knew she wasn't his wife. Yet he'd made love to her and had taken advantage of her in the most calculating way imaginable.

Although she didn't wish to be gentle, she was as she tied the last knot. He was injured and she could no more let him bleed to death than she could a wounded animal. The bleeding stopped. She didn't realize how hard she was concentrating and how tense she'd gotten until she finished and looked straight into his eyes.

They shimmered with unspoken words. He assessed the brush of her hair against her face, the upturn of her lips.

The pain of looking at him was unbearable.

Abruptly, she pushed herself away from him, gathered herself and walked to the winding river to wash her hands of blood and refill the canteens. Her fingers shook. The toll of his injury and the shock of his disclosure were difficult to shoulder.

She felt as though she'd just been through a battle and had lost. She returned to his side, where he was sitting against a tree. She handed him his canteen. "Drink."

He followed her orders.

"Give me the canteen and I'll tie it to your saddle."

He did so again without question. She returned from the horse, about to help him up.

He was already standing, a broad figure of a man who looked as if nothing could topple him. But he had lost a good quantity of blood, and no one was invincible.

"Let's make this perfectly clear, shall we?" she said with a catch to her throat. "I'll go with you to Rattler Peak, but I'm my own person and I make my own decisions."

"Understood."

"You can be as charming as you like. It won't work."

"Not me."

"I want my granddad's watch mailed to me as soon as humanly possible."

"Absolutely."

She turned to look back at the hills and vales they'd come from. "Which trail do you think we should take?"

He pointed. "We'll head east along the river, then up through the shortcuts from there."

She cupped a hand to her face against the warming sun. "Are you strong enough to ride?"

He nodded. "Don't worry about me, Natasha," he said softly with a twinge of remorse.

I'm not, she told herself. *Never again.* "Let's go."

Chapter Twenty

Spending time with the man who had hurtfully deceived her wasn't the most pleasant way to spend a morning. What a far cry, thought Natasha, from the dreams and hopes she'd had in Chicago. She tried not to think of her disillusionment as the late-morning sunshine beat into her gloved hands. The horses beneath them splashed through the riverbed, thudded across grassy acres and clomped on the narrow, craggy trail on the mountain.

Everything her granddad had ever warned her about strangers was coming true. She shouldn't have trusted this man, Garr, with any bit of her heart.

They reached the first small village. She spotted a roadhouse ahead. It looked like a barn, crudely put together with sawn timber and rough doors. A painted sign announced that it was Camden's Eatery. Several horses were hitched outside, but none of them belonged to McKern or Fowler.

"Did you escape with any money, Jar—" she cut herself short from saying the wrong name "—Mr. Garr?"

"Please, Natasha, it's Simon."

She looked away.

"Got a wad right here in my pocket. I always keep extra in my boot, too."

She shuddered at how prepared for danger and escape he must always have to be. What a life. She was relieved that after today, she'd never have to worry about this man again. But even as she thought it, her throat constricted. She had been naive to believe she could simply send out a letter to find a husband and that the perfect one would respond.

Perfection was an impossible goal.

"I think food would serve you well," she said to him. "Simon." His eyes flickered. The name felt odd on her tongue. "You need your strength. And so do I."

They stopped at the far side of the dining hall. He slid off his horse and helped her to her feet. He clenched his injured arm to his side, favoring it over the other. But he seemed much stronger now that he'd had some water and a rest.

"I'll wait here," she said. "Perhaps you can bring some food outside. I don't think it's safe to stay in one place for too long."

"Agreed. You got your gun?"

She'd tucked it into the back of her skirt so that it was hidden beneath her jacket and wasn't too uncomfortable as she rode.

"I'll be right back," he said.

"I'll take the horses around those shrubs and wait for you there."

Simon agreed. Would she ever get used to his new name? Not too long ago, she'd told him that he seemed like a very different man from the one who'd written the letters. She'd been so right! He'd had every opportunity to tell her then and there that her observations were correct, but he'd declined. How easily he'd tricked her.

He went inside as she gingerly walked to the edge of the rising cliff. They weren't too high yet, but it afforded a pretty view of the green valley below. A large bird floated by and she recognized it to be a vulture. Goodness, it was ugly. The first she'd ever seen. It had a crooked neck and hooked beak, and a wingspan of six feet. Another vulture circled beside it, scavenging for food.

She heard a shush of footsteps in the weeds behind her. Alarmed, she took out her gun and swung around.

"It's me," said Simon. He held out a wrapper made of newspaper, filled with a clump of bread and roasted fowl. "Duck meat."

She ate. "It's good."

It didn't take them long to finish and get back on their horses.

"Did you speak to anyone in there?" she asked from atop her horse.

"There was an old man sitting at the bar. Says he runs the place with his son. Said no strangers came in today that fit Fowler's or McKern's description."

"Where do you think they are?"

"Either looking for us or headed to Rattler Peak to get the loot. All we can be fairly sure about is that they didn't stop at that dining hall."

"So it's hard to say if our shortcuts through the valley caused us to be here sooner or later than them."

"If you see them, Natasha, I don't expect you to wait around and say goodbye to me. Just leave. I appreciate your help. I'll take it from there."

"How? You're right-handed and that arm's injured."

"I can shoot just as well with my left," he assured her. "Years of practice from the age of ten. That's one of the reasons the agency hired me."

The knowledge of his skills made her feel somewhat better. But the age of ten? That was awfully young.

"If your contacts are here somewhere, Jar—Simon—" she stumbled over his name "—how would I recognize them? What do they look like? Do they wear badges?"

"You won't recognize them. That's the whole point."

"How do I tell them apart from the contact that Jarrod Ledbetter likely has up here?"

Simon shook his head. The tips of his blond hair skimmed his collar. "Leave that to me. If it gets to be a sticky situation, if anyone confronts us, I want you to ride out of here as fast as you can."

She tried not to let her jitters take over. "Hopefully, we'll get to the village before anyone else. You can locate your treasure, and we can escape down the other side of the mountain on a different trail."

"We did make excellent time. I believe we're well *ahead* of McKern and Fowler, not behind."

"I agree."

Despite her personal objections and anger at how deceptive Simon had been to her, she recognized that he was on the right side of the law. The death of his friends must've been an awful image for him to see. She shuddered at the gruesome violence. And then she wondered how Jarrod Ledbetter must've died. To think, he was stone-cold dead before she'd even left Chicago.

She admitted she wanted Simon to apprehend the rest of the Ledbetter gang, but she could never forgive him for his personal use of her as a pawn.

They rode uphill for another half hour, past another

hamlet. The cliffs got steeper, the vegetation sparser, the path narrower. Simon took the lead. They wove around large boulders and tall white pines. The air smelled pure.

Eagles soared overhead. She twisted in her saddle to look. A massive eagle's nest, its structure overflowing with a crisscross of branches and leaves, sat perched on top of a rocky cliff. More eagles circled in the sunshine.

"So many eagles," she said, breathless.

"They're here for the rattlers," Simon said matter-of-factly. "Eagles are the snakes' natural predators."

"Why'd you go and tell me that?" she said. "I hate snakes, and I never would've known they're here. I would've been quite happy to sit here and enjoy the view."

"I told you for your own protection. Rattlers come up here in August and September. They like to sun themselves on the cliffs. And their young hatch this time of year. So if you see a lot of eagles in a particular spot, they're after the newborn serpents, so steer clear of that spot."

"Mercy," she said. "I thought they were just pretty birds flying overhead."

"Lots of predators attack rattlesnakes. Eagles, hawks. Badgers love rattlers, if you can believe it. I saw one jump out and ring a rattler's neck once. Another time, I was fishing and caught a big trout. When I gutted it, I found a small rattler inside. Must have been swimming and the trout thought it was a worm."

Her eyes widened in horror. She was stricken by this information. "If I see a rattler, I'm leaving. Sorry."

He looked back at her and grinned for the first time

in hours. It was unexpected and powerful and made her stare.

"Did you eat the trout?" she asked.

"Nah. I didn't have the stomach for it. I tossed it."

She tried to suppress a smile of her own. He wasn't always as tough as he appeared. But she still didn't like him.

When they twisted around another bend in the trail, Simon halted his horse. He peered ahead through the trees, but all she could see was vegetation and rocks.

"We're here," he said quietly as fear rumbled up her spine again. "Rattler Peak."

Simon leaned forward in the saddle and studied what he could see of the village through the branches ahead.

It had a wide main street. A boardwalk ran along a few shops on the right side. The building directly in front and to the left of them was a livery. There were people tending to horses in the corral outside, and a man walking on the boardwalk. It seemed like any other small town. Folks made their living here, Simon assumed from mining claims. Most towns this size had no sheriff and no jailhouse. They'd have to be careful.

But he had a good feeling that he and Natasha had arrived well ahead of McKern and Fowler. He'd seen no sign of them on the trail, no indication that they or their horses had come this way. If Simon could simply locate the loot—not necessarily take it with him, for he could leave that decision to his superiors and he didn't want to take extra chances having to protect Natasha due to his injured right hand—he'd be satisfied that his mission was complete.

But how could he be certain the loot was even here?

There was only one way to find out.

"Follow me and do what I do," he told Natasha. "I'll ride slowly through town, and you tell me if any image conjures up something Ledbetter might have written in his letters."

She tossed the loose hair off her shoulder and nodded in the sunshine. Her features were set in determination.

She'd blossomed into a real asset.

"Ready when you are."

He was grateful for her cooperation. And that was all he allowed himself to think at this moment. If he started examining what his chaotic feelings were for her, they'd never survive this. He'd seen it time and time again. When it came to a criminal showdown, an emotional display always tugged a man's heart in the wrong direction. Simon was well trained and well equipped to detach his mind from his heart.

Her cool demeanor was making it easier for him. It was likely *better* that she no longer believed they were husband and wife. She had less to lose, therefore, and would look after herself and herself only in a crunch.

He urged his horse into a slow walk along the side of the livery and turned left onto the main street. Natasha came up beside him, which would lead most folks here to believe they were partnered up in some way, either married or courting.

They rode slowly through town. Some folks on the boardwalk or coming out of shops looked their way.

Only a few nodded in silent greeting.

Some men tipped their hats and offered a cordial, "Howdy."

"I don't see any women," whispered Natasha.

"Women are few and far between in these parts," said Simon. "But seeing none is unusual."

What did that mean for the town? he thought. Was no one here interested in starting a family? What kind of men were these? Outlaws and miners?

There was a saloon at the end of town, sandwiched between a casket maker's and a mining outfit. The tall steeple of a church rose from behind the saloon. Simon turned to Natasha and discreetly indicated that they should make their way to the church.

Simon lifted his throbbing right arm and tried to rest it comfortably on his thigh. The gun in his left holster shifted on his other side, giving him reassurance that a weapon was within easy reach. His dagger was still neatly tucked inside his cowboy boot.

A man with a heavily scarred face came out of a building labeled Rattler Peak Mining Office. He stopped when he noticed them and leaned against a post. He stared at Natasha, his eyes narrowing, not moving a muscle.

Two men in overalls were sawing a large log at the lumber mill. They looked like muscled strongmen, both with red hair and freckles and seeming to be brothers. They straightened up, unfriendly, and swiped their hands on their trousers to stare.

Pinpricks rose at the back of Simon's neck. Still no women. No children. How strange.

They passed what looked like a general store that doubled as a post office and bank. When the front doors of the building swung open and a customer exited, Simon could make out a teller's cage inside. A man of Spanish descent with a long black mustache and sombrero swung his head in their direction, then turned down the boardwalk and pocketed some change.

All the men were wearing guns. What the hell for? Simon swallowed. He didn't like this place. Discreetly, he turned to signal Natasha. Had she seen anything that triggered any memories?

She shook her head no.

Frustrated, he kept riding, hoping that all his hard work and risk would amount to something. He stopped his horse in front of the church. Natasha did the same.

"What now?" she whispered as they dismounted.

"We'll spend no more than thirty minutes, then move on."

"But this is the town."

He shook his head and insisted, "No more than thirty minutes." Sometimes staying in a place where you didn't belong was counterproductive. It only gave more time to alert those who might want you dead. If he couldn't uncover the information he was looking for in thirty minutes, he had to get Natasha out of danger. McKern and Fowler might be following.

Before they had the opportunity to enter the church, Simon noticed that nearby, the casket maker came out of his shop. He was as skinny as one of the planks he used in his caskets, and missing a front tooth. He did, however, have massive hands, which he was wiping with an oily rag. "Howdy, missus. Mister." He assumed the two were married. Why correct him? "Need some help?"

"Not looking for a casket," said Simon with humor, trying to be friendly.

"No one ever is," said the casket maker with a chuckle. "Just passing through?"

Simon nodded. "We're on our way to Pickton to stake

a claim. I hear the copper vein they struck there runs a mile long."

"Good luck to ya."

"Thanks."

Simon ushered Natasha toward the side door of the chapel. He noted a cemetery in the back with several tombstones. It was a wide-open, sunny place overlooking a cliff. "This has to be the place Ledbetter wrote to you about. It's the only church in town."

Natasha nodded.

Once inside, Simon removed his hat. Natasha walked down the center aisle and entered a pew. Simon followed. It afforded him time to survey the inside. Simple church, altar at the front, woodstove to the side, two stained-glass windows shining down from above. There was a second story above them, he'd noted from the outside.

At the sound of heavy footsteps, Simon put his hand on his gun and pivoted.

A well-aged minister, roughly sixty, in a long black robe and clerical collar approached. "Welcome to the Lord's home. Can I help you folks?"

Simon rose to greet the cordial man, while Natasha finished a prayer and then also joined them.

"We were riding through on our way to Pickton," Simon explained. "We never ride past a church without stopping in. Sorry we missed the services on Sunday."

"Ah, but perhaps you'll be in town for the next one. They always take place from eight to nine on the Sabbath morning."

"Afraid we're not staying, Reverend." Simon nodded. "I'm Archibald Norton," he said smoothly, feeling a healthy dose of guilt for lying directly to a minister. "This here is my wife, Dora."

"Reverend Samuels," the man introduced himself. He thrust out his hand and they shook. Simon winced at the slight pressure to his right hand.

The reverend seemed to notice his discomfort. "You all right, son?"

"Just a twisted arm. Riding mishap."

"You best take care of that."

Natasha nestled into Simon's side. "I keep telling him not to overdo it."

"My wife and I have a keen interest in churches," said Simon. "We're antiquity buffs. Been to every church from Washington to San Francisco. Have you ever seen the cathedral in New Orleans, Reverend?"

"Can't say I've had the pleasure."

"Well, it is difficult to see them all. Which ones do you recommend in the area?"

The man blinked and seemed to falter. Now, why would a man of God not be able to name a single beautiful church or cathedral?

"There are so many," said Reverend Samuels. "I'm from Santa Fe myself and not as accustomed to this area yet as I should be."

Simon nodded and looked to the tall stained-glass windows, not wishing to make the man uncomfortable. "May we go outside and have a look at the window relief?"

"Sure, go on. Just watch your step around the front. They're repairing the boardwalk."

"Thank you kindly," said Natasha as she passed by.

While they weaved their way to the side door that led to the cemetery, Simon heard a chair slide on the floor above. There was someone up there. Protectively, he took Natasha by the elbow and led her outside. The sun blazed on the grassy cemetery plots. Some of the slabs were old and turned over. Two eagles were circling the tombstones from high above. He took a minute to survey the area.

"Did you see anything while you were inside?" he asked her. "Anything jog your memory?"

She shook her head. "I think we came to the wrong place. I don't think it's here."

"Oh, it's here all right," said Simon, getting that prickle up his spine again. "That was no minister."

"How can you be sure?"

He tilted his hand and replanted his hat. "He dances with his answers." Simon caught the glint of something from the periphery of his eye. When he saw what it was, a cold feeling spread through him.

She frowned at his expression. "Simon? What is it?"

He kept his voice low and cool. "Someone on the upper floor of the church just slid a rifle out the window and is pointing it at us."

Chapter Twenty-One

Natasha's blood chilled at the petrifying words. She was unable to move for fear of what might happen to them.

Simon whispered quickly, "Stick to the wall of the church where the gunman can't see you. Then stay under the trees where he can't aim, and run to your horse. Okay? On the count of three—"

"But what are *you* doing?"

"Keeping them from you—"

"No, let's stick together—"

"To your horse! One, two, three!"

He pushed her to the stone wall of the church and she slammed against it. He lunged beneath a line of trees that ringed the graveyard.

Rifle fire rang out above her head, blasting through the sunny sky, sending the soaring eagles fluttering their wings. Simon kept racing beneath the trees. He clutched his revolver in his left hand, trying to get a shot at the rifleman.

She was safe here against the wall. Panting, she removed her revolver from the back of her skirt, cocked the trigger and raised it slowly at the rifle poking out from the window above her head. She could see the man's right hand, and he wore a bulbous golden ring. She pulled her trigger.

Her bullet hit the rifle with a loud zing. The rifle dropped out of the window. Glass shattered over her head with a painful thump, and someone above her growled curses. Her scalp stung. Flicking glass particles out of her hair, she raced out to snatch the rifle in victory and then looked to Simon.

"Oh, no," she muttered at the sight of more armed men crossing the street, aiming at him. The group included the casket maker and the two red-haired brothers she'd seen at the sawmill. Dirty gunslingers.

They fired at Simon and she dived behind a four-foot-high tombstone. Simon was in dire trouble, alone to face all these men. A bullet ricocheted off the granite slab by her hand. They were shooting at her, too!

Her throat clamped with mortal terror.

She peered out. Coming up the other side of the street was the man with the heavy scars on his face whom she'd seen at the mining office, and the Spanish man in the sombrero. They were aiming their revolvers at the men who were firing at Simon and her. Undercover lawmen? Undercover help?

Simon's message must've gotten through to his contacts!

A door opened at the side of the church. The reverend poked his head out. He seemed frightened, the wrinkles around his eyes deepened, the disgust on his face evident. "Brutal killers, miss. Come inside." He motioned to her.

But whose side was he on? She flattened her back

against the tombstone and weighed her options. She felt something on her hand, looked down, and to her horror, a slender baby rattlesnake slithered over her fingers.

Panting, she jumped out of the way but more serpents came crawling out from beneath the warm, sunny rocks.

She cringed. That was why the eagles were soaring above.

Panicked, she sprang to another tombstone, shielding herself from the minister, too.

"This way!" the reverend repeated.

And then she noticed the bulbous golden ring on his right hand.

He was the rifleman who'd fired at them from upstairs! Not a minister at all!

Stunned for a moment, she heard more gunfire blast behind her and the sound of voices she didn't recognize.

"Watch out!"

She heard a man's body thudding to the grass. She prayed it wasn't Simon's.

More voices called.

"Over here!"

Another body fell.

She closed her eyes at the bloody violence. She didn't know who was winning, but Simon would want her to take care of herself.

Then suddenly the man with the heavy scars leaped out from a tombstone beside her and quick as pie raised his gun to aim at something behind her. She pivoted and saw him shoot the so-called minister.

She groaned as the would-be minister fell, holding a revolver. Another man raced out from behind him in the church doorway, brandishing a gun, and the heavily scarred man shot him, too.

"You best get out of here, miss, while you have the chance," the scarred man told her.

Balancing the weight of her gun, she sprinted to the nearest tree but didn't make it there. To her utter repugnance, two familiar faces stood in her path, newly arrived to the gunfight. Kale McKern, sweaty as a pig, and Woody Fowler, leering at her from behind a mass of oily skin.

"Well, lookee, lookee," McKern said with a sneer. "What do we have here?"

"One damn stupid female on her way out of a cemetery," Fowler answered.

"No need to run, *Mrs. Ledbetter,*" McKern emphasized in disgust. "We've got a nice plot for you right here."

His tall partner, Fowler, raised his weapon but she raised hers first. She aimed for his thin chest but in total trepidation that she could not do such a bloody deed, she shot him in the leg instead.

"Aaah!" Fowler keeled over, clutching his bloody limb and hollering in pain.

In a burst of fury, McKern grabbed her by the hair, kicked her gun out of her hand and dived behind a tree, dragging her with him. She stumbled. Her scalp throbbed with a million jolts of pain. Her fingers felt broken.

Fowler fired at someone but the person fired back. Fowler recoiled, blood oozed from his chest, and he fell straight to the ground. Dead for sure.

Gunfire ceased. Simon's voice called out, "McKern, come out with her. I won't shoot. Just come out with her."

"Look who's begging who now," McKern called.

"Let her go and I'll tell you where the real Ledbetter is."

McKern shoved her out into the sunshine, but he remained behind the gnarly trunk of the cottonwood.

She regained her balance. She rubbed her sore fingers and tried to ease the ache in her scalp and the rest of her body from the rough handling.

Simon was the only man left standing. Thank God. She looked away from the horrible sight of bodies tumbled over the tombstones. What a loss. What a waste.

But he was left standing. And she desperately wanted him to remain alive. She shook her head at him, signaling not to risk his life for hers, but he remained undaunted.

"Talk!" McKern hollered from behind the tree.

"You're right about me," Simon said calmly. "I was hired to recover the stolen goods you took from the good people of the Union Pacific."

McKern chuckled in sick glory. "It's in a place you'll never find." His voice shifted in a devious undertone. "Where's Ledbetter?"

Natasha could hear McKern reloading his gun. Nausea welled up inside her. Then she heard a soft rattle.

It took only a second till she understood what it was. A rattlesnake. She turned her head and noticed one large mottled snake recoiled and ready to strike on the other side of the tree trunk, waiting patiently for McKern. Smaller snakes were slithering around the area. There was likely a den nearby. But McKern was reloading and talking and seemed unaware.

"I said," McKern repeated with a cruel twist of his mouth, "where the hell is Jarrod Ledbetter?"

Crouching low to the ground, McKern peered out

from around the tree, and the rattlesnake struck him on the throat. His eyes bulged in panic, he dropped his guns to allow his hands to reach for the snake, clutching and grabbing unsuccessfully. He fell to the ground fighting it. The snake did its job and slithered away.

Simon raced to her side, holding her with utter relief, and then protectively whisked her to stand behind him as he pointed his gun at McKern.

Groggy, terrified and stunned from the snakebite, McKern rose to his knees. With a whimper, he reached for his weapon to shoot, but a bullet hit him in the chest.

It hadn't come from Simon.

She and Simon looked to the south end of the cemetery. The man with the heavily scarred face, holding an injured shoulder, had shot Kale McKern dead.

"Natasha," Simon gently said to her an hour later when things had settled, "you need to rest a while longer." With an ache in his throat, he wondered what more he could do for her, and calculated how quickly he could get her out of here.

Simon had had to watch her awful torture and hadn't been able to do a thing to help her. She had bloody cuts all over her face from the shattered glass of the church window, and her scalp was bleeding in places from where McKern had pulled her hair. Her palm was bruised and her skirt was torn.

Pale and trembling, she sat with her feet up in the church pew, wrapped in a blanket. A dozen townspeople milled about them, including some women who'd finally ventured out of their homes. All were answering the questions of two more detectives, and two railroad tycoons with several assistants who'd all come to claim their treasure. Except that treasure was nowhere to be found.

"I'll be fine," Natasha murmured.

"Have some more tea." He brought it to her hands and helped her raise it to her lips. Her fingers didn't seem broken, but they were swollen and tender.

"Did you find the stolen property?" she asked.

He shook his head sadly. A sense of disappointment so deep that he couldn't even speak whispered through him. He'd put her through hell and all for nothing.

Everything that anyone had ever told him about having a lover involved in his life was true.

He was ashamed that he was the cause of this brutality in her life. She could have died, and for what? Who knew how much time she'd need to recover from her shock, from her memories of him and this awful day?

He should have told her from the beginning who he was. He had been as awful to her as his father had been to his mother. Dismissing her concerns, leaving her out of his decisions, letting her cope alone with whatever he saw fit to deliver.

"What now, Simon?" she asked.

"We get you back to Cheyenne, and the only thing you have to worry about is getting better."

"I have no place to stay. I won't go back to those cabins."

"I've given the men directions to put you up at the Mountain Hotel. Finest room they have."

She lowered her gaze to her steaming tea. "How did the detectives and the other officials know where to find us? How did they know to wait for us in Rattler Peak?"

"They didn't. Apparently they planted thirty men along the Eastern Ridge road in various locations and villages. They figured we'd turn up with the treasure in one of those places."

"Smart."

He tilted his head in agreement.

"I'm sorry this mission didn't turn out how you planned," she whispered.

"I should have told you from the beginning who I was."

She gauged his face. Her delicate cheeks, bloodied from glass, lifted in a sorrowful expression. "Yes, you should have."

He took a deep breath, trying to forgive himself but knowing that he never would.

"Miss?" interrupted a gentle older woman. "More tea?"

And this was how their relationship would end, thought Simon, easing himself out of Natasha's space so that she could rest and eat, easing himself out of her life, he vowed.

"I've come to say goodbye, Simon." Outside on the cemetery grounds two hours later, Natasha tugged her blanket tighter around her frame. The warmth gave her comfort, and the food and drink she'd taken had helped her strength. She was still exhausted from the gunfight and looking forward to getting away from all of this and back to some semblance of control in her life. "There's a team of men from the railroad who have a buggy," she explained to Simon, "and they're taking me back."

"Good," he said, straightening up in the cemetery. She noticed he'd been reading the names on various tombstones.

The cemetery was almost back to looking normal.

The bodies of the deceased men had been cleared out of the grassy place and brought to the doctor and undertaker one block down the street.

"I'm sorry nothing jogged my memory," Natasha murmured.

"Please," he said, looking deeply tortured, "don't concern yourself with this."

He was standing at a well-groomed gravesite at a wide double plot. The old grass had been neatly shorn and the names and dates of the couple's deaths neatly etched into a block of gray granite.

She looked down and read the names. "Mr. and Mrs. Arnold Ledbetter." She shook her head. "Jarrod Ledbetter's parents. It seems either he, or someone he paid, took good care of his parents' plot."

"Hard to believe that man cared for anything."

This was the tombstone she'd hid behind when the minister had hollered to her from the door. The same tombstone that the tiny snakes had crawled out of. "Careful, Simon, I saw snakes around here earlier."

They moved away from the spot and strolled along the far edge. He kept his distance, not a touch or a flicker between them. She grappled with how to say goodbye. There was so much and so little to say.

Perhaps she needn't say anything. Who knew where he was heading next? What job, what town, what state? She had meant so little to him that he hadn't even acknowledged his true self to her in all the time they'd shared.

She turned to the gravestones again, and something popped into her mind. "Simon, there is one thing Ledbetter did mention in his letters. It's probably nothing…"

"Tell me anyway."

"He mentioned that he might someday like to be buried next to his folks."

"That desire never happened. The authorities already took care of his body, burying him in the spot he died."

She shrugged. "I had the feeling that was likely, but thought I would mention it."

He turned. "So then you're ready to go?"

She frowned. "Simon, have you read all of the writing on all of the tombstones here?"

"Most of them." He rubbed his chin. "But not all," he said, suddenly realizing what she was suggesting. Why not check every single one while they were here?

They struck out, reading the names as they passed. "S. Moulton, Mr. B. Hassalbie, Mrs. Darlene—"

"Here." Simon pointed to a newly dug grave. "What's going on here?"

Natasha looked aghast and read the name on the wooden cross. "J. Ledbetter?"

"But he can't have been buried here."

"Unless…"

They stared at each other.

Simon barked out orders at the other men beneath his command. "Get a shovel here! Stand aside! Call the others, please! More shovels!"

Natasha stepped aside and let the men do their work. It took them seventeen minutes to dig to the bottom of the grave marked J. Ledbetter. When they were finished, they hauled out a fortune of gold bricks, cases of precious jewels and bankrolls of money, all in total worth over three hundred thousand dollars.

Chapter Twenty-Two

Natasha hadn't seen Simon for two weeks. His absence felt like a sore ache inside her bones that never seemed to go away.

At first, the days went by and she told herself that she was happy that she didn't have to deal with the aggravation. He'd done what he thought necessary in the line of duty, and she had been an easy target to latch on to in his hopes of gaining more information about Ledbetter.

It had been difficult for her to think of other things besides Simon as she lay recuperating in her hotel bed. The railroad was happy to put her up until she got stronger and was able to travel back to Chicago, the two officials had told her when they visited.

"The ticket's on us, miss," they'd said appreciatively. "Just a few more questions about your interaction with misters Ledbetter, McKern and Fowler…"

The following week hadn't been any easier to forget Simon.

She'd been busy with the Dooligans, as they'd asked her to help them find a cabin to rent. Their money had come through from Boston and they were eager to begin their lantern business. To her chagrin, they'd been shocked, then delighted, to learn that Simon Garr was an undercover detective.

How grand for him, thought Natasha, that everyone thought so highly of him. The Dooligans had quickly picked up on the fact that she didn't wish to mention him.

However, they'd all read about him in the papers. It was all the town could talk about. Headlines screamed:

Railroad Recovers Stolen Loot.

Detective Unearths More Glittering Gravestones across the Country.

Natasha stared down at this latest headline as she sat on a folding wooden chair in her tent among the market stalls. Early-morning customers strode past the open flaps, their boots squishing on spongy grass as they shouted hellos to one another and barked out prices.

The article in the paper went on to explain that Ledbetter had left instructions to several gang members he'd been working with, not only McKern and Fowler, to bury his stolen loot in scattered cemeteries where he could easily retrieve the jewels and gold.

She studied the photo of Simon, standing proudly beside an elderly man. She read the caption: Detective Simon Garr Returns Wedding Lapel Pin to Ninety-Year-Old Man.

The papers had clearly identified Simon by name. His secret identity was no longer secret. She tried not to wonder, but the familiar ache went throbbing through her chest again as she wondered what place he'd be traveling to next.

"Good luck," she whispered to his slightly grinning face in the photo.

She opened the woodstove in the corner and dropped the newspaper into the flames. It would burn for a little while and keep her warm.

It was time she focused on her own plans.

She turned and stacked the other newspapers she'd collected for the fire. When she'd first confided her business idea to the Dooligans last week, they were entirely enthusiastic. She was coming to like them very much, and they were treating her as if she were family.

When she'd asked if she could rent a part of their tent here in the market so that she could start a small jewelry business, Mrs. Dooligan had nearly wept.

"What a splendid idea," the woman had declared. "We'll have our lanterns on one side, and your jewelry pieces on the other. Only, mind you, until business grows and we get a proper store. And I'd also like to add some cooking pots and utensils. I'm having some specially designed in copper from the coppersmith two tents down."

Natasha was starting out small.

She was holding on to her personal jewelry pieces in the event she ever needed to sell them in an emergency and was working to build up some capital to invest in new pieces. The railroad officials had told her two weeks ago when they'd visited that they were working on locating her grandfather's pocket watch and would get it to her once all their evidence had been documented and returned to their proper owners.

"Miss O'Sullivan!" Mrs. Dooligan called now as she walked into the tent.

Natasha turned to greet her. The kind woman brought a timid young couple with her. They were dressed in working clothes and seemed out of their element, distracted and intimidated by all the people walking past the tents, hollering for crates and wagons, and hammering out bargains.

"Allow me to introduce you to Mr. and Mrs. Peabody from Mississippi," Mrs. Dooligan declared. "They arrived yesterday and are looking to invest in gold chain necklaces. I told them they really should invest in hiring you for an hour or two first. That you might save them a lot of headache and cost."

"Absolutely." With confidence, Natasha held out her hand to welcome them. They shook. "Are you looking for domestic gold or imported?"

"Please, what might be the difference?" asked the young woman.

Natasha explained, "Gold from some of our new mines, such as those from California, is of the utmost quality. If you wish to invest in Victorian gold, you have to be careful of the date. Pieces before 1854 are generally eighteen to twenty-four karat, which I'm sure you know is very pure. But after that date, gold purity in England was allowed to go as low as nine or twelve karats. You really must look to see if the piece is hallmarked and stamped with the karat marking—"

"Oh," the young lady said in relief, "I'm so glad we found you."

"Didn't I tell you?" Mrs. Dooligan beamed. "Hiring her is like having your banker with you as you shop."

As they discussed what jewelry stores they wished to stop at first, Natasha noticed a gentleman barely visible, standing outside and listening at the side of the tent flap, black hat in hand.

She knew that hat. She knew the man.

Simon.

Her pulse tore off in a crazy rhythm and she seemed to have no control over her breathing.

When he took another step closer, she stared up into his inquisitive, probing face.

He seemed to have aged five years since she'd last seen him. There were worry lines beneath his eyes, and his mouth ruffled as though he was deeply concerned about something. From his photos in the papers, he'd seemed pleased and satisfied with life. Had something gone wrong with his mission?

She didn't need to worry about this man any longer. He could worry about himself, as he always had. She had her own plans, her own worries.

What did he want from her? Why couldn't he leave her alone?

The moment tensed between them, neither saying a word.

Heat stung the back of her eyes, yet she held the welling tears at bay. And then she was angry at herself for her lapse in strength. She would not let him affect her.

Gathering every bit of fortitude she had, she placed a hand on the waistline of her skirt and tried to remain outwardly detached.

The conversation had stopped inside the tent. Mrs. Dooligan was looking from Natasha's stricken face to Simon's.

The older woman patted her gray bun and directed the young couple. "Shall we take a walk and have a glimpse at the stores? Natasha? Meet you there within an hour?"

Natasha nodded. "Yes, I'll be along."

"It's awfully nice to meet you," the young man said, tipping his hat. "It's our lucky day."

They left, and Simon took a few steps inside the tent.

They were alone, save for the hustle and bustle of people walking past the tent.

Simon took the lead. "You've gained many admirers, it seems."

"Does it? It seems to me that not all my admirers are lasting."

With a sharp expression of regret, he glanced down at his hat.

She sighed, instantly regretting her choice of words. What was the use of fighting? She didn't wish to be confrontational, nor spiteful. She didn't want to hurt him. What had happened, had happened. Perhaps she was partly to blame. How many times had he rebuffed her, but she had pressed her company upon him? He'd turned her away physically but she had demanded his touch on more than one occasion.

Simply put—what did he want now?

He played with the brim of his hat. "You're not going back to Chicago?"

"I thought about it. Very carefully. Then I thought about the true reasons I came to Wyoming Territory and how much they involve me, not just the husband I was seeking." She smiled in relief, trying to let the past go. "I learned a lot about myself, Simon. I learned that I'm capable of looking after myself and being independent. That I've developed some true friends here—namely Mr. and Mrs. Dooligan—and that I have valuable skills I can use in the jewelry trade."

The soft corners of his mouth turned upward into a gentle smile, yet he seemed contemplative and wistful. "I always thought you were remarkable. And I hear you're staying with the Dooligans for the time being?"

"Who told you that?" She looked to the passing figures outside her door. "Who else," she said with a dose of humor, "but Mrs. Dooligan."

"She also told me that you had a concussion for three days that we didn't catch."

Natasha shook her head in embarrassment that her private business was being leaked. "She shouldn't have mentioned it. It was over very quickly. I'm fine now."

He pointed to his brow. "There's still a little scar on your forehead from the shards of glass from that church."

She rubbed the spot. "Hardly noticeable. Look, if you've come to drag this out—"

"No," he interrupted. "I'm not here to bother you. I wanted to tell you that things got settled with the railroad. We were carefully watching to see if this big heist they'd planned on a shipment of jewelry from San Francisco might still happen…and apprehended three more men in Ledbetter's gang. The last of them."

"That's a relief, Simon. Did you ever uncover any jewelry stores that Ledbetter actually owned?"

"No," he said, "it was all a big lie."

She shrugged. At least the nightmare was over.

He shifted his weight on his large cowboy boots. "Natasha, I also came today because I…I wanted to give you this." He reached into his leather jacket and removed a golden pocket watch.

Her eyes stung again with welling tears. Her granddad's watch.

"Your granddad would be proud of you," Simon whispered. "Your being hired as a jewelry expert, no less."

She reached out and took the watch from his grasp.

The metal was cold but soon heated beneath her fingers. Smooth and shiny and slightly scratched. Beautiful. She clutched it to her heart.

He watched her with hawklike concentration. "You were right. It does keep good time."

She nodded, too moved to speak without a tremor.

"Thank you," she said hoarsely. "You said you'd bring it back, and you kept your promise."

She blinked away her emotion as best she could and placed the watch in her skirt pocket. It lobbed to one side because of the weight, but she loved the feel of it.

She tried to ask lightly, "What are your plans? Everyone seems to know your name and position with the agency, so I dare say you can't work undercover anymore. Where do you go from here?"

He patted the sleeve of his right arm. "They're giving me some time off to completely heal."

Suddenly concerned for his health, she wondered if that was why he looked so aged. "How is that injury? It's not giving you any trouble, is it?"

"It's fine. Doc says it'll be as good as new."

"That's good." She nodded. "Very good."

He wasn't forthcoming with any more news, and to tell the truth, her heart was too troubled and confused to listen to his private plans. Perhaps forgetting him would be easier if she couldn't picture where he was and what he was doing. If she were lucky, she thought with a tremble, he might be stationed on the West Coast, as far from her as possible.

There didn't seem to be anything more to say.

Awkwardly, they stared at each other. His green eyes flickered and the breeze tousled the length of his blond hair across his shoulders. She would like to remember him this way.

Filled with melancholy, she turned a shoulder to him and pretended to be occupied arranging some of the Dooligans' crates on the tables. "It was very nice of you to stop by, Simon. Good luck to you."

He was silent behind her.

She didn't intend to cause either of them any grief; she intended to lessen their pain by allowing him to leave without another painful conversation.

She set down another crate and turned as he retreated. He removed his black hat in a gesture of respect. "So long, Natasha."

And then he was gone.

The emotion welled then and was simply too much to handle. She crumpled to the chair, placed her elbows on the table and rocked her forehead in her hands.

She didn't realize how difficult it would be to see him. Nor how difficult it would be to say goodbye.

Both of them had been too proud to speak freely.

With a soft gasp, she tried to hold herself together. Finally, after several minutes, she regained her composure, lifted her face off her hands and leaned back in her chair.

She had things to do, she thought, trying to get into a more cheerful frame of mind.

Something on the corner of the table caught her attention. She turned to look.

It was a little wooden bird. She picked it up. Where had it come from? And then suddenly she knew. Simon had left it behind for her as a parting gift.

She turned it around in her hands. It was a whittled piece of wood, very aged, and someone had painted the wings with streaks of blue.

A whittled bluebird.

It was the bluebird Simon's father had whittled for him when he was a young boy. The one Simon had kept on his windowsill for years, hoping that his abusive father would someday return.

In all the lies and deceptive things Simon had said to her, she had assumed that he'd lied about his father, too, that it had been a sad, made-up story to gain her sympathy and trust.

Simon had told her the story during their wedding night and had said that it had been the "real" him she'd gotten to know. She had refused to believe him. She had discounted everything he'd said.

She rubbed her cheek. She'd been wrong about him on several points.

With a blinding need, she rose from her chair and bounded out of the tent.

Simon readjusted his hat and strode through the marketplace of tents and shacks. God, it had nearly felled him to see Natasha again.

She seemed to be blossoming in her newfound position. In her newfound decision to remain in Wyoming Territory. She was healthy and strong and thriving just fine without him.

Good for her, he thought sincerely. She deserved to find some peace and happiness.

As for himself…he sighed at how stupid he'd been.

"Simon!"

He heard the faint call but didn't at first notice.

"Simon!" called the female voice again. "Simon, stop! Please!" That was Natasha's voice.

He wheeled around, surprised to see her.

"You forgot this," she said, holding out the little blue-bird. Her long hair was windblown over her slender shoulders and her face flushed.

"I don't need it anymore," he said gently. "You helped me work through a few things, Natasha, and I don't need it anymore. You helped me gain a better understanding, a clearer perspective on the past."

"Oh," she said with a tremulous smile.

"And maybe even the future," he added.

"The future?"

"Seems to me I've been doing a lot of running away from things. I've decided I'm going to start running to things instead."

"How do you mean?"

"The agency said they'd back me. I'm heading up a new division of training here in Cheyenne. Seeing that my cover's blown, I had to think of something. And that's when I decided that after twelve or so years as an undercover agent, I have a few things to say about the way things are done around here. Things that other detectives coming up through the ranks might find help-ful to know."

He took out a letter from his jacket. "And I got a let-ter from Clay's widow, Sarah. And their young son, Tucker." Simon's voice crackled, but he couldn't help it. It had been the most heartfelt letter—from a young boy who was roughly the same age Simon had been when he'd been tortured about his own father and what had become of him. "Anyway...Tucker thanked me for my letter telling him how brave his father was and what a smart detective he'd been..."

This time, Simon couldn't go on. Emotion choked him. But he figured that Natasha got the gist of what he was trying to say. He tucked the envelope back into his jacket.

"I made many mistakes in my life, Natasha. The biggest one was you. I thought if only I could control everything, everyone, my life would be better. That your life would be better if only you wouldn't resist me and simply do everything I thought was best. I was wrong."

"Oh, Simon, I'm sorry, too."

"You are one person who does not need to apologize to me." He pointed to her forehead. "You've got permanent scars from our time together."

"I know," she said, feeling much lighter and hopeful. "That's why it's crazy that I want it to continue."

His green eyes flashed at her. He searched her face.

She held up the bluebird. "I thought you were lying about everything," she whispered. "I dismissed everything you tried to tell me."

"You have every right to be angry and unforgiving."

"I don't want to be unforgiving," she confessed. "I don't want to be that kind of person. I'm not that kind of person."

"And so?" he asked with fear that he was reading more into this than his broken heart could handle. "What are you saying? Is there hope for us?"

She nodded. "Absolutely, yes."

With a moment of stunned silence and pleasure, he took her in his arms. "I promise to listen and to treasure every word that passes between us."

She whispered in his ear, "I shut myself so firmly against you, Simon, I—I promise never to be like that again. Whatever the problems, I'll try to speak my mind and try to work things out."

"I will never, ever deceive you again, Natasha."

She let go and looked up at him. Her dark lashes flashed against the creamy tone of her skin.

"My love," he whispered. "I love you, Natasha. I think I fell in love with you the moment you stepped off the train, cussing at your trunk."

"I love you, too," she whispered. "I fell in love with you when you told me the story behind the bluebird."

He kissed her throat. She was heaven.

"These last couple of weeks have been so difficult, Simon. First I was angry that you might show up to see me…"

"I wanted to, but I was ashamed…and deep down, scared that you'd send me away."

She touched his hair. "And then I was convinced that I didn't want to see you, that I was thrilled that you weren't coming around."

"And now?" he asked gently.

"And now I realize that I never would've gotten over you. I love you, Simon. I love the man you are. Heroic and honorable and valiant in defending your fallen friends."

He was deeply moved by her words. "I'll protect you, Natasha, for as long as we both shall live. If you'll have me." He reached down to cup her beautiful, soft face. Her lovely eyes filled with sentiment.

"Hey, mister," said a passing farmer with a crateful of squawking chickens. "Would you and your wife mind turning a bit so I can get these birds past you? Thank you…. Oh, hey, aren't you that detective?"

Simon and Natasha smiled at each other, ignored the question and kissed for all the world to see.

Epilogue

One month later

The first-class sleeper coach on the train headed to New York City jostled beneath Simon as he lay in bed with his new wife. It was dark outside, the shade was pulled, the door was locked and the hum of the tracks muted the sounds of their lovemaking.

Simon rose on an elbow and stared at her lovely, naked body.

She had one hip turned toward him, one slender leg draped beneath a sheet, the other resting on his bare, muscled leg. She twirled her fingertips erotically over his belly, making his skin tingle.

He ran a finger along her neck and over the silky turn of her beautiful breast. He swirled his gentle thumb over the arc of her pink swells.

"Such a lovely picture you make," he murmured.

She laid a hand on his shoulder, and he loved the feel of her.

She kissed the upturned side of the forearm he was resting his head on.

"Has anyone ever told you that you are a very handsome man?"

"There was a woman once," he teased. "She must've had an affliction for schoolteachers.... She was about twenty years my senior...."

She smiled. "You went undercover as a schoolteacher?"

"Mmm-hmm." He drew another lazy O around her other breast and beneath the plump mound.

"You'll have to give me some private lessons, then, sir...."

He patted her bare leg. "I have something for you, darlin'."

He reached into the outer pouch of his luggage, rummaging over the slender golden pocket watch she'd tenderly given him again. He understood the love behind her gesture and was grateful for it. He wished he'd been around to meet her granddad, since the gent had meant so much to Natasha.

Simon's fingers hit what he was looking for in his luggage. He pulled out a square, shiny black cardboard box and presented it to her.

"What's this?" She grasped it between careful fingers and sat up on her pillow. Her breasts swayed, making him love her even more. He didn't think it was possible to be filled with this much joy.

He shrugged playfully at her question. "Why don't you have a look?"

She'd agreed to marry him three weeks ago. They'd married two days afterward with only the Dooligans present, and the local minister, Reverend Ericson, who'd returned from his trip and was especially caring to hear about their struggle together as a couple. It had meant a lot to Natasha—and to Simon—that they'd been married in a church.

Mrs. Dooligan had managed to help Natasha remove all the wine stains from her fancy wedding gown, and the picture Natasha had presented on their wedding day would be one he'd hold in his dreams till the day he died.

Natasha lifted the lid of the box.

On a square of cotton wadding sat a gorgeous necklace with a silver locket, embedded with pearls and sapphires and opals in a very carefully shaped design of a heart topped by a crown.

The symbolism and hidden message in the design weren't lost on her. He knew it wouldn't be.

"A crowned heart," she said with a pleasing lilt. "It symbolizes love triumphant."

"I had it specially made."

"It's breathtaking."

"May I?" He indicated that he would like to help her clasp it.

She swung around with her gorgeous back to him, a ripple of lovely naked flesh and curves. She lifted her glossy brunette tresses and he affixed the necklace.

She dropped her hair.

His arms came up around her, stroking the sides of her rib cage down to her waist, then up to cup her breasts from behind.

"Mmm," she moaned. "If we get started again, we may miss our stop and never get to Europe."

London. Paris. Vienna. They were planning to see it all.

Amused at her words, he kissed her upturned shoulder. "That's what honeymoons are for."

She turned around on the slender bed.

He planted a large tanned hand on her white hip to anchor her from falling over, and glanced down at the sparkling locket dangling between her breasts.

"It suits you. I think you should wear it like that, all day long."

"With no clothes? I think the other passengers might object."

"Not the men," he said with humor.

She smiled, laid her head back on the pillow, slid her arms around his waist and pulled him closer.

"Simon, I think it was our destiny to meet."

He patted her lovely thigh and marveled at the power and truth of her words. And then he glanced at her necklace again and the beautiful shape of her body, and he was lost again as they headed for Grand Central Station. They still had twenty minutes to go, more than enough time for him to show her how he felt.

* * * * *

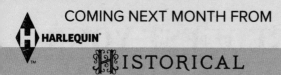

COMING NEXT MONTH FROM

HARLEQUIN®

⚜ISTORICAL

Available April 15, 2014

NOTORIOUS IN THE WEST
by Lisa Plumley
(Western)

Infamous Boston businessman Griffin Turner may have a reputation for being ruthless, but when Olivia Mouton sees a new side to him, will she believe the gossip, or trust her heart?

UNWED AND UNREPENTANT
by Marguerite Kaye
(Victorian)

Lady Cordelia Armstrong and Iain Hunter have a pretend engagement. But as the lines between fantasy and reality blur, will either of them want to walk away once their deal is done?

YIELD TO THE HIGHLANDER
The MacLerie Clan • by Terri Brisbin
(Medieval)

Fearsome warrior Aidan MacLerie's heart remains restless, until he meets Catriona MacKenzie. She is a married woman, so he can never truly possess her, yet he seeks her surrender one kiss at a time....

RETURN OF THE PRODIGAL GILVRY
The Gilvrys of Dunross
by Ann Lethbridge
(Regency)

Drew Gilvry must do his utmost to protect the widowed Lady Rowena MacDonald. But his honor is about to be tested—because on a perilous journey across the Highlands, their attraction to each other becomes impossible to resist....

YOU CAN FIND MORE INFORMATION ON UPCOMING HARLEQUIN® TITLES, FREE EXCERPTS AND MORE AT WWW.HARLEQUIN.COM.

HHCNM0414

REQUEST YOUR FREE BOOKS!

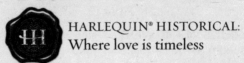

HARLEQUIN® HISTORICAL:
Where love is timeless

2 FREE NOVELS PLUS 2 FREE GIFTS!

YES! Please send me 2 FREE Harlequin® Historical novels and my 2 FREE gifts (gifts are worth about $10). After receiving them, if I don't wish to receive any more books, I can return the shipping statement marked "cancel." If I don't cancel, I will receive 6 brand-new novels every month and be billed just $5.44 per book in the U.S. or $5.74 per book in Canada. That's a savings of at least 16% off the cover price! It's quite a bargain! Shipping and handling is just 50¢ per book in the U.S. and 75¢ per book in Canada.* I understand that accepting the 2 free books and gifts places me under no obligation to buy anything. I can always return a shipment and cancel at any time. Even if I never buy another book, the two free books and gifts are mine to keep forever.

246/349 HDN F4ZY

Name _____ (PLEASE PRINT) _____

Address _____ Apt. # _____

City _____ State/Prov. _____ Zip/Postal Code _____

Signature (if under 18, a parent or guardian must sign)

Mail to the **Harlequin® Reader Service:**
IN U.S.A.: P.O. Box 1867, Buffalo, NY 14240-1867
IN CANADA: P.O. Box 609, Fort Erie, Ontario L2A 5X3

Want to try two free books from another line?
Call 1-800-873-8635 or visit www.ReaderService.com.

* Terms and prices subject to change without notice. Prices do not include applicable taxes. Sales tax applicable in N.Y. Canadian residents will be charged applicable taxes. Offer not valid in Quebec. This offer is limited to one order per household. Not valid for current subscribers to Harlequin Historical books. All orders subject to credit approval. Credit or debit balances in a customer's account(s) may be offset by any other outstanding balance owed by or to the customer. Please allow 4 to 6 weeks for delivery. Offer available while quantities last.

Your Privacy—The Harlequin® Reader Service is committed to protecting your privacy. Our Privacy Policy is available online at www.ReaderService.com or upon request from the Harlequin Reader Service.

We make a portion of our mailing list available to reputable third parties that offer products we believe may interest you. If you prefer that we not exchange your name with third parties, or if you wish to clarify or modify your communication preferences, please visit us at www.ReaderService.com/consumerschoice or write to us at Harlequin Reader Service Preference Service, P.O. Box 9062, Buffalo, NY 14269. Include your complete name and address.

HH13R

*Get swept away by Marguerite Kaye's sizzling
Victorian tale of a convenient engagement, and a highly
inconvenient passion...*

"You prefer to make your own decisions. As do I." Iain grinned. "We're likely to have some interesting clashes, my wee love."

"I am not your *wee love*."

Iain slipped his arm around her waist and pulled her up against him. "For the time being, that's exactly what you are."

Her heart began to beat erratically. She had that feeling, that her corsets were too tightly laced. She wished he would not smile at her like that, because it was nigh on impossible not to smile back at him.

His fingers were stroking the skin at the nape of her neck. His mouth was curved into a smile that was blatantly sensual. It was there again in his eyes, that heat, and she was pretty certain it was there in hers, too. "Iain, we are just pretending to be engaged."

"Aye, but there are other things we've no need to pretend about. You know I still want you, Cordelia."

"Did you have this in mind when you suggested our engagement?"

"No, and I won't change my mind if you're not interested. I think you are, though."

"I think I've already mentioned that you've a very high opinion of yourself, Mr. Hunter."

Iain laughed softly. "I don't want to play games, Cordelia. Knowing that you want me as much as I want you—have you any idea what that does to me?"

His voice was low, making the hairs on her skin stand on end. No man had ever been so—so blatant before. "You do not subscribe to the belief that men shall hunt and women shall be hunted?" she asked.

His expression darkened momentarily. "I told you, I'm not interested in playing games. I don't want you subservient to my desires, Cordelia—I want my desires to be yours. Yours to be mine."

His words were a low stomach-clenching growl. "My desires to be yours," she repeated, mesmerised.

She had only to make the tiniest movement and he would let her go, but she didn't want to. She wanted him every bit as much as he said, and she wanted not to want him every bit as much. Cordelia smiled, deliberately provocative. And then she kissed him.

Follow Iain and Cordelia's story in
UNWED AND UNREPENTANT
Available from Harlequin® Historical
May 2014

Look for more in this miniseries about
THE ARMSTRONG SISTERS *in*
INNOCENT IN THE SHEIKH'S HAREM
THE GOVERNESS AND THE SHEIKH
THE SHEIKH'S IMPETUOUS LOVE-SLAVE (Undone!)
THE BEAUTY WITHIN
RUMORS THAT RUINED A LADY

HISTORICAL

Where love is timeless

COMING IN MAY 2014

Notorious in the West

by *USA TODAY* bestselling author

Lisa Plumley

Infamous Boston businessman Griffin Turner may have a reputation for being thoroughly ruthless, but underneath it all he hides a painful past. He's determined to keep the world at bay, and the last thing he expects is to discover a light in his eternal darkness—in the form of smart, sassy Olivia Mouton.

Morrow Creek's resident beauty Olivia is determined to stand up to Griffin—no matter how terrifying the stories that precede him! But when the notorious businessman reveals a side that no one else has seen before, soon Olivia is reconsidering everything she's ever heard....

Available wherever books and ebooks are sold.

COMING IN MAY 2014

Yield to the Highlander

by

Terri Brisbin

Fearsome warrior Aidan MacLerie may be brave and unquestionably loyal to his family and clan, but his heart remains restless. Until he meets stunning Catriona MacKenzie. She is a married woman, so he can never truly possess her, yet he seeks her surrender one kiss at a time….

When her loveless husband falls on the battlefield, Cat is left homeless, destitute and with her reputation in tatters. Aidan is the only man with the power to protect her now. All Cat has to do is yield to this insatiable highlander.

Love the Harlequin book you just read?

Your opinion matters.

Review this book on your favorite book site, review site, blog or your own social media properties and share your opinion with other readers!

Be sure to connect with us at:
Harlequin.com/Newsletters
Facebook.com/HarlequinBooks
Twitter.com/HarlequinBooks